Alice-Miranda at School was shortlisted for the 2011 Australian Peace Literature Award.

'Alice-Miranda has a beguiling ability to enchant those around her and an enthusiasm for helping people in need. This new series, with its sprightly, resilient heroine, who is sweet without being cloying, offers readers a lively blend of humour and intrigue.'
Kirkus Reviews

'Alice-Miranda's optimism and determination is infectious. An immediately lovable character that young girls are going to want to be or be with.'
Deborah Abela, bestselling author of *Max Remy*

'What's the worst thing about reviewing kids' books? When you find a book so enchanting that you want to ignore your own child to keep reading it! A modern story with a touch of the classics about it.'
Megan Blandford, Kids' Book Review blog

'Full of humour and with very likeable characters, this book sets a benchmark for a fantastic new series.'
Donella Reed, Read Plus blog

Alice-Miranda
in New York

Jacqueline Harvey

RANDOM HOUSE AUSTRALIA

For Ian and Sandy and Linsay

A Random House book
Published by Random House Australia Pty Ltd
Level 3, 100 Pacific Highway, North Sydney NSW 2060
www.randomhouse.com.au

First published by Random House Australia in 2012

Addresses for companies within the Random House Group can be found at
www.randomhouse.com.au/offices.

National Library of Australia
Cataloguing-in-Publication Entry

Author: Harvey, Jacqueline
Title: Alice-Miranda in New York / Jacqueline Harvey
ISBN: 978 1 74275 114 6 (pbk.)
Target audience: For primary school age
Subjects: Girls – Juvenile fiction
           Manhattan (New York, N.Y.) – Juvenile fiction
Dewey number: A823.4

Cover and internal illustrations by J.Yi
Cover design by Mathematics www.xy-1.com
Internal design by Midland Typesetters, Australia
Typeset in 13/18 pt Adobe Garamond by Midland Typesetters, Australia
Printed in Australia by Griffin Press, an accredited ISO AS/NZS 14001:2004
Environmental Management System printer

Prologue

Hugh Kennington-Jones stared at the yellowed piece of paper in his hand. He scanned the extravagant lettering and read aloud: *'It's not fair to Master Hugh. He should know the truth.'*

The rest of the characters danced on the page. 'What truth? What does it mean?' Hugh murmured.

Opposite him, across an acre of desk, sat a silver-haired man. 'I wish I knew, sir. I've asked the solicitor in charge of her affairs if there were any personal effects. There may be some clues.'

Hugh Kennington-Jones exhaled deeply. 'I suppose so, but it's unlikely. I imagine it's all been dumped by now or sent to the charity shop. There was no family, as far as I understand.' Hugh stood up and walked towards the door.

The older man rose to his feet and followed.

'Thank you and I . . . I appreciate your discretion, Hector.' Hugh reached out and firmly shook the man's hand. 'I suppose we'll just have to wait and see what turns up.'

'Very good, sir. I'll be in touch if there's anything else.' The man retreated from the office and closed the door behind him.

Hugh Kennington-Jones held the page in front of him. 'You always were a strange one, Father. And now this.' He carefully folded the letter, strode back to his desk and placed it at the very back of the top drawer, which he locked. There it would stay, for now.

Chapter 1

'It's not fair! I don't know why you have to go,' Jacinta grouched. 'We've only been back at school for a month.' The fair-haired girl and school's former second best tantrum thrower sat cross-legged on the end of Alice-Miranda's bed, watching as Alice-Miranda packed.

The tiny child smiled. 'Please don't be cross, Jacinta. It's a wonderful opportunity. Miss Grimm said I should make the most of it and I know Mummy and Daddy are terribly excited. Besides,

I told you ages ago. It's just come forward a couple of weeks, that's all.'

'You said you were only going for *two* weeks and now it's *much* longer,' Jacinta griped.

Alice-Miranda folded a pair of jeans and placed them neatly at the bottom of her suitcase.

Millie rolled over on her bed beside them and propped her elbows under her chin. 'Who's going to ride over and visit Miss Hephzibah with me now?'

'Don't look at me,' said Jacinta, curling her lip. 'You know I hate horses and I certainly won't be going near that pony of yours, Alice-Miranda. He's a nasty little beast.'

Alice-Miranda grinned. 'Bonaparte just has a mind of his own, that's all. And it's only for a month or so. Not even the whole term.'

'But that's for*ever*,' Jacinta sighed.

'I'm sure Susannah will go riding with you, Millie,' Alice-Miranda assured her friend. 'And really Jacinta, I'll be back before you've had time to miss me.'

'I wish we could come. I'm sure there'll be loads of movie stars and celebrities at the opening party.' Jacinta sprang from the bed and sauntered across the floor, as if she was walking a red carpet.

Millie looked at her and laughed, then jumped up and pretended that she was taking Jacinta's photograph.

'Jacinta, over here, this way, look at me,' Millie ordered like a mini paparazza. 'Gorgeous, amazing, you're a star!'

Jacinta smiled and struck a pose with her hand on her hip.

'I wish you could both come too,' Alice-Miranda said.

'Hey.' Jacinta's smile turned to a frown as a thought suddenly struck her. 'My mother had better not be invited. It's just the sort of thing she loves – a fancy department store being re-launched.'

'Oh, ugly, ugly, Jacinta, what's with the face?' Millie grimaced. 'Those pictures are not going anywhere near the cover of *Gloss and Goss*.'

Alice-Miranda giggled.

'As if I'd ever want to be on the cover of that rubbish.' Jacinta rolled her eyes. 'That would mean I was turning into my mother.' She launched herself off the make-believe red carpet and onto Millie's bed.

'I thought you and your mother were getting on much better,' Alice-Miranda commented. 'Hasn't she rented a cottage in the village so she can spend some time with you on the weekends?'

'Yes, but I've only seen her once,' Jacinta said. 'And I haven't been near the cottage because she's having it repainted. I don't know why she's bothering. It's not as though she's going to come and live here permanently.'

'At least it's a start,' Alice-Miranda smiled.

There was a sharp knock at the door. 'Hello girls.' Mrs Howard's voice drifted ahead of her into the room. 'Whatever are you doing there, young lady?' she said with a glance at Alice-Miranda's open suitcase.

'I thought I'd get a head start,' the girl answered.

'But you're not off until the weekend are you?' Mrs Howard enquired. 'I've set aside a couple of hours to do all that for you.'

'I don't expect you to pack my bags, Mrs Howard. That wouldn't be fair at all,' Alice-Miranda frowned.

'Goodness, you don't know where I can get some more just like this one, do you girls?' Mrs Howard's eyes wrinkled as her lips turned upwards.

'Oh, you wouldn't want that, Howie,' Jacinta replied. 'If we were *all* like Alice-Miranda you'd be completely bored and have nothing to complain about.'

'Jacinta!' Millie rebuked. 'Howie doesn't complain about us, do you?' Millie looked up at the housemistress, who rolled her eyes and changed the subject.

'I know someone who's going to miss this little one very much.' The sturdy woman strode over and pulled a pink cardigan from the tall chest of drawers, folded it with military precision and placed it into the suitcase.

'Oh, Mrs Howard, of course I'm going to miss you too.' Alice-Miranda wrapped her arms around the old woman and rested her head against her tummy.

'And what's all that for?' Howie enveloped the child in return.

'Just because,' Alice-Miranda replied. A plump tear formed in the corner of the housemistress's eye. She tried to blink it away but it fell heavily onto the top of Alice-Miranda's head. 'Mrs Howard, you're not crying are you?' Alice-Miranda stepped back and looked up.

The older woman snatched a handkerchief from her apron pocket, wiped her eyes and blew her nose noisily.

'Oh, goodness no. Hayfever, my dear. I think

I need to give this house a good going over. Must be a layer of dust in here.' Mrs Howard glanced around; the room was spotless, its surfaces gleaming.

'But you cleaned our room yesterday,' Millie said.

'I must have missed a spot.' Mrs Howard blew her nose again.

'We don't want Alice-Miranda to go either,' said Jacinta with a pout. 'It's going to be so dull without her.'

'And no one to talk to at bedtime,' Millie frowned.

'Well, I have a surprise for both of you.' Alice-Miranda's voice fizzed.

'A surprise?' Jacinta bounced up and down on the bed. 'You're not really going and this is all just a big joke?'

'No, even better, we *are* coming with you!' Millie exclaimed.

'Well, neither, I'm afraid.' Alice-Miranda bit her lip. 'But I asked Miss Grimm if you could share a room while I'm gone and she said yes.'

'Oh.' Jacinta stopped her bouncing. 'Is that all?'

'Jacinta Headlington-Bear – where are your manners?' Howie gave her a frosty stare. 'You know

Miss Grimm is not one for moving girls willy-nilly so I think you might be a little more grateful.'

'I didn't mean it like that,' Jacinta protested.

'Thanks, Alice-Miranda. You know Jacinta and I have been getting on just fine since you arrived.' Millie turned her attention to the older girl. 'But you'd better be tidy, Headlington-Bear. I like living with "Miss Nothing Out of Place" here,' she said, nodding towards Alice-Miranda, 'and I don't fancy having to dodge your dirty undies all over the floor.'

'I don't leave my underwear on the floor,' Jacinta snapped.

Mrs Howard gave Jacinta a meaningful look. 'Oh, really, young lady? Is that so?'

'Well, I don't do it on purpose. And I didn't mean to sound ungrateful, Alice-Miranda. Thanks. You really do think of everything.' Jacinta leapt up and hugged her friend.

'Just promise me that you'll be kind to each other,' Alice-Miranda grinned.

Mrs Howard folded her arms. 'Oh dear, that will be the day.'

'No it won't, Howie. You wait and see. We'll be perfect friends,' Jacinta insisted.

'I'm looking forward to seeing that.' Howie pulled a dusting cloth from her apron and ran it quickly along the top of one of the chests of drawers opposite Alice-Miranda's bed and then marched out the door.

'Come on then, Jacinta. I want to look at how much junk you're planning to move in here,' said Millie as she walked towards the door.

'I don't have any junk, thank you very much,' the blonde-haired girl retorted. 'And why do I have to move in here? Why can't you come to my room?'

Alice-Miranda chuckled at her friends.

Jacinta followed Millie out the door, the pair of them trading questions all the way.

Chapter 2

The next two days flew by. Alice-Miranda made sure that she said goodbye to all her friends and promised to write every week. On Saturday morning she did a sweep of the campus to say some final farewells and then, followed by a group of well-wishers, she walked out of the boarding house to meet her parents. Alice-Miranda was tingling with excitement about the trip.

It seemed almost the entire school had gathered to see her off, despite her protests that they would hardly have time to miss her and she'd be back before they knew it. 'Goodbye,' Alice-Miranda called through the open window of the back seat of her family's silver Range Rover.

A rowdy chorus of 'goodbye, farewell, *au revoir* and travel safely' rang out from the assembled crowd as the car crunched down the long gravel driveway.

'You know, I must be the luckiest girl in the whole world,' Alice-Miranda informed her parents as her father turned onto the main road. 'I have the most wonderful friends and Winchsterfield-Downsfordvale truly is the most beautiful school – oh, and look at this.' She pulled a tiny guidebook from her pocket. 'Mr Grump gave it to me. It's got a map and loads of information about the city.'

Cecelia Highton-Smith leaned around to look at her daughter.

'That's lovely, darling. You know, I think I'm the luckiest mother in the world to have you all to myself for four whole weeks. It's perfect. You'll be at school from eight until three-fifteen and then Daddy and I plan to meet you every afternoon and we can explore the city together.'

'But won't you have to be at the shop, Mummy?' Alice-Miranda asked.

'Well, we're scheduling as many meetings as

possible during school hours, so I hope we can get away, but if I'm caught up, Daddy should be okay to play tourist. There would have been no reason to drag you halfway around the world if we couldn't spend time with you, darling,' her mother replied.

The 'shop', Highton's on Fifth Avenue, was renowned as one of the world's most beautiful department stores and considered the jewel in the Highton's empire. Alice-Miranda's great-great-grandfather, Horace Highton, had been a visionary man, establishing three stores in his lifetime. Over ninety years the business had grown to twenty-five stores in major cities around the globe.

For the past six months, the New York store had been closed for business while undergoing a complete renovation. Cecelia had been back and forth several times and she and Hugh had decided to take Alice-Miranda with them in the lead-up to the reopening. Their trip had been brought forward a couple of weeks due to some unexpected hiccups.

'I doubt I'll be needed terribly much at all,' Hugh Kennington-Jones added. 'Gilbert and your mother will have everything under control. The building works are nearly complete and the schedule is, well, *almost* back on track.'

'What are you going to do when I'm at school, then, Daddy?' Alice-Miranda asked.

'I thought I might do some research,' her father replied.

'Research?' Cecelia raised her eyebrows. 'On what?'

'Just a bit of history,' Hugh replied.

'It says here that there are hundreds of museums in New York City so that should keep you very busy, Daddy.'

Cecelia's phone rang. She retrieved it from her handbag and answered the call.

'Hello Gil, yes, we're just on our way now. Really? That's very odd. Did Tony know anything about it? Okay, see you soon,' Cecelia rang off.

'Something the matter? Hugh asked.

'That was Gilbert. Apparently the toilet suites for the ladies' powder rooms mysteriously arrived at Highton's Chicago this morning so now they won't get to the store until after the weekend. Just another hold-up,' she sighed.

'What did Tony have to say about it all?' Hugh asked.

'He couldn't understand it. He placed the order himself.' Cecelia shook her head.

'Who's Tony, Mummy?' Alice-Miranda asked.

'He's our building contractor, darling. He oversaw all the renovations to the apartment a few years back and he's marvellous. But I can't help thinking there is something strange going on over there.'

'What do you mean, Mummy?'

'There have been so many problems getting things finished off. Deliveries going astray, tradesmen who were booked not turning up, just general confusion, actually. Poor Gilbert needs as much support as I can give him,' Cecelia said, frowning.

'Is Mr Gruber all right?' Alice-Miranda was asking after Gilbert Gruber, the General Manager of Highton's on Fifth. 'He's so adorable. I loved it when he came to stay last Christmas. He and Granny are such fun together.'

'He says that he's fine but I know this refurbishment has tested his patience. There are so many regulations with the building and on top of the strange happenings at the store he's had difficulties with the city authorities over the most ridiculous things,' Cecelia replied. 'But he is a darling man and my father knew exactly what he was doing when he appointed him to look after Highton's on Fifth all those years ago.'

'Well, I can't wait to see the store,' Alice-Miranda beamed.

'Me too,' her father replied.

'You're going to love the toy emporium,' Cecelia began. 'There's a giant tree house in the middle of the floor and all sorts of cubbies and hidey-holes.'

'That sounds amazing,' said Alice-Miranda. 'Is Aunt Charlotte coming over? And Uncle Lawrence and Granny?'

'No darling, I'm afraid not. Lawrence has only got a month between film shoots so he's taking Charlotte on a belated surprise honeymoon. He was being very mysterious and wouldn't tell anyone what he had planned,' Cecelia replied.

'That's so romantic,' Alice-Miranda said.

Cecelia's younger sister Charlotte and the handsome movie star Lawrence Ridley had recently been married in splendid style on board the Royal Yacht *Octavia*. The ship was owned by Aunty Gee, Alice-Miranda's grandmother's best friend and godmother to Cecelia and Charlotte. Aunty Gee was otherwise known as Queen Georgiana.

'And I'm afraid your grandmother is begging off too. She's going to Aunty Gee's birthday party –

which is the very same night as the opening,' Cecelia explained.

'It's a *special birthday*,' Hugh winked at Alice-Miranda in the rear-vision mirror.

Alice-Miranda grinned. 'Gosh, I hadn't realised that Aunty Gee was turning forty.'

'Ha, more like ninety,' her father laughed. Cecelia gave him a playful smack on the leg. 'Darling, don't be so mean. You know a lady never reveals her age. And she's nowhere near ninety, you rude thing!'

With the help of Aldous Grump's guidebook gift, the trio spent the rest of the journey to the airport planning all the spots they would visit in New York City. Hugh said that he and Cecelia hadn't played tourist there since they were in their early twenties and it would be a novelty to hop on the sightseeing trail.

'Can we ride the subway, Daddy?' Alice-Miranda asked.

'Oh, I don't know about that,' her father replied. 'I'm not sure that it's safe.'

'"The subway is a perfectly good option for getting around the city",' Alice-Miranda read from her guidebook.

'But darling, we have a town car at the store,' her mother frowned. 'And there's the Highton's limousine as well.'

'That's lovely, Mummy, but I want to experience the real New York and I'm certain not everyone has a town car or a limousine. Please, can we go on the subway?' Alice-Miranda begged.

Hugh glanced at his wife and then at his daughter in the rear-vision mirror. 'I'm game if you are.'

'And I think we should go to the Empire State Building and the Top of the Rockefeller Center and Staten Island and . . .' Alice-Miranda began.

'Slow down, darling,' her mother laughed. 'Why don't we take a proper look at that book of yours on the plane?'

Hugh parked on the edge of the tarmac. 'Looks like we're nearly ready to go.' He hopped out of the car and was greeted by Cyril, their multi-skilled pilot who not only flew the family helicopter but also *Kennington 1*, the company jet.

'Good afternoon, sir, good to see you,' said Cyril, offering his hand.

'And you, Cyril,' Hugh replied. 'How are we looking?'

'Very good, sir. Should be ready for take-off in about thirty minutes.'

Alice-Miranda leapt from the car and raced over to her father.

'Hello!' She rushed forward and gave Cyril a hug.

'And hello to you too, miss,' the pilot smiled.

'Come on, sweetheart,' Cecelia called as she collected Alice-Miranda's suitcase from the back of the four-wheel drive. 'Let's hop on and get settled. Dolly must be on board already. Ambrose was dropping her off. Daddy and Cyril need to talk.'

'Leave that, ma'am,' the pilot nodded at the luggage. 'I'll take care of it.'

'Thank you, Cyril.' Cecelia took Alice-Miranda's hand and mother and daughter boarded the plane.

Alice-Miranda couldn't wait to get to New York and start their adventures, although she had a strange feeling that there was going to be a lot more excitement on this trip than she had first imagined.

Chapter 3

Lucinda Finkelstein glimpsed her reflection in the hall mirror. Despite an hour of torturous straightening, her hair was already rebelling back to its natural state of frizz. Lucinda's mother Gerda had silken black tresses, which her older brothers, Tobias and Ezekiel, had inherited. Lucinda, on the other hand, took after her father. Morrie Finkelstein was proud of the fact that he had never owned a hairbrush or a comb. His wiry greying locks sat atop his head like a Brillo pad.

'Lucinda, hurry up, your father wants to see how beautiful you look,' her mother called from the sitting room.

Lucinda tried in vain to flatten the rogue ringlets that were appearing around her forehead but the more she pulled, the more they escaped, mocking her with their springiness.

'I'm coming, Mama,' the girl sighed, and headed for her appraisal. But she didn't need to anticipate her father's reaction. Morrie Finkelstein was nothing if not predictable. Lucinda would walk into the room where her father would be drinking a strong cup of tea with today's *New York Post* on the side table next to him. He would look up and gasp and then he would say the exact same thing that he said every Saturday at 2 pm, just before Lucinda and her mother took the town car to the store for afternoon tea in the Salon, with the usual gaggle of twenty or so of her mother's friends and their daughters.

Each week her father would say, 'Oh, Lucinda. Look at you, my gorgeous girl. That's a lovely dress – you know, I picked it out myself. Come and give Papa a kiss, and you and your mother enjoy your afternoon tea.'

Lucinda entered the room. She looked around expecting to see her mother but she wasn't there. The gangly child stood a few metres inside the doorway and waited for her father to greet her. His steaming cup of tea sat idle beside him. Morrie Finkelstein had his head buried in *The Post*. He didn't set the paper aside nor did he look up.

'Hello Papa,' Lucinda said quietly.

But there was no response. Lucinda frowned. Every weekend for as long as she could remember, her father had arrived home on a Friday evening with a new dress from the store and admired her in it on Saturday afternoon. The routine was only broken twice a year, when the Finkelsteins went on holiday to their estate in Southampton.

'Papa? Are you all right?' Lucinda tried again.

Morrie finally looked up. 'Oh, I didn't hear you come in, Lucinda.' He folded the paper and put it to the side.

'Is everything all right, Papa?' Lucinda's stomach twisted. By this time her father should have been midway through his usual farewell speech.

'Everything's fine, Lucinda. Now run along. You don't want to keep your mother waiting, do you?'

Lucinda walked towards her father, leaned down and kissed him on the forehead. The knot in her stomach tightened. It felt strange not to have her father comment on her appearance. And while her hair was misbehaving, her dress was particularly lovely and, she thought, quite flattering for someone whose limbs were growing way too quickly for the rest of her body.

As she turned to leave, her father picked up the newspaper and in a loud voice said to no one in particular, 'Just like your father, your grandfather before that and your great-grandfather too. We'll see who's boss of this town, Cecelia Highton-Smith!'

Lucinda was puzzled by his outburst. She knew that the Finkelsteins and Hightons didn't get on for some reason but her father's voice was angry. She retreated to the doorway and peered back inside to see him depositing the newspaper into the huge fireplace, where the glowing embers erupted into flame. Lucinda scurried along the hallway to the apartment's grand foyer to wait for her mother. Her father was acting strangely, for sure.

Chapter 4

Alice-Miranda sat in the back of the limousine as it snaked its way from Teterboro Airport to the city.

'Oh, Daddy, we can't be far now!' she exclaimed as the car approached the signpost for the Lincoln Tunnel.

'No, not far, but I suspect the traffic in the city could slow us down a little,' her father replied.

'But it's not bad at all,' said Alice-Miranda as the car sped through the tunnel and emerged onto West

38th Street and straight into a bank-up of cars a mile long.

'Oh, I think I spoke too soon.' Alice-Miranda stared wide-eyed out of the window at the lights of Manhattan. On the flight she and her parents had made lots of plans about the places they would visit and sights they wanted to see. She'd made Mrs Oliver promise to come with them as often as she could, too.

'Look at all those yellow taxis, Mummy,' Alice-Miranda observed as their car turned into Sixth Avenue, heading towards Central Park. As far as the eye could see, yellow cabs clogged the street, peppered with black town cars. 'Does anyone drive their own car in New York?' Alice-Miranda was trying to spot other vehicles among the bumblebee-coloured swarm.

'No, most New Yorkers don't bother with a car. There's hardly any parking and what there is costs a king's ransom,' her father replied.

A group of pedicabs darted by, weaving their way in and out of the traffic, their young drivers shouting offers of cheap rides to the pedestrians on the foot-paths.

'That looks like fun. Are you game, Mrs Oliver?'

Alice-Miranda pointed at the bicycles with their pedestrian carts behind.

'Count me out, my dear,' Dolly replied, shaking her head. 'I prefer my arms and legs attached.'

'Excuse me, Mr O'Leary, do you know what the hold-up is?' Alice-Miranda asked the uniformed driver.

The kindly man glanced at Alice-Miranda in the rear-vision mirror and said in his lovely Irish lilt, 'Oh lass, this is just the regular Saturday night. This place never stops, you know. Three o'clock in the morning and there are still thousands on the streets.'

'It's electric!' Alice-Miranda bubbled. 'There's something about this city. I can't wait to start school on Monday.'

'I know Jilly is looking forward to it too,' Cecelia replied.

For the next month or so, Alice-Miranda would be attending Mrs Kimmel's School for Girls, on East 75th Street. The headmistress just happened to be an old friend of Cecelia's from her own school days. With a diplomat father, Jilly Hobbs grew up attending schools in several different countries before returning to the United States to go to college. Jilly had made a career teaching girls in New York

City and was now headmistress of the prestigious Mrs Kimmel's.

The car continued up Sixth Avenue and into Central Park.

'Oh, Mummy, look at the carriages. Aren't the horses beautiful? Can we ride in one? Please?' Alice-Miranda begged.

'Don't you remember? We did that last time we were here,' her mother replied.

'Yes, but that was when I was only four,' Alice-Miranda reminded her. 'And now I'm almost eight.'

'Of course,' her mother smiled. 'It doesn't seem that long since we last came together but, yes, you're right.'

The car wound its way through Central Park, exiting at the 65th Street Transverse and crossing Fifth Avenue. Veiled in scaffolding, Highton's department store took up the entire block between East 64th and East 65th, with its frontage on Fifth Avenue. A grand set of gates at the rear of the building opened automatically. Hidden behind the gothic facade, a circular driveway led through a formal garden and spiralled downwards. Another set of elaborate metal gates, adorned with cherubs and vines and other creatures among the ironwork, slid open to reveal a private parking garage and equally decorative subterranean entrance to the building.

'Well, here we are.' Cecelia Highton-Smith slid forward and gathered her handbag and jacket. Seamus O'Leary held open the door as the group alighted from the vehicle.

'Good evening all.' An impeccably dressed man emerged from the entrance. He had a shock of wavy white hair and wore a red polka dot bow tie.

'Mr Gruber!' Alice-Miranda raced towards the gentleman and immediately launched herself at his middle.

He lifted her up in one swift action and Alice-Miranda gave him a smacking great kiss on the cheek.

'Oh, my dear girl, you do make an old man happy.' Gilbert Gruber put Alice-Miranda back down. 'I think you are just the tonic I've needed.'

'I'm so excited to be here, Mr Gruber. I'm starting school on Monday and then Mummy and Daddy are going to take me all over the city after school and we're going to ride the subway and pedicabs and have the best time ever and I think Mrs Oliver might even let me eat hot dogs from the street stalls and giant pretzels and we're going to the Museum of Natural

History and the Met and I don't remember where else but I'm not going to waste a minute.'

'Whew! I'm tired just hearing it,' Gilbert grinned.

Cecelia Highton-Smith greeted the old man with a kiss on each cheek. He embraced Mrs Oliver like a long-lost friend and firmly shook Hugh's hand.

'How are you, Gil?' Hugh Kennington-Jones slapped the old man on the back.

'Well, I have to be honest, Hugh, I think this renovation has almost done me in. I suspect that daughter of yours will give me just the boost I need, although I might require a vacation once you've gone.'

The group laughed.

'I imagine you'd like to head straight upstairs?' Mr Gruber offered.

'Actually, Gilbert, I wondered if you might give Hugh and me a quick tour. I'm dying to see what you've done with the ground floor since I was last here,' Cecelia Highton-Smith suggested. 'Dolly, why don't you take Alice-Miranda upstairs and get her settled.'

'May I come with you instead, Mummy?' Alice-Miranda asked.

Dolly Oliver nodded at Cecelia. 'I'll go up and put the kettle on.'

'All right, we won't be long,' Cecelia smiled.

'Are you sure you don't want to wait until Monday?' Gilbert asked Cecelia.

'No, of course not,' she shook her head. 'It can't be that bad.'

The old man frowned. He led the family through a long hallway and up a short flight of steps. Gilbert pushed open a large door and spread out in front of them was a muddle of counters, boxes, signage and general disarray. Lights not yet attached to the ceiling dangled from long cables and there seemed to be a whole wall of plasterboard missing.

Down among the muddle, the high-pitched whine of a drill started up.

'Goodness, someone's working late,' Alice-Miranda said.

A head popped up from beside a counter.

'Haven't you got a home to go to George?' Gilbert joked with the young man.

The man seemed startled. 'Oh, hello Mr Gruber. I . . . I just thought I'd get a couple of things done before heading off,' he called back.

'George, you know Cecelia, of course,' Gilbert began, 'and this is her husband Hugh and daughter Alice-Miranda.'

'Hello.' The fellow waved. Alice-Miranda and her father waved back.

'George is Tony's site foreman,' Gilbert explained. 'I think that man works harder than anyone.'

George held his drill aloft. 'If you don't mind.'

'Of course not. Don't let us hold you up,' Gilbert replied. He turned to Cecelia and noticed that her face had drained of colour. 'It's a work in progress, Cee,' he said gently.

She gave a clenched smile.

'Is that what you call it, Gil? I'd say it's a dirty great mess,' Hugh laughed.

'I'm sure it will come together,' Alice-Miranda said and slipped her hand into her mother's.

'I hope so,' Cecelia whispered.

'Don't worry, dear. You know we'll get there,' Gilbert reassured her.

'Let's go upstairs, Mummy. You look like you could do with a cup of tea.'

The four of them walked back through the large door and into the private corridor towards the elevator.

'Tony assures me that George will have all trades on deck first thing Monday, and I guarantee you won't know the place by the afternoon,' Gilbert said.

'I'm not concerned,' Cecelia protested. 'Really, I'm not.'

'Then what are those?' Hugh reached out and touched his wife's forehead. 'They look like worry lines to me.'

'Don't be silly.' Cecelia smiled and the lines disappeared. 'Goodnight Gilbert,' she said and kissed the old man.

'Goodnight all,' he replied.

Alice-Miranda reached out and pressed the elevator button. There was only one option for the carriage they stood in front of: P for penthouse.

Chapter 5

Alice-Miranda's eyelids fluttered open.

'Good morning, sleepyhead, we thought you were going to snooze the day away.' Hugh Kennington-Jones drew back the curtains and sunlight flooded the room.

The Highton-Smith-Kennington-Joneses' penthouse covered the two top floors of their iconic department store. Built almost one hundred years ago, the building was hailed as a stunning example of gothic architecture along what was then called

Millionaires' Mile. The glorious apartment, which had been part of the original design of the building, boasted six bedrooms and as many bathrooms, a formal sitting room, dining room, chef's kitchen and a media room complete with home theatre. There was an enormous library and study too. On the rooftop a small garden gave a wonderful view of Central Park.

Alice-Miranda's bedroom was decorated with the palest of lemon and pink striped wallpaper. Floral curtains adorned the two double-height windows and a silk Chinese rug covered the bare polished boards. Two single beds jutted out from the long wall opposite the door and a bookcase packed full of Alice-Miranda's favourite volumes stretched half the length of the room. A cedar armoire and antique chest of drawers contained a lovely set of clothes her mother had chosen especially from Highton's on Fifth's new collection. There was an ensuite off the end of the room with a deep roll-top bath and a shower. The apartment had undergone a major renovation only a couple of years before and was headquarters for Cecelia and Charlotte or their mother Valentina whenever they were in town.

'Ahhh.' Alice-Miranda yawned and stretched her arms above her head. 'Good morning, Daddy.'

Her father sat down on the side of her bed and stroked his daughter's hair. 'So, what would you like to do today?' he asked. 'What about a tour of the New York City Sanitation Depot?'

'I don't remember *that* being on my list,' Alice-Miranda frowned. 'I thought we were going to the park.'

'Of course we are – I was just teasing,' her father smiled.

'Do you have to work?'

'No, darling. Today Mummy and I are all yours,' Hugh smiled.

Alice-Miranda leaned forward and hugged her father.

'Well, come along. Why don't you hop out of bed and have a quick shower to help you wake up. Dolly will fix you some breakfast and then we can get moving.'

After a delicious stack of fluffy pancakes drowned in maple syrup, Alice-Miranda and her parents headed across the road to Central Park. First stop was the Central Park Zoo, a small but perfectly formed animal kingdom in the heart of one of the largest parks in one of the biggest cities in the world.

'See here, it says that there are over 1400 animals in the zoo from 130 species. Look, Daddy!' Alice-Miranda exclaimed. 'There's a polar bear.' Alice-Miranda ran towards the enclosure, scanning for its inhabitant. 'His name is Gus and it says here that he loves to show off for visitors.'

Just as Alice-Miranda spoke, the enormous snowy bear sauntered into the pool. The girl giggled with delight. The polar bear swam right to the far end of the pool, turned and locked eyes with Alice-Miranda through the glass.

'Isn't he gorgeous?' Alice-Miranda remarked.

'Yes, and he'd happily eat you for lunch,' her father smiled.

'I don't think he'd mean to, though.' Alice-Miranda stretched her hand across the glass. 'It's just what bears do, isn't it?' The giant white beast swam towards her, then reached up and placed its hairy paw on the other side of the barrier.

A group of visitors milling around were watching the encounter wide-eyed.

'Goodness, look at that,' a portly man said, grinning at the huge bear and the tiny girl. Cameras snapped away, capturing the tender moment.

'I think that daughter of yours must have a way with animals,' said a man standing beside Cecelia Highton-Smith.

'I think you might be right. She seems to have a way with most everything and everyone else,' her mother smiled.

In his best bear-like voice, Hugh Kennington-Jones teased, 'Hmm, you look like a very tasty little girl. In fact, I think I could eat you up right . . . now!' He grabbed Alice-Miranda from behind. She shot into the air with a squeal.

'Daddy, stop!' Alice-Miranda giggled as Hugh twirled his little daughter up onto his shoulders, where she dangled over his back.

'Come on, you two,' Cecelia admonished with a smile. 'There's a lot more to see so we'd better get a move on.'

'Goodbye Gus,' Alice-Miranda called and waved.

It was hard to believe that a couple of hours had flown past by the time the family left the zoo and headed out into the park.

'Well, I don't know about you ladies but I'm feeling rather peckish,' her father advised. 'What about lunch at the Boathouse?'

'Daddy, couldn't we just have a hot dog from that man over there?' Alice-Miranda squeezed her father's hand and pointed at a vendor with his mobile cooking station. 'If we go to the restaurant it will take much longer and there are so many more things to see.'

Alice-Miranda's parents exchanged glances.

'I'm game if you are,' Cecelia smiled.

'All right, hot dogs it is,' Hugh replied.

The family purchased their lunch and went to sit on a bench in the middle of a patch of green lawn. The smell of food brought some other critters out and soon two squirrels were playing hide-and-seek up and down and around a tree beside them.

'They're so cute,' Alice-Miranda declared.

'Yes, but don't touch,' her mother warned. 'They're still wild animals and people shouldn't feed them or they can become a problem.'

Alice-Miranda just loved watching the way they would sit still for a few seconds, twitch, and then run away at lightning speed.

'Well, you know, sweetie, that was the best hot dog I've ever tasted,' her father declared as he ate the last bite.

'It's probably the *first* hot dog you've ever tasted.' Cecelia Highton-Smith arched an eyebrow at her husband.

'Of course you must have had hot dogs before, Daddy. That was simply scrumptious,' said Alice-Miranda.

'Well, not for a very long time, I have to admit,' her father replied.

'I'll be back in a minute.' Alice-Miranda leapt from the bench and ran along the path back in the direction they had come.

'Darling, don't go far,' her mother called.

Alice-Miranda reached the hot dog vendor, who was sitting on a folding chair reading the newspaper. His face was lined with the stories of life and his hair had the misfortune of having fallen out in a perfectly round circle on the top of his head. A bushy moustache stood guard over his upper lip.

'Hello, my name is Alice-Miranda Highton-Smith-Kennington-Jones,' she said, smiling at the man.

He looked at her quizzically. 'And to what do I owe this introduction?'

'Do you have a name, sir?' the child asked.

'Yes, of course, it's Lou. Lou Gambino,' he replied slowly.

'Well, Mr Gambino, I just wanted to say that was the most delicious hot dog I've ever tasted. Thank you very much.'

The man smiled. 'Really? It was good?'

'Oh yes, delicious,' Alice-Miranda replied.

'Would you like another one?' he asked.

'I would but not today if that's all right. I couldn't fit another thing in.'

'Maybe you can come back and see me again sometime,' he offered.

'I surely will,' Alice-Miranda replied. 'I'm staying in the city for a month and I'm starting school tomorrow and I can't wait.'

The man shook his head. 'You're a breath of fresh air if you ask me, Miss Alice-Miranda and I can't remember the rest.'

'It's Highton-Smith-Kennington-Jones,' she replied.

'Highton,' he mused, looking up over the trees in the direction of the store.

'Yes, sir, my mummy and daddy are here to oversee the reopening.'

He grinned. 'Boy, it must be my lucky day, talking to royalty almost.'

'Oh no, Mr Gambino, we're not royalty, not at

all.' Alice-Miranda looked up at him with her brown eyes as big as saucers.

'You're the closest thing to it I've ever met.' Lou Gambino glanced up and saw another vendor pushing a pretzel cart towards them. 'Hey, Geronimo, over here! Come meet my new friend,' he called.

'All right, all right, I'm coming. These legs don't move as fast as they used to,' the older man yelled back. He pushed his cart slowly. 'So, who's your new friend?' he puffed.

'Hello Mr Geronimo, my name is Alice-Miranda Highton-Smith-Kennington-Jones and I'm very pleased to make your acquaintance.' The tiny child offered her hand.

'She's a Highton – like the store. And what's more she told me that I made her the best hot dog she's ever tasted,' Lou Gambino boasted.

The older man reached down and took Alice-Miranda's hand in his. She looked into his crystal blue eyes and smiled. 'Well, miss, you're something else. You just wait until you taste my pretzels. They leave his dogs for dead,' the man grinned. The skin around his eyes folded into soft creases and his whole face lit up.

'That sounds delicious, Mr Geronimo, but I don't think I can eat another thing today,' Alice-Miranda replied. 'I'll definitely see you again soon though, and then I'll try your pretzels.'

Cecelia Highton-Smith called out to her daughter.

'I'd best go or Mummy will start to worry,' Alice-Miranda declared. 'It's been lovely to meet you Mr Gambino, Mr Geronimo. See you soon.'

And with that Alice-Miranda spun around and scampered back up the hill to her parents.

Lou nodded his head. 'She's a cutie.'

'Worth a fortune too,' said Harry Geronimo. 'And not like some of the kids around here – wouldn't give you the time of day. No, that little girl's a special one.'

Harry set up his stall beside Lou's. A folding table appeared and Harry produced a chessboard from a cupboard on his stand. The two old friends sat opposite each other.

'You know, Harry, this is a good life,' Lou smiled. 'A very good life indeed.'

Chapter 6

Alice-Miranda and her parents spent the rest of the afternoon sailing remote-controlled boats in the inaugural Highton-Smith-Kennington-Jones family regatta. In the end Hugh managed to beat his daughter, taking out the championship by just half a boat length. Cecelia told him off for being so competitive but Alice-Miranda said that she didn't mind a bit. Her father had better skills and that was that.

As the late afternoon sun slanted through the trees and warmed Alice-Miranda's face, she told her mother and father that she couldn't have imagined a more perfect day. Hand in hand the family walked out of the park and back across Fifth Avenue to their temporary home, where they found Mrs Oliver midway through making dinner.

'That smells delicious.' Alice-Miranda sped through the hallway to the kitchen.

'Yes, it does, if I might say so myself,' Mrs Oliver replied. 'How was your day?'

Alice-Miranda pulled over a stool, and used it to climb up onto the end of the kitchen bench. She sat with her legs dangling in the air as she told Mrs Oliver every last detail.

'Saints preserve us, slow down and take a breath, young lady,' Mrs Oliver tutted. 'From all that, I'd say you've already befriended half of New York City.'

'Oh no, Mrs Oliver, that's just silly. There are over a million people in Manhattan alone and I only met about twenty of them today.' Alice-Miranda stared up at her.

Dolly Oliver shook her head and smiled. 'But if I know you, at the end of four weeks that won't be the case.'

Alice-Miranda offered to set the table for dinner. Dolly had spent the afternoon perfecting a huge pork loin with the crispiest of crackling, baked potatoes and honey-glazed carrots, sautéed green beans with slivered almonds and a homemade apple sauce to top it all off.

For dessert there was chocolate pudding with praline ice-cream.

'That's an awful lot of food just for us,' Alice-Miranda remarked as she busied herself finding cutlery and carrying it through to the dining room next door.

'Your mother invited Mr Gruber to dinner,' Dolly replied, as she stirred the thick brown gravy on the stovetop.

Alice-Miranda dashed back to the kitchen to locate the salt and pepper pots. She pulled a pair of crystal shakers with shining silver tops from the sideboard and grabbed an extra knife, fork and spoon while she was there.

'Thank you, darling girl,' said Mrs Oliver to her young assistant. 'Now, why don't you run along and have a bath and pop one of your pretty dresses on.'

'That sounds like a very good idea,' Cecelia Highton-Smith agreed as she entered the room, fresh from the shower herself.

'You smell delicious, Mummy,' her little daughter remarked.

'Thank you, darling.'

Cecelia Highton-Smith wore a smart pair of white trousers and a lovely deep-aqua silk blouse. Her patent aqua pumps were perfectly matched.

Dolly Oliver glanced at Cecelia as she pulled the potatoes from the oven. 'That's a great colour on you, ma'am.'

'Thank you, Dolly. I rather like it too. Is there anything I can do to help?'

'No, it's all under control. Alice-Miranda set the table and the dinner's almost done,' Mrs Oliver replied.

Cecelia busied herself locating a bottle of champagne from the wine cooler in the walk-in pantry. Being fourteen floors up, it was a little tricky to have a cellar attached to the penthouse; instead, Cecelia's great-grandfather had included a very large walk-in butler's pantry off the kitchen. The recent renovations had included the installation of a wine fridge and climate-controlled 'cellar' for the reds.

A plate of smoked salmon and chive crème fraîche blini and another of the tiniest roast vegetable tarts were transported by Mrs Oliver to the sitting room where the family would gather before the main meal.

'Now Dolly, can you join us for a drink before dinner?' Cecelia asked as Mrs Oliver walked back into the kitchen having delivered the trays.

'Why not?' the old woman grinned. 'Everything's under control in here and I just have to serve up when we're ready. So long as you don't mind, ma'am?' Mrs Oliver enquired.

'Oh Dolly, you're family. And it will be lovely to catch up with Gilbert and find out what on earth has been happening here,' Cecelia put her hand gently on Mrs Oliver's shoulder and gave it a light squeeze.

'Don't go worrying yourself about the store.' Dolly reached over and patted the younger woman's hand. 'Cecelia, if I may say, dear, you are the most organised person I've ever met. You could run a country, never mind just the Highton's empire. In fact, if I think about it, Highton's and all its staff around the world probably are equivalent to a small country.'

'Thank you, Dolly,' Cecelia smiled. 'You always know just the right thing to say.'

Dolly winked at Cecelia. 'I learned that from the little one.'

At exactly 7 pm the buzzer rang, signifying the imminent arrival of Gilbert Gruber. Alice-Miranda, in a pretty white dress tied in the middle with a large lemon bow, ran to the hallway to greet their guest. The elevator bell chimed and the doors slipped open. Mr Gruber barely had time to exit the compartment before the tiny child rushed forward.

He bent down and Alice-Miranda pecked him on the cheek.

'Don't you look gorgeous, young lady,' Gilbert admired. With a pirouette of his right index finger, Alice-Miranda twirled like a ballerina. 'You're getting taller, my dear. I'm sure that you've grown at least an inch since last I saw you.'

'Well, that's silly,' Alice-Miranda giggled. 'I only saw you last night. I couldn't possibly have grown an inch.'

'Oh, you cheeky little thing – I meant since I saw you at Christmas at the Hall,' Gilbert replied. 'But your mother is always sending photographs and news about your exploits. I hear you've made quite an impression on that school of yours.'

'I love it!' Alice-Miranda beamed. 'It's beautiful and I have the most wonderful friends and the teachers are so clever.'

'It must be taking quite a deal of courage to come here and try a new school, even if it is just for a month or so?' Gilbert Gruber leaned down to meet Alice-Miranda's gaze.

'Oh no, not at all. I can't wait to start tomorrow. And besides, it's not as if I don't know anyone. I mean, the headmistress is one of Mummy's best friends. I'll miss everyone at home but it's not permanent and really there aren't too many girls who have the opportunity to try out school in another country.'

Gilbert Gruber smiled at this child with her cascading chocolate curls and eyes as big as saucers. He'd known her mother and aunt since they were small girls too, but he couldn't help marvelling that Alice-Miranda seemed to have inherited the elegance of her mother with the no-nonsense, loving heart of her aunt.

'That's a very handsome tie, Mr Gruber,' said Alice-Miranda, admiring the old man's green polka dot bow tie. Bow ties were his signature look and she couldn't remember a time when he wasn't wearing one.

'Thank you, dear. I rather like this one. And I have something for you.' Gilbert passed Alice-Miranda a beautifully wrapped parcel. 'And I thought your mother might like these.' In his other hand was a stunning bouquet of roses.

'Thank you. May I open it later? I want to share the surprise with everyone.'

'Of course you may,' Gilbert Gruber replied. 'All right, lead the way.'

Alice-Miranda took him by his free hand and together they walked down the hallway to the sitting room.

'Gilbert, darling, how are you?' Cecelia Highton-Smith walked through from the dining room just as the pair arrived.

'These are for you. Beautiful flowers for a beautiful lady,' Gilbert winked. Cecelia leaned forward and kissed the old man on both cheeks.

'You know you don't have to bring gifts,' she frowned. 'But they are stunning. And if I didn't know better I'd say that they're an apple blossom pink hybrid tea rose called Audrey Hepburn.'

'I'm impressed. You certainly know your roses, Cecelia,' Gilbert smiled.

'Thank you, Gil, but I've cheated a bit. That's the variety I was planning to fill the ground floor with for the opening,' Cecelia replied.

'Oh Mummy, that will be heavenly,' Alice-Miranda said.

Hugh Kennington-Jones entered the room from the hallway. 'Ah, there you are, Gil, I thought I heard the elevator. How are you?' He strode forward and the two men shook hands.

'All the better for seeing this one,' said Gilbert, glancing down at Alice-Miranda.

'Well, she's kept her mother and me on our toes today,' Hugh smiled.

'You'll have to tell me what you got up to over dinner,' Gilbert invited.

'Be warned, Mr Gruber, once she gets started you'll be hard pressed to stop her,' Mrs Oliver added as she joined the group.

'Hello Dolly, lovely to see you.' Gilbert kissed Mrs Oliver on the cheek.

'And you too, Gilbert. You must be relieved that the renovations are almost complete,' Mrs Oliver commented.

'Absolutely. This has been the longest six months of my life and the staff are very keen to get the doors open again.'

The unmistakable sound of a popping champagne cork got everyone's attention.

Hugh Kennington-Jones poured four flutes and filled another with pineapple juice from the small bar cabinet in the corner of the room. Cecelia delivered the drinks to Gilbert, Dolly and Alice-Miranda.

Hugh proposed the toast: 'Here's to a wonderful reopening and a fantastic time in New York!'

'Hear, hear,' the rest of the group chorused.

Chapter 7

Alice-Miranda slept well, exhausted after her big day out in the park. But she had set her alarm for 6.30 am and still managed to wake before it began to beep. There were a few butterflies teasing her tummy.

Her mother appeared at the door just as she was sitting up in bed.

'Goodness, you're up early. I thought I'd have to wake you.'

'Oh no, Mummy. I'm far too excited,' Alice-Miranda slipped out of bed and scampered over to her walk-in closet where she retrieved a plaid skirt, white shirt and lilac blazer. She hung the clothes on the handle of the armoire. 'Are you taking me to school, Mummy?'

'Of course, darling, I wouldn't miss it. And I'm going to have tea with Jilly while you're getting settled,' her mother replied, while she took Alice-Miranda's school shoes from the closet.

Alice-Miranda was ready in no time. She packed her brown leather satchel with her pencil case and the lovely notebook that had been her gift from Mr Gruber. The notebook was covered with a silk-screened Japanese design of brilliant pink cherry blossoms interwoven with gold and green. Alice-Miranda thought it was beautiful.

During the evening Mr Gruber had told them of some of the challenges he'd faced with the renovation. There had been some truly odd difficulties, including the Finkelstein's Parade being given permission to divert down Fifth Avenue the very same day they had the enormous crane in place to lift several art installations up to the sixth floor home wares department. Strangely, a number of their stock deliveries had gone missing too, only to be located at the Finkelstein's dock several days later. And now some of their key suppliers seemed jittery about committing to exclusive contracts. The project was running two weeks behind schedule, with some odd requests from the planners at City Hall. Cecelia said that it was all just an unfortunate coincidence until Mr Gruber revealed that he had received an invitation at the end of last week to the Finkelsteins' opening of their Grand Salon, which was on the very same day as the gala re-launch of Highton's.

Cee decided that she would phone Morrie Finkelstein and see if they could meet for a coffee. Obviously there was something going on. Morrie was never easy to deal with but this was pushing the boundaries even for him.

Mr Gruber's stories gave Alice-Miranda a strange feeling but this morning she didn't want to think about that at all.

In the kitchen Mrs Oliver had prepared Alice-Miranda's favourite: French toast. Her mother and father joined her for breakfast.

'Oh, look at you, young lady,' said Hugh, glancing up from the paper. 'I like the plaid.'

'It's lovely, isn't it?' Alice-Miranda replied. 'But it's nowhere near as formal as my uniform at home. And the girls in middle school wear the skirt with whatever blouse they like, and then in the senior years there's no uniform at all.'

'Well, I suppose the school is encouraging girls to be individual – or at the very least more comfortable,' her mother added.

Cecelia poured a weak milky tea for her daughter and a much stronger brew for herself.

Alice-Miranda had worked out the night before that they should leave the apartment at 7.45 am to walk the ten blocks to school to be there in time for the start of class. Her mother had suggested they take the car but Alice-Miranda thought that was silly. It wasn't far and besides, her mother could have Mr O'Leary pick her up later if she wanted.

So, at precisely 7.40 am, having kissed her father and Mrs Oliver goodbye, Alice-Miranda and her mother stood in front of the lift. Five minutes later they were on Fifth Avenue making their way further uptown.

The streets were alive with the almost constant beeping of horns from the black and yellow vehicles. Several yellow school buses added to the tapestry of morning traffic and Alice-Miranda tingled with the excitement of it all.

'Do you know, Mummy, I don't think there's

anywhere in the world like New York.' Alice-Miranda looked up at her mother and smiled.

'I think you're right about that, darling. I've always loved the city, ever since your grandmother and grandfather brought me here when I was little. It reminds me of a giant, and the streets and traffic are the blood running through its veins.' Cecelia's eyes sparkled.

'Oh, that's exactly what it's like,' Alice-Miranda agreed.

Mother and daughter trotted along in the morning sunshine, past the mansions and apartment buildings opposite Central Park and the magnificent Frick Collection in its grand old building. Cecelia decided they should head towards Madison Avenue as there was more to see and then turn right into East 75th Street.

'Look at that!' Alice-Miranda stopped to admire thousands of pink roses, which were providing the backdrop to some high fashion in the windows of Finkelstein's.

'They're beautiful –' Cecelia drew in a sharp breath. She peered in closer. 'And I think they're the very same roses I was planning to use to decorate Highton's for the reopening.'

'I'm sure the Finkelsteins won't mind if you use the same roses,' Alice-Miranda replied.

'I think they might,' Cecelia sighed. 'Morrie Finkelstein has never been our greatest fan. In fact, I'd say openly hostile has been his mode of operation ever since I've known him.'

'But why?' Alice-Miranda asked, wide-eyed.

'I don't really know, darling, although I've heard whispers of a long-standing grudge. Something to do with when the stores were first established in the 1920s. Apparently, Great-Grandpa Highton and Morrie's great-grandfather were the best of friends and they were all set to go into business together but something happened and the deal soured at the last minute. They both went it alone. From the day the Finkelsteins opened their store they declared war on Highton's and it's been that way ever since. I don't understand it at all. We've both got beautiful stores that make handsome profits – it's just a nonsense.'

'But Mummy, have you ever asked Mr Finkelstein what the problem is? Maybe it could be solved and you could be friends,' Alice-Miranda suggested.

'Oh darling, I've tried to extend an olive branch to that man on many occasions. In the early days, when your grandfather was still in charge and

Morrie's father Joseph was running Finkelstein's, your father and I were determined that the next generation would get past whatever the problem was. So we invited Morrie and his wife Gerda to dinner, we had them over to the apartment for drinks, I wrote notes to congratulate Morrie whenever he did something fabulous at Finkelstein's. In fact, I still do. My father told me I was wasting my time and that the Finkelsteins would hate the Hightons forever – it was just a fact of life. Like breathing. But I wanted to prove your grandfather wrong.'

'And did you?' Alice-Miranda asked.

'Apparently not. Look, Morrie Finkelstein can be charming and Gerda's lovely – apart from her voice, it's a little on the high side – but just when I think things are fine between us, he does something nasty to put me back in my place. No matter how many times I ask him to explain what the problem is, he just says, "Cecelia, you know what your family has done." And really, I have no idea – and neither does your grandmother. We've even hired someone to look into it for us and they said that all of Morrie's great-grandfather's personal effects were destroyed in a fire that devastated their store back in the thirties and there didn't seem to be anything in Great-Grandpa Horace's things that gave us any leads either.'

'Oh well,' Alice-Miranda replied. 'Perhaps one day Mr Finkelstein will want to be friends.'

'You are an optimist, sweetheart.' Cecelia tightened her grip on Alice-Miranda's hand and they crossed into East 75th Street.

'Well, here we are,' Cecelia pointed towards an inconspicuous brownstone building across the street. In small brass letters on the wall, a sign said: *Mrs Kimmel's School for Girls.*

A yellow school bus pulled up and out tramped a long line of girls, some wearing plaid skirts in lilac and blue with white shirts and navy blazers, and others in an array of casual clothes. A cacophony of chatter accompanied the students as they jostled into school. Alice-Miranda studied the group from behind. She couldn't wait to meet them all. A tall girl with blonde hair parted perfectly in the middle and tied up in matching pigtails with lilac bows was talking intently to a smaller child beside her. The body language indicated that the shorter girl had done something that displeased the taller one. There were lots of hand signals and inflated gestures and raised voices. Alice-Miranda thought for a moment that her actions looked familiar, but she dismissed the notion from her mind.

Alice-Miranda and her mother waited on the other side of the street until the girls disappeared through the doorway.

'Come along, darling. Let's go and see Jilly,' said Cecelia Highton-Smith as she led her daughter across the road.

Chapter 8

Mrs Kimmel's School for Girls was one of the oldest in the city. There had been a long line of headmistresses before Jilly Hobbs, who was the sixteenth woman in charge of the revered institution.

A middle-aged man with thinning grey hair and a substantial mid-section welcomed Alice-Miranda and Cecelia at the top of the short flight of steps. A thick black belt held his trousers in place and he wore a blue shirt with an extravagant K embroidered on the pocket.

'Good morning, ma'am, miss,' he greeted the pair.

'Good morning, sir, my name is Alice-Miranda Highton-Smith Kennington-Jones, and I'm very pleased to meet you.' She held out her hand which the man shook vigorously.

'Good morning,' Cecelia echoed her daughter, and shook the man's hand too.

He nodded at Cecelia, then kneeled down and grinned at Alice-Miranda.

'Well, aren't you just as cute as a button. I'm Whip Staples, at your service.'

'I'm just starting today, Mr Staples. And it's only for a month but I can't wait to meet everyone. School in New York is quite a different adventure to my boarding school back at home. May I ask what you do here?' Alice-Miranda enquired.

'Well, for a start, please call me Whip – all the girls do – and I guess I look after everything from security to sanitation and a whole lotta things in between.' The man's grey eyes twinkled as he spoke.

'Do you take care of the garden?' Alice-Miranda asked.

Whip glanced at the window boxes along the front of the building with their bright red geraniums, and at the two square pots of standard roses that stood guard either side of the front door.

'Well, I suppose I do,' he smiled. 'Have to admit, though, it doesn't take me long.'

He held open the door.

'See you soon, Mr Whip,' said Alice-Miranda.

A small rectangular entrance hall lined on one side with a cabinet full of polished silver trophies opened out into a circular reception area. There were overstuffed antique chairs positioned around the room and a spiral staircase which rose up for at least four floors. A patterned carpet runner in shades of green and blue snaked its way up the middle of the stairs and was held in place by polished brass rods. A sparkling crystal chandelier adorned the lower ceiling and in the centre of the room, way up high at the very top of the building, an enormous K, the same as on Whip's shirt, was replicated in a glass skylight.

Alice-Miranda's jaw dropped open as she took in her surroundings. 'Oh Mummy, it's so lovely,' she whispered.

A young woman sat behind the reception desk. She greeted the pair warmly and directed Cecelia to sign in.

Alice-Miranda introduced herself in the usual way and proceeded to ask all manner of things about school. Where the classrooms were and what time they had lunch and where the girls went to play.

'Sweetheart, you really mustn't ask so many questions,' her mother chided.

'But Mummy, I only have a month so I need to know everything as soon as possible,' Alice-Miranda buzzed.

The young woman, whose name was Miss Cleary, telephoned through to the headmistress whose office was immediately off the reception area.

'Miss Hobbs will be right out, ma'am,' Miss Cleary announced. 'Please take a seat. I'm sure she won't be long.'

'Look, Mummy,' Alice-Miranda said as the pair sat down on two chairs opposite the reception desk. 'There's Aunt Jilly.'

Through a large oval-topped glass door with the Kimmel K etched into the centre, Alice-Miranda could see Jilly Hobbs engaged in an animated discussion with three small girls. They were sitting on a couch and she was leaning forward on a chair opposite them, smiling and laughing at whatever it was they were sharing.

'I love that Aunt Jilly has a glass door on her office – she must be very welcoming to her students and the staff,' Alice-Miranda observed. 'I must tell Miss Grimm about that when I get home.'

'I'm sure Miss Grimm will love hearing about it,' said her mother with a raised eyebrow. Given that Ophelia Grimm had only recently come out of ten years hiding from her students and staff, Cecelia smiled to herself at the thought of Alice-Miranda suggesting Ophelia install the same in her own study.

The door opened and the three girls giggled their way out of the office, followed by a portly labrador dog wearing what looked to be a neck scarf.

'Goodbye girls, thanks for stopping by,' Jilly Hobbs called after them from inside the office.

The girls disappeared through another archway off the reception hall.

Miss Cleary glimpsed the dog as she ambled across the hallway towards Alice-Miranda. 'Where are you off to, Miss Maisy?'

'She's lovely.' Alice-Miranda scratched the labrador's ears. Maisy immediately rested her head in the child's lap and began to drool.

'You scratch her ears like that and she will be your friend for life,' the receptionist smiled.

'Hello you two.' Jilly Hobbs walked out of her office. Cecelia stood up and the two friends warmly embraced. Alice-Miranda waited her turn.

'Hello Aunt Jilly.' Alice-Miranda hugged Jilly tightly around the middle. 'I'm so excited to be here.'

'And I'm thrilled to bits that you're going to join us – for a little while, at least. I see you've met Maisy.' The headmistress leaned down and gave the dog a scratch.

'Is she your dog?' Alice-Miranda asked.

'Technically yes, but if you ask any of the girls, they'll tell you she belongs to everyone at Mrs Kimmel's – at least until she does something to disgrace herself.'

'She's lovely,' Alice-Miranda smiled.

Maisy put her nose in the air. 'She's hungry,' Cecelia observed.

'Oh dear, can you smell lunch cooking? Maisy, don't you dare go down to that kitchen. You'll have us shut down by the city,' the headmistress berated. 'Why don't you head up and visit the ladies in the library? They've always got a treat for you.'

On hearing the magic word 'treat', Maisy shuffled across the parquetry floor towards the staircase.

'Good girl, you go get some exercise. Come on in.' Jilly ushered Cecelia and Alice-Miranda into her study and closed the door.

Chapter 9

Alice-Miranda had the most wonderful morning. After a short chat with Aunt Jilly, who they all agreed she would call Miss Hobbs when she was at school, Alice-Miranda was taken to meet her home room teacher Mr Underwood. Jilly decided that Alice-Miranda should spend the next month in the fifth grade – her academic ability was beyond doubt and the fifth grade had several exciting projects planned which Jilly thought would enhance Alice-Miranda's New York experience. It was also where she had a gap in the enrolments but that was information she preferred to keep to herself.

Rake thin with a goatee beard and shaggy hair grazing his collar, Felix Underwood had been a teacher at Mrs Kimmel's for nearly ten years. He welcomed Alice-Miranda into the classroom.

'Why don't you tell us a little bit about yourself,' Mr Underwood directed.

The tiny child stood in front of the class.

'Good morning everyone, my name is Alice-Miranda Highton-Smith-Kennington-Jones and I'm very pleased to be here. I can't wait to meet you all.'

Several girls in the front row smiled.

Alice-Miranda told the class that she usually went to boarding school and that she had come to New York because her parents were there on business for a little while.

The girls were keen to ask questions about her school and were especially intrigued that she lived there all the time.

'Do they serve, like, gruel for lunch?' a bright-eyed blonde girl in the front row asked.

'Do you have to study until bedtime?' another girl wanted to know.

'Is your headmistress, like, a witch or something?'

'I'm sorry to disappoint you,' Alice-Miranda replied. 'But the answer is no, no and no.'

'I'm sure that over the next month you can ask Alice-Miranda all about her school,' Mr Underwood grinned.

Alice-Miranda was directed to sit next to a girl with a tight mop of black curls in the second row.

'Hello,' Alice-Miranda said happily as she slid in behind her desk. The girl gave Alice-Miranda an awkward metal-clad smile.

'What's your name?' Alice-Miranda spoke in a hushed tone, aware that the classroom had fallen silent.

'Lucinda,' she whispered.

'Well, it's nice to meet you Lucinda,' Alice-Miranda smiled.

The time until recess flew by. Maths was followed by spelling (which Alice-Miranda found a little bit challenging, seeing as where she came from 'colour' contained a 'u') but it didn't take too long to get the hang of things.

'And after break I want you to get your sketchbooks and pencils and meet me at the back door,' Mr Underwood advised.

'Excuse me, Mr Underwood, where are we going?' Alice-Miranda asked.

'We're heading over to the Met for art class,' the man replied.

'The Met!' Alice-Miranda exclaimed. 'Really? That's wonderful!'

The rest of the class giggled and stared.

Alice-Miranda had read all about the Metropolitan Museum of Art in her guidebook. Renowned as one of the finest galleries in the world and housing an extensive collection of art and antiquities, it was on her list of places to visit.

'We go there every week,' Lucinda whispered to Alice-Miranda. 'It's not a big deal.'

'Well, I'm glad someone apart from me thinks that it is.' Felix Underwood's bionic teacher ears overheard Lucinda's comment and he grinned at his new student. 'I love your enthusiasm, Alice-Miranda. If you keep it up we might just trade one of the girls here for you – permanently. I'm sure they'd just love boarding school.'

The rest of the class groaned. 'Sir!'

'Lucinda and Ava, can I entrust Alice-Miranda to your care for break time?' he asked.

'Yes, sir,' the two girls chorused.

'Hey, what about me?' demanded another girl with black hair braided into cornrows and tied in a ponytail.

'Okay, you too Quincy, but don't you go leading this young one astray,' the teacher advised.

'Not yet, Mr Underwood. I'll wait until lunch-time,' Quincy replied cheekily.

An ear-splitting bell rang through the school, quickly followed by the thundering feet of hundreds of girls as they raced along the hallways. Mrs Kimmel's was set over six floors, including two in the basement which housed the gymnasium and the cafeteria. A rooftop terrace jutted out from the rear of the third level, with the tiniest of playgrounds.

'Where do we go?' asked Alice-Miranda. She was swept along with her new friends down several flights of stairs, where they were brought to a halt by the long line in the cafeteria.

Despite being in the basement of the building, the space was light and airy with tables for six along the walls and some booths tucked around the corner from the serving area. Fake windows were painted on the walls with real shutters attached, giving the impression that there was a garden just outside.

'I hope you like fruit,' Quincy turned around and informed her new friend, 'because Miss Hobbs is on a health food drive.'

Ava smiled at Alice-Miranda. 'That's not true at all. The student council voted for it. And there are cheese and crackers too. And it's fruit kebabs, actually.'

The girls proceeded along the edge of the counter. Alice-Miranda picked up a fruit stick and a napkin and followed her new friends.

'Come on, let's get a table before they're all gone.' Quincy urged the girls towards a booth on the edge of the room. The cafeteria was crowded with girls chatting and eating their morning tea.

Ava slid into the bench with Lucinda beside her and Alice-Miranda sat opposite, next to Quincy.

'So, do you have a cafeteria like this at your school?' Lucinda asked.

'No, we have a dining room where all of the girls come together at breakfast, morning tea, lunch, afternoon tea and then again for dinner. Mrs Smith is our cook and she makes the most delicious food – although the girls tell me she's improved quite a lot in the past little while. I have to say her chocolate brownies are probably some of the best anywhere in the world. She packs them with walnuts and they have exactly the right amount of squishiness.'

'Mmm, yum, I love brownies. Can she send over a box – or make that two?' Quincy licked her lips. 'Better still, maybe she can come and work at Mrs Kimmel's for a little while,' Quincy suggested. 'Cos we're on starvation here.'

'Mrs Smith would love that. Her grandchildren live in America.' Alice-Miranda picked up the fruit stick, devouring the strawberries, banana and watermelon along the line. 'And this is delicious.'

'So where are you staying while you're here, Alice-Miranda?' Quincy asked.

'We have an apartment above the shop,' Alice-Miranda replied. 'It's about ten blocks away.'

Lucinda Finkelstein's ears pricked up.

'Do your parents own a store?' she asked, already quite sure of the answer.

'Yes. Well, it was started by my great-great-grandfather but now Mummy's sort of in charge since Grandpa passed away. Aunt Charlotte works with her too and Daddy helps out but he's quite busy with his own work,' Alice-Miranda replied.

'Which one is it?' Ava locked eyes with their new friend.

'It's called Highton's on Fifth,' Alice-Miranda smiled.

'Highton's on Fifth. Oh my gosh, that's my favourite store in the whole city!' Ava gushed. 'No offence, Lucinda, but Highton's is so beautiful and I can't wait until it reopens. My grandmother takes me there so we can look at all the window displays each season. We love how they always have themes. Last year there were fairies in the garden for springtime. They looked so real I could have sworn I saw them moving.'

'I didn't see that.' Alice-Miranda shook her head. 'I haven't been here since I was four. But it sounds wonderful.'

'My mom always takes me to see Santa at Highton's,' Quincy added. 'Their Christmas Cave is the best.'

Alice-Miranda wished that she could see the store throughout the year – it sounded like everyone loved it. At least she could learn about it from her new friends.

'What about you, Lucinda? Do you ever visit Highton's?' Alice-Miranda asked.

Lucinda fiddled with a rogue strand of hair. She took a bite of banana and did her best to avoid the question, praying that the bell would go.

'It's all right, Lucinda. I completely understand if you don't. Shopping isn't everyone's cup of tea – a lot of the time I prefer just to look at the beautiful displays. Like on the way here this morning, Mummy and I walked past Finkelstein's and they had the most gorgeous show of roses in their windows. There were hundreds and hundreds of them. Mummy and I just stopped and stared for at least five minutes.'

Lucinda felt her stomach knot, just like it had on the weekend when she heard her father talking to the newspaper article.

'I don't go,' she mumbled, her tongue probing at the mashed banana that was now firmly stuck in her braces.

'Come on, Lucinda. Tell Alice-Miranda the truth. Your father would kill you if you walked within a block of Highton's,' Ava revealed.

'Why?' Alice-Miranda was wide-eyed. 'Is it in a dangerous part of the city?'

'No.' Ava grinned and shook her head.

'Well, if it's not dangerous then why aren't you allowed to go there?' Alice-Miranda asked.

'It seems the same rules don't apply for your family, Alice-Miranda,' Ava began. 'I wonder what your father would think, Lucinda, knowing that Alice-Miranda and her mother were admiring your window displays?'

Lucinda looked up at Alice-Miranda.

'I'm not allowed to go there because my father forbids it,' Lucinda offered. 'Because I . . .' she faltered. 'I'm a . . .'

Lucinda and Alice-Miranda said it together: 'Finkelstein.'

'But that's wonderful,' Alice-Miranda smiled.

'How?' Lucinda wondered how much trouble she would be in if her father knew Alice-Miranda was in her class, let alone that she'd been assigned to look after her. 'We're not supposed to be friends.'

'Do you know why?' Alice-Miranda asked.

Lucinda shook her head. 'I've got no idea. I just know that I'm not allowed to go to your store and my father *really* doesn't like your mother.'

'Oh dear. Apparently there's some long-running family feud between the Hightons and the Finkelsteins that dates back to when the stores were first opened. Mummy was telling me as much as she knew this morning. And no one really knows what it's about – well, except I think your father might. But he won't give Mummy a straight answer. So this is perfect,' Alice-Miranda gushed.

'This is a disaster,' Lucinda corrected her. 'You're just another friend I can't have.'

'What do you mean?' Alice-Miranda asked.

'If anyone tells my father that I've met you, let alone that we're in the same class, he'll be so mad, he'll phone Miss Hobbs and demand that you be moved. He'll yell at me.' Lucinda's eyes glistened.

'But that's just silly. Whatever problem our great-great-grandfathers had with each other has nothing to do with us. And if anything, our being friends is the best possible thing in the world,' Alice-Miranda replied. 'Perhaps together we can solve that silly old mystery. But why did you say "another friend"?'

Ava and Quincy exchanged glances.

'Lucinda's not allowed to be friends with us either,' Quincy started.

'We're not on the same social scale as her,' Ava added.

'I don't understand,' Alice-Miranda replied. 'What do you mean?'

'Well, her mother and father have carefully selected her friends for her and they go every Saturday afternoon to their salon at Finkelstein's to meet up,' Ava explained.

'And we're not invited,' Quincy added. 'We're not the right kind of people.'

'The right kind of people?' Alice-Miranda frowned. 'But you're good friends at school?'

Lucinda nodded. 'Quincy and Ava are my best friends in the world.'

'Come on, Finkelstein.' Quincy looked at her. 'We're your *only* friends in the world. We love you no matter how weird your parents are.'

'But I don't understand why you can't be friends,' said Alice-Miranda. 'You go to the same school and you live in the same city.'

'Yes, but Ava's here on –' Quincy and Ava glanced at each other, and then Quincy whispered – 'scholarship, and my parents own a jazz club.'

'We're really inappropriate,' Ava added.

'But that's wonderful!' Alice-Miranda fizzed. 'Mrs Kimmel's is a lovely school and I'm sure that it's very expensive so it's important to have scholarships so lots of girls get to come here. And owning a jazz club sounds amazing.'

'Gee, I wish everyone thought like you,' Ava grinned.

'We have girls on scholarships at my school at home. It would be terribly dull if everyone was exactly the same,' Alice-Miranda explained.

'My father wants me to be friends with people who are just "like us",' Lucinda put invisible quotation marks around her words in the air.

'So why don't you spend time with the girls from the salon at school?' Alice-Miranda asked.

'Because I don't think they like me very much and that's okay because I don't like them either. Some of them go to other schools and the ones who come here, well, we just say hi but we don't hang out,' Lucinda replied.

'Well, that's just silly. You and me probably have the most in common when it comes to our families, Lucinda, and you've just told me that your father wouldn't allow us to be friends because of some ridiculous old family feud,' Alice-Miranda shook her head.

The shrill ringing of the bell interrupted the girls' conversation.

'Come on.' Quincy slid out of the booth, followed by Alice-Miranda. On the opposite side Ava and Lucinda did the same.

The girls raced upstairs to their lockers to grab their sketchbooks and pencils, and then headed for the back door.

Chapter 10

'Excuse me a moment.' Hugh Kennington-Jones walked away from the group of staff he had been discussing floor layouts with and answered his phone.

'Hello, Hugh Kennington-Jones speaking. Oh, hello Hector.'

Hugh stood behind a male mannequin dressed in a dapper cream sports jacket and navy pants.

'What do you mean you're in New York? Oh.' Hugh paused for a moment. 'I'll meet you there in fifteen minutes.'

Hugh terminated the call and walked back towards the group.

'I'm terribly sorry, folks, but I have to duck out for a while. Can I leave the rest of the decisions in your capable hands, Marcel? It's looking great – product placement's very logical. I'm sure Ralph and Calvin will be pleased.'

A dark-haired man in a smart pinstripe suit nodded.

'Of course, sir. Thank you.'

Hugh wove his way through the racks of clothing that were scattered around the floor. A lone carpenter was putting the finishing touches on one of the designer showroom areas, screwing the last sign into place.

Hugh exited the shop floor and ducked through to the private elevator in the rear passageway. He hopped in and rode it down to their parking garage.

'Seamus, could you give me a lift?' he called to the chauffeur who was sitting inside the workshop with his head buried in *The Post*.

'Of course, sir, where would you like to go?'

'The Carlyle.'

Seamus held open the rear door and Hugh got into the vehicle.

Within a few minutes the limousine turned into Park Avenue and then travelled a handful of blocks uptown.

'I wonder how the little one is enjoying her first day at school.' Seamus glanced in the rear-vision mirror.

Hugh didn't answer. He appeared lost in his thoughts. 'Sorry, what did you say?' he apologised after a moment.

'Miss Alice-Miranda – I said, I wonder how she's enjoying her first day,' the driver repeated.

Hugh managed a tight grin. 'If I know my daughter, she's probably running the place by now.'

'She knows her own mind that one,' Seamus replied.

'Yes, you're right there,' Hugh replied.

The limousine pulled up in East 76th Street opposite Hugh's destination.

'Isn't that her there?' The driver was studying a group of schoolgirls exiting a building just in front of the vehicle. A tall man with a goatee beard led the children to the traffic lights on the corner.

Seamus O'Leary opened the driver's door.

'Wait,' Hugh urged. 'I'd rather not distract

her. In fact, I'd prefer that we keep this excursion between ourselves.'

'Of course, sir,' Seamus watched as Alice-Miranda skipped across the road surrounded by a gaggle of girls, all laughing and talking as they went. 'Would you like me to wait for you, sir?'

'No, I'll make my own way back,' Hugh advised. He opened the rear door and hopped out.

Hugh checked the traffic and scurried across the street to the side entrance of The Carlyle. There in the foyer, Hector was waiting for him. The two men shook hands vigorously and Hugh suggested they sit in the Bemelmans Bar, where the booths were private.

'So what have you found that has brought you all the way to the US?' Hugh scanned the old man's face looking for clues.

'Well, after we spoke, I took a trip back to the village to see if the charity shop had received anything from the estate. I don't think the old woman running the place thought much of me at all, but there was a naive young thing working alongside her who answered my questions. Lo and behold, she found an ancient tin trunk out the back with the initials MAB. I offered to buy it on the spot without even a glimpse inside as I couldn't risk opening the thing in front of her, and besides it was padlocked. She wasn't keen to let me have it without knowing the contents and it took some convincing, but I managed to persuade her to sell it to me as is – for a price.'

'And what *did* you find?' Hugh leaned in closer.

'I took the trunk home and mangled the lock off and I found –' Hector snapped open the locks on his briefcase beside him – 'this.' He handed Hugh a thick book.

Hugh ran his fingers along the plain brown cover. There was nothing on the outside to hint at its contents but as he opened the first page, the same swirly script from the letter identified its owner.

This diary belongs to Martha Annerley Bedford, Pelham Park, Dunleavy.

The address was crossed out and underneath was written:

Nutkin Cottage, Tidmarsh Lane.

Hugh looked up. 'And?'

'And I think you will find its contents compelling

to say the least, sir. But I'm afraid the old girl wrote in rather a cryptic fashion and there are still many unanswered questions. There was this too.' Hector handed Hugh a much smaller book.

'Oh, you've got to be kidding me.' Hugh took the delicate volume. 'My brother made this for me. I loved it.'

'It's lovely artwork, sir. He had quite a talent,' Hector said admiringly.

'I used to have Nanny read it to me every night. I adored all those fanciful drawings of dragons and knights. There were other things hidden in the illustrations too. See?' Hugh pointed. 'There's a turtle in there. She must have had it all those years.' Hugh turned his attention back to the diary. 'Does she mention the "truth" that she talked about in the letter to my father?' Hugh asked.

'Well, sir, I believe that has something to do with your brother Xavier,' Hector advised. 'But we'll need to do some more digging – literally.'

'What do you mean?' Hugh stared at his companion.

'We need to check the crypt at Pelham Park,' Hector replied.

Hugh was aghast. 'The crypt! What on earth

does that have to do with anything?'

'It will tell us for certain,' said Hector, 'that your brother isn't dead.'

✴

Hugh Kennington-Jones decided to walk the ten blocks back to Highton's via Central Park. He needed time to think. The diary was wrapped in a shopping bag and Hugh was eager to decipher its contents for himself. Amid the mothers' groups and their parades of prams, tourists with their cameras and folks taking a break from the chaos of the city, Hugh spotted an empty bench in the middle of a patch of lawn.

His stomach grumbled. He checked his watch and saw that it was just after 1 pm. Further along the path he spotted a street vendor and walked over to see what he might buy.

'Hot dog please, with mustard and cheese,' Hugh requested.

'No little one today?' the man asked.

'I'm sorry?' Hugh frowned.

'Your little girl. You were here yesterday. Sweetest little miss I ever met,' the man replied.

'Oh, you've got a good memory.' Hugh's grin was

brief. 'You must meet hundreds of people.'

'When you've got all the time in the world, mister, you pay attention,' the older man said, nodding. 'And your daughter – she made me smile.'

'She's at school, actually. Started today,' Hugh replied as he was handed his lunch.

'Of course. She mentioned that yesterday. Well, you tell her that old Lou said hello and I'm looking forward to seeing her again soon.'

'Yes, I will.' Hugh thanked the man for his hot dog and walked back to the bench.

As he sat there, slowly chewing his food, Hugh wondered if what Hector told him could possibly be true. Hugh's memories of that time were sketchy to say the least. He was only five when it happened. And almost straight afterwards he'd been sent away to school and the topic was barely spoken of again.

Hugh finished his lunch and pulled the book from its covering. He opened it to the first page and scanned the ornate script, wishing that it was easier to read. The dates were most helpful. Martha Annerley Bedford had been employed by his parents as a nanny to their first-born son Xavier some fourteen years before Hugh's arrival. The early years seemed to document mostly happy times, helping with the baby and then as he grew into a toddler. As time passed it seemed his brother and father did not always see eye to eye; Nanny Bedford spoke of terrible rows and times when the master did not speak to his son for days on end. But his mother adored him.

Hugh's impending arrival sent the household into a spin. A new baby was apparently the last thing anyone expected. By the time Hugh was born, his brother had been away at boarding school for many years, so the two had little to do with one another, except when Xavier came home to Pelham Park for the holidays – and Hugh couldn't remember much about their time together.

On a terrible rainy night, Hugh had stood in the window of the nursery and watched the lights of the car flashing down the drive. He hadn't wanted his mother to go. She had seemed sad and he wanted her to stay close. He could still remember her perfume – that musky scent that stayed with him for years after her death. He hadn't seen his brother get into the car, but in the morning, Nanny Bedford, whose red eyes were rimmed from the hundreds of tears she had already shed, took Hugh to his father's study, where he was informed that his mother and his brother would not be returning to Pelham Park.

Hugh had asked his father where they had gone. The old man had blistered with rage.

'They are dead, you stupid child, dead!'

Hugh could still remember those words ringing in his ears. He had run towards his father and thrown himself at his knees.

'Take the boy away,' his father had instructed Nanny, his voice icy, his touch even colder.

Hugh sobbed for days, taking comfort from the one person who he felt loved him at least as much as his own mother.

On a bitter day, he stood beside his father and Nanny as they lowered his mother and brother into the ground on the hill overlooking the estate. Almost immediately his father had a lavish crypt built over the gravesite. The memorial to his mother recounted his father's devotion. His brother warranted only a name and a date.

Hugh's heart pounded as he scanned Nanny Bedford's private recollections. She had disappeared from his life not long after his mother and brother. Hugh was sent away to school where his days were brightened by a slew of clever teachers and a kindly housemistress, Mrs Briggs, who dedicated herself to her young charges and was particularly fond of her youngest.

Holidays had been spent roaming the estate at Pelham Park, hunting and fishing, often with friends who preferred to spend their break with Hugh rather than brave going home to their own families. Hugh had grown into himself without the aid of parents.

His father remained a distant figure until Hugh's thirteenth birthday, when he decided that it was time for the young lad to be taken into the family fold. From that time on, Hugh had spent his school holidays working alongside his father at Kennington's, learning the grocery business from the ground up. Hugh had loved it from the very first day. And his love for Kennington's inspired more attention from his father than he had ever known.

On the few occasions that Hugh felt confident enough to ask his father about his mother and brother, his queries had always been met with a sharp rebuke, as though the mere pronouncement of their names tore open a wound that had never healed.

Hugh felt like a thief as he read Nanny Bedford's most private thoughts. In the weeks and days leading up to that terrible time, she recounted fearsome rows between his father and brother with his mother standing between them.

They have been at it again tonight. Master Xavier and his father arguing over the boy's future: the lad wanting to find his own way, his father insisting upon a path already trod. I fear it won't end well.

Hugh had known nothing of this. He'd spent his days in the nursery, unaware of the war going on downstairs.

Somewhere in the distance a phone was ringing. Hugh looked up from the diary and saw that the sun had dipped behind a bank of fluffy white clouds. He finally realised the ringing phone was his. It was his wife.

'Hello darling,' he answered. 'Of course. No, I hadn't forgotten – just delayed. I am sorry. Please apologise. I'll be there in ten minutes.' He closed the diary and returned it to its plastic bag. He'd forgotten all about their meeting with the business manager to go over the accounts for the renovations.

Hugh stood up. Nanny Bedford's secrets would have to wait for now.

Chapter 11

Felix Underwood led his class up Madison Avenue, turning left into 81st Street before weaving across the pedestrian lights to the museum.

'Is this your first visit to the Met?' Mr Underwood asked Alice-Miranda as they climbed the stairs to the entrance.

'Yes. I've read all about it and I can't wait to see inside. The girls are so lucky to have their lessons here every week. My school is in the middle of a village, miles from the city, so if we go to a gallery or museum it takes a whole day,' Alice-Miranda replied.

The pair stopped at the top of the stairs and waited for the rest of the group to catch up. Alice-Miranda looked around at the array of visitors scattered across the steps: backpackers, families, well-dressed business men and women and at least three other groups of school students. People were eating and talking on their telephones and some were just lying back enjoying the sun. Of course, there were lots of people taking photographs of the museum's exterior with its Corinthian columns and enormous banners announcing the current travelling exhibition of Impressionist painters.

'Hurry up, girls, we haven't got all day,' Felix Underwood called out to three stragglers.

The trio scooted up the steps and joined the rest of the group.

'Sorry, sir,' they chorused.

'Okay, you know the drill. We need to head inside and get our badges and our stools and boards. Lucinda, can you show Alice-Miranda what to do?' the teacher asked.

'Yes, Mr Underwood.' Lucinda flashed a smile at her new friend.

'Today we are going upstairs to the west galleries to continue our study of European art. You have your sketchbooks and pencils and I want you to take your time selecting a work that really appeals to you. You need to give each painting a chance so I want you to take a good look around. Don't just choose the first thing you see. And Harriet and Isabelle, don't bother about finishing early. You're not going to the Met Store, no matter how much you nag me.' Two girls who were standing beside each other with their hands in the air quickly put them back down and exchanged dirty looks.

'We will be staying in the European area so please don't go wandering off. You have a whole hour to sketch your version of whichever artwork you select. And another thing, girls, remember that the gallery has tutors positioned near the exhibits so if you need any assistance just ask, and of course I'll be around to see how you're all going as well. Are there any questions?' Felix Underwood glanced at the group.

'Excuse me, Mr Underwood,' Alice-Miranda said. 'Do you want us to draw the artwork exactly as it is or how we see it?'

'Good question, Alice-Miranda. Sorry, I forgot

that you weren't here last week. I'd like you to interpret the piece, so it doesn't need to look exactly the same,' the teacher replied.

'Which is just as well,' Lucinda whispered to Alice-Miranda, 'because last week I tried to draw a Renoir painting of a mother and her children and they ended up with heads like frogs.'

Alice-Miranda giggled.

'All right then, girls, let's go. We'll meet back here at 12.45 pm.'

Lucinda and Alice-Miranda walked behind Ava and Quincy as the group followed Mr Underwood through a range of exhibits to their destination.

'I hope I do better than last week,' said Ava. 'I chose a still life because I thought that would be easy. I mean, how hard is it to draw a bowl of fruit?' She thumbed through her sketchbook and showed her drawing to Quincy.

'Very?' Quincy wrinkled her nose.

'Thanks for the encouragement.' Ava rolled her eyes.

'It's not that bad. Well, except maybe that bit that looks like a bottom,' Quincy giggled.

'It's meant to be a peach,' Ava protested.

Alice-Miranda was awestruck as she took in her

surroundings. A large group of tourists, betrayed by their cameras and bumbags, was moving, swarm-like, through a piazza brimming with ancient Greek statues. A grey-haired woman in a smart white pants-suit was talking loudly about the various antiquities. Her comments were greeted with many 'oohs and ahhs' and the almost continual snapping of photographs.

'Make the most of that now,' she said, nodding at one rotund fellow with his camera slung around his neck, 'because there are lots of places where it will just have to go away.'

He smiled enthusiastically and clearly hadn't understood a thing she had said.

When the class reached their destination, Alice-Miranda found a suite of smaller galleries playing host to the style of paintings that adorned the walls of her home, Highton Hall. Grand Old Masters' portraits of people, some alone, some with their families, others on horseback. There were later landscapes too; a gorgeous Monet and another Turner painting of Venice with the most subtle light dancing on the water between the buildings.

Alice-Miranda and Lucinda stayed together for the first few minutes before the girls' natural curiosity split them up. The class was scattered throughout the galleries, each student searching for her favourite work. Alice-Miranda found herself lingering in front of several paintings, trying to work out which she liked the most.

Fifteen minutes later she found herself completely drawn to a painting by Edgar Degas called *The Dance Class*. Alice-Miranda unfolded her stool, sat down in front of it and opened her sketchbook, wondering how she would capture the movement, the characters, the feeling of the dance class and all those beautiful white tutus.

Before long she was engrossed in her task and doing a much better job of it than she had expected to. Her perspective was good and she found drawing people relatively easy, although achieving just the right expressions on their faces was tricky. Her dancers seemed a little cheekier than Mr Degas's.

Behind her, a tall man with a thick head of salt-and-pepper coloured hair watched. He observed the Degas and then the small child in front of him as she carefully sketched what she saw. He was impressed with her light touch and the texture she achieved with her pencils.

She added a little dog that wasn't in the original painting. He smiled.

Alice-Miranda held her work out in front of her.

The man spoke. 'That's very good.'

'Oh.' Alice-Miranda spun around. 'Do you think so? I know I haven't got the faces quite right. That man there –' she pointed at her sketch – 'looks quite cross, but I think in the real painting he just seems aloof. And this girl –' she pointed at a ballerina in the foreground – 'she doesn't look serene like she does up there. Mine looks like her ballet shoes are two sizes too small.'

The man put his forefinger to his lip and nodded.

'But I do like your dog,' he added.

'Oh, well, Mr Underwood said that we could add our own interpretations and I rather liked the idea of a fluffy white dog among the dancers. He sort of matches their tutus, don't you think?' Alice-Miranda replied. 'Perhaps I should put a bow around his neck.'

'Or you could move his head a little so it looks as though he's about to dance as well,' the man suggested.

'I hadn't thought of that. Thank you.' Alice-Miranda began to erase the dog's head and reposition it. 'I am sorry, it was rude of me not to introduce myself properly –' Alice-Miranda spun around and was surprised that the man had disappeared.

She stood up and searched the room but he had moved on.

Alice-Miranda checked her watch. She could hardly believe that it was already twenty to one and she wasn't nearly finished her work. Other girls from her class were beginning to stand and close their sketchbooks. She did the same, then picked up her folding stool and walked to the entrance. The galleries flowed from one to another. She caught sight of Ava in the next room and walked over to her.

'That was an hour of torture wasn't it?' Ava pulled a face. 'What did you draw?'

'*The Dance Class* by Mr Degas in the next room,' Alice-Miranda replied.

'Well, come on, let me see,' Ava insisted. She put her own sketchbook down on her chair and took Alice-Miranda's from her. 'That's neat!'

'Do you think so?' Alice-Miranda asked. 'It's not finished yet.'

'It's way better than this.' Ava flicked open her own sketchbook to reveal a rather square head.

Alice-Miranda looked at the painting on the wall, then back to Ava's interpretation.

'You know, I think you've drawn that like Picasso would have, in his cubist phase,' the tiny child admired.

'Except that it was painted by Renoir,' Ava observed, 'and his people look like people and mine just look like they're related to Spongebob Squarepants.'

'Mr Underwood said that it didn't have to be exactly the same. I think it looks great,' Alice-Miranda nodded. 'We'd better go find Mr Underwood, hadn't we?' She turned to leave.

'Oh goodness, that's an amazing painting.' Alice-Miranda stared at a colourful medieval canvas on the wall near the doorway.

Ava studied the myriad creatures. 'Weird, I'd say.'

'No, I think it's terribly clever. Can you see?' She pointed. 'There's a bear and a lion. It's one of those pictures that I'm sure the longer you look at it, the more secrets it will share.' Alice-Miranda wished they had more time. 'Come on, we'd better get moving.' She picked up her things and headed for the exit.

Chapter 12

The group tripped their way back to school just in time for lunch, and were greeted at the back door by Maisy.

'She thinks she's a sniffer dog.' Lucinda smiled as Maisy thrust her nose against the girls' skirts looking for snacks.

'I think she's adorable.' Alice-Miranda reached down and gave her a friendly pat. 'But going by the size of that tummy, I think she must have a very good sense of smell.'

The girls raced upstairs to deposit their books and pencils into their lockers. Ava and Quincy had to run an errand for Mr Underwood and said that they would meet Alice-Miranda and Lucinda in the cafeteria.

Alice-Miranda and Lucinda were walking through the sixth grade corridor when Alice-Miranda spotted the girl from the bus with the pigtails and lilac bows. She was standing side on, staring into her open locker. As Alice-Miranda and Lucinda reached her, the girl closed the locker door and spun around.

'Alethea!' Alice-Miranda exclaimed. 'I thought you looked familiar when I saw you getting off the bus this morning. But I could only see you from behind, so I couldn't really tell.'

The taller girl stood with her mouth wide open, gaping like a giant cod.

'Do you know each other?' Lucinda asked, looking from Alice-Miranda to the taller girl.

'Yes,' Alice-Miranda replied.

The taller girl closed her mouth and stared at Alice-Miranda, her tanned face taking on a sickly pallor.

'I don't know you,' she finally said in a thick

southern twang. She threw her pigtails over her shoulders one at a time.

'Of course you do. You're Alethea Goldsworthy. We were at school together at Winchesterfield-Downsfordvale and then you left at the end of my first term. You were the head prefect.'

'No I wasn't.' Alethea shook her head.

A smaller girl who was standing behind Alethea stepped forward. She had just deposited an armful of books into the next locker.

'Her name's Thea Mackenzie,' the child offered. 'She's from Alabama.'

'Oh.' Alice-Miranda was surprised to hear it. She could have sworn that the girl in front of her was Alethea Goldsworthy, except for the accent. 'I'm sorry,' Alice-Miranda apologised. 'But you look exactly like a girl I know.'

'No, you definitely don't know me.' The girl narrowed her eyes.

'Then I should introduce myself. My name's Alice-Miranda Highton-Smith-Kennington-Jones.' Alice-Miranda held out her hand to the taller girl. She took it and squeezed so hard that Alice-Miranda felt her knuckles grind together.

The tiny child recoiled. 'Ow.'

'Sorry, don't know my own strength sometimes,' Thea grinned. 'Must be all that fried chicken my mama likes to feed me.'

There was an awkward silence.

'I'm Gretchen,' the smaller girl beside Thea spoke.

'It's nice to meet you, Gretchen.' Alice-Miranda held out her hand which, to her relief, Gretchen shook gently.

'This is Lucinda Finkelstein.' Alice-Miranda motioned towards her new friend.

Lucinda smiled.

'Eww, gross,' Thea grimaced.

'What . . . what's the matter?' Lucinda had no idea what was wrong but right at that moment she wished that the floor would open up and swallow her whole.

'Are you friends?' Thea asked.

'Well, we've only just met today but I'm sure that we're going to be good friends,' Alice-Miranda replied.

'I don't think I'd trust her to be my friend,' said Thea to Lucinda, while glaring at Alice-Miranda, 'because you've got something really gross stuck in your braces and your good friend here hasn't even bothered to tell you. Gretchen would be unfriended immediately if she let me walk around with something that disgusting stuck in my teeth. But then again, I don't have a mouth full of metal to contend with, you poor thing. That must be so uncomfortable. Ugly too,' said Thea sweetly.

Lucinda spun around and looked at Alice-Miranda. 'Do I really have something stuck in there?' She smiled as widely as she could.

'Well, there's a tiny bit of, I think it's a strawberry seed, maybe, but you can hardly see it,' Alice-Miranda replied.

'Hardly see it. You're kidding, aren't you?' Thea screwed up her face. 'I'd be getting myself to the bathroom quick smart.'

Lucinda's face had gone from pink to fire-engine red. 'I'll be back in a minute,' she said and dashed away.

'Gretchen, why don't you go with her and make sure that it's all gone?' Thea suggested.

Gretchen nodded and scurried off after Lucinda. As soon as both girls were out of sight, Thea leaned in and with outstretched arms shoved Alice-Miranda's shoulders against her locker.

'Ow!' Alice-Miranda protested. 'What did you do that for, Thea?'

'What are you doing here?' Thea's twang disappeared completely, replaced by clipped vowels.

'Sorry?' Alice-Miranda frowned.

'Why are you here? You ruined my life. It was all your fault I had to leave that school and move – to another country!' Alethea stamped her foot. 'So why are you here?'

'Oh, Alethea, I knew it was you!' Alice-Miranda slipped out of the bigger girl's grasp. 'I know people say that we all have someone who looks just like us out there in the world– you've only got to see Mrs Oliver and Aunty Gee to know that's true – but I thought I must have been going mad. You were simply too good a twin not to be you. But why are you called Thea Mackenzie? I suppose Thea is just a short version of Alethea. But Mackenzie? I don't understand.'

'You don't need to understand anything, you little brat. You don't know what it's like to be me,' Alethea hissed.

'Of course I don't,' Alice-Miranda smiled. 'That would be impossible – to know what it's like to be anyone other than myself.' Alice-Miranda stopped for a moment. 'I thought when you left Winchesterfield-Downsfordvale that you went to Sainsbury Palace School.'

Alethea's whole body tensed. 'I did, but then I had to move again and it's all your fault.'

'I can understand if you were cross about the boat race at Winchesterfield-Downsfordvale but I'm sure that you didn't have to leave. You should have talked to Miss Grimm. You could have worked something out. She's really a wonderful person – she was just heartbroken and sad when you were there, that's all. And I really don't see how I could have had anything to do with you leaving Sainsbury Palace. I've never even been there for a visit,' Alice-Miranda explained.

'As soon as I met you my life started to fall apart. The last thing I need is you coming here and ruining everything – *again*.' Her blue eyes filled with tears. 'I've made friends here and people like me. And no one knows anything . . . about Daddy,' Alethea whispered.

Alice-Miranda began to understand. Of course, Alethea's father had recently been in quite a bit of trouble at home. She remembered her father saying something about his being charged with tax evasion and fraud and there was a huge criminal court case going on.

'It's all right, Alethea. I'm glad that you've made friends and that you're enjoying yourself. I won't

tell anyone your real name if that's what you want.'
Alice-Miranda looked up at the older girl.

'You'd better not, or you're dead.' Alethea grabbed Alice-Miranda's wrists and twisted as hard as she could.

Alice-Miranda tried to pull away. 'Ow, Alethea, that hurts. Please let go. I promise I won't tell anyone who you are. I'm only here for a month until Highton's reopens and then I'm going home to Winchesterfield-Downsfordvale.'

'You'd better not be lying to me – or else,' Alethea threatened. 'So, what's my name?'

'Thea Mackenzie,' Alice-Miranda replied.

'And where am I from?' she demanded.

'Alabama,' Alice-Miranda confirmed.

Alethea finally let go of Alice-Miranda's arms, leaving blotchy red marks.

'You'd better rub that,' Alethea warned. 'Don't want anyone thinking you've hurt yourself now, do you?'

Lucinda and Gretchen reappeared.

Alethea smiled at Lucinda. 'Everything okay?'

'Yes,' Lucinda frowned.

'Well, you'd better go to lunch, girls. Don't want to miss it, do you?' Alethea flashed a toothy grin.

'Of course not,' Alice-Miranda replied. 'Goodbye Thea, goodbye Gretchen. It was lovely to meet you.'

'That was weird,' Lucinda said as the pair scurried along the hallway towards the stairs.

'What do you mean?' Alice-Miranda asked.

'Thea made it sound as though I had half a strawberry mashed into my braces but you were right, it was hardly anything – and then she sent Gretchen along to check that it was all gone. I almost felt like she was trying to get rid of me. Either that or she's just very caring,' Lucinda observed.

'Yes,' Alice-Miranda was lost in her own thoughts. 'That must be it.'

Alethea had always been tricky at Winchesterfield-Downsfordvale and as much as Alice-Miranda was a firm believer in second chances, she had a feeling that her time at Mrs Kimmel's was about to become a whole lot more interesting than she had first thought.

Chapter 13

Lunch was served in several sittings, with each grade given half an hour before they went out to 'play'. Some days that meant time in the gymnasium or the library or on the tiny rooftop terrace, but at least two days a week the girls trekked across Madison and Fifth avenues to Central Park where they could run around properly.

Alice-Miranda's stomach grumbled. She eyed her serving of cheesy lasagne and followed Lucinda to a table where Ava and Quincy were already halfway through their lunch. Alice-Miranda put Alethea out of her mind. She wasn't planning to tell anyone her secret.

Quincy was munching on a crispy iceberg lettuce leaf. 'What took you so long?'

Lucinda spoke first. 'Alice-Miranda saw a girl in the sixth grade that she thought she knew.'

'And did you?' Ava asked.

'No, she just looked like someone I know,' Alice-Miranda replied.

'Too bad.' Quincy stabbed at her last bite of lasagne. 'It must feel weird being at a new school with no friends. It might have been nice to see a familiar face.'

'Who said I have no friends?' Alice-Miranda smiled. 'I've got the three of you, haven't I?'

Lucinda grinned. She'd known Alice-Miranda for less than four hours but already felt as if they could be friends for life.

Quincy nodded. 'Point taken.'

Alice-Miranda asked her new friends if they had any brothers or sisters. Ava and Quincy said they had one each and Lucinda had two brothers. Ava's was younger but Quincy and Lucinda's brothers were all older. When Alice-Miranda told them she was an only child they groaned with envy.

'You're so lucky,' Lucinda grouched. 'I wish I was an only child. Toby and Zeke get to do everything they want and because I'm the only girl, Papa treats me like a princess in an ivory tower.'

'I'm sure there are much worse things in the world than being treated like a princess,' Alice-Miranda replied, chewing daintily on her salad.

'I know that's true but you don't understand. I'm not allowed to do anything. I feel like I'm in prison – I'm either at school or at home or at some activity that Papa says is suitable for a "girl like me". I just want to escape and have some adventures of my own – ones that don't involve play dates at my mother's friends' places or afternoon tea at the salon.' Lucinda's forehead was puckered into a frown.

'You should come home with me,' Ava grinned. 'Every day's an adventure there.'

'Where do you live?' Alice-Miranda asked.

'East Harlem. It's north of the park – and I think it's an awesome neighbourhood. There are so many different nationalities and the food is amazing.' Ava loaded her fork with lasagne.

'Do your parents work in the city?' Alice-Miranda asked.

'My mom is a detective downtown. My dad lives in Hong Kong but I get to see him sometimes in the holidays. He hasn't been around since I was little,' Ava explained. 'We live with our grandma too. She helps look after me and my brother.'

'A detective? That sounds dangerous.' Alice-Miranda's eyes widened.

'Yeah, it is. I really worry about her sometimes.'

'I'd love to meet her,' Alice-Miranda said. 'She must be very brave.'

'I think she is,' Ava agreed.

'I'll ask Mummy and Daddy if we can invite your family to the opening of the store,' Alice-Miranda suggested. 'Your parents too,' she said, glancing at Quincy and Lucinda.

'I don't know if my family would fit in with the people your parents are used to hanging out with.' Ava stuffed a chunk of bread roll into her mouth. 'You know where we come from; it's different to the Upper East Side.'

'I don't come from the Upper East Side either,' Alice-Miranda said. 'Is your mother a good person?'

'Of course she is,' Ava replied, breadcrumbs sputtering from her mouth.

'And what about your brother and your grand-mother? Are they good people?'

Lucinda and Quincy had no idea where Alice-Miranda was going with her line of questioning but they gave her their fullest attention.

Ava swallowed before she spoke. 'Sure they are.'

'So why wouldn't my parents want to know them?' Alice-Miranda asked. 'I don't care where you live. In fact, I'd really like to come and visit you one day after school, if you'd invite me.'

'That would be great,' Ava grinned. 'But I bet your parents wouldn't let you ride the subway home with me.'

'I think they might. Daddy knows that I want to experience the real New York and riding around in a town car or a limousine is not how most people get about. Riding the subway is on my list of things to do,' Alice-Miranda replied. 'I read in my guidebook that it's perfectly safe so long as you're sensible and don't go to out-of-the-way places after dark.'

'What about you ride the subway with me and then another time we can go out somewhere in your limousine. This experience thing, it works both ways, you know?' Ava nodded and raised her eyebrows.

'What about you Quincy? Do you live far from school?' Alice-Miranda asked.

'I go in the other direction downtown to Hell's Kitchen,' Quincy explained.

'And I've never been to either of those places, or ridden the subway,' Lucinda griped. 'I've never been anywhere.'

Alice-Miranda wondered what Lucinda meant by anywhere.

'Well, of course you must have been to lots of places, Lucinda. Manhattan Island is not that big. I'm sure you could actually walk from one end of it to the other in a day if you wanted to. My headmistress at home, Miss Grimm, well, her husband Mr Grump gave me the most wonderful guide book and it has this fantastic little map and on the way over I went through it with Mummy and Daddy and we marked all the places we're going to explore while we're here. We're going to Broadway and Madison Square Garden to watch a Knicks game and I'd love to see a baseball game at Yankee Stadium and walk along the High Line and visit the Statue of Liberty and Ellis Island. There are so many places to see.' Alice-Miranda was fit to burst. 'And I've heard about this place called Serendipity 3 which has frozen hot chocolate – I can't imagine how good that must taste.'

'Oh, it's awesome,' Quincy nodded.

Lucinda's face fell. 'I know you think I should have been to all of those places, but trust me, I'm not lying when I tell you that I haven't.'

'None of them?' Alice-Miranda quizzed.

'Well, I visited Serendipity 3 with Dolores our housekeeper one day when Mama and Papa were out of town. And frozen hot chocolate tastes every bit as good as you imagine. But I wasn't allowed to tell anyone at home because Dolores said that she would get into trouble for taking me there.'

'What about the park and the zoo?' Alice-Miranda asked.

'I go to the park with school but I've never even been to the zoo,' Lucinda replied.

Alice-Miranda thought that was very odd.

'I can't go because my father is allergic to fur and so he says that I'll probably be allergic too. It's stupid, I know – I pat Maisy all the time and I don't get a rash.'

'Do you live in the city, Lucinda?' Alice-Miranda wondered if perhaps the Finkelstein residence was out of town somewhere.

'Fifth Avenue, just opposite the Met,' she replied.

'She lives in a mansion,' Quincy nodded. 'You should see it. It used to belong to the Rockefellers a long time ago.'

'So you live in New York City but you don't live in the city at all.' Alice-Miranda was shocked. 'That's just silly.'

'I told you. My father wraps me in cotton wool. I can't wait until I'm eighteen and I can do whatever I please.' Lucinda placed her knife and fork neatly together on her empty plate.

'Surely you don't have to wait until then.' Alice-Miranda smiled at her. 'I'll speak to your father as soon as I can.'

Lucinda's face drained of all its colour. 'Oh no, Alice-Miranda, you can't. That would only make things worse. My father doesn't appreciate anyone interfering with our family. He'd be so mad,' she pleaded. 'I think he'd lock me in my bedroom and throw away the key.'

'But you have to live Lucinda,' Alice-Miranda explained. 'My granny always says that we should make the most of every single day, not just look forward to things in the future.'

Lucinda had a gnawing feeling in her stomach. Alice-Miranda was right. She had to let her father know that she wanted to do more and she didn't want to wait until she was grown up. She knew if her father found out about Alice-Miranda he'd put a stop to their friendship immediately. But there was something about this tiny girl, with her cascading chocolate curls and eyes as big as saucers, that made Lucinda feel just that little bit braver.

Chapter 14

The rest of the afternoon whizzed by. At 3.15 pm the bell rang proclaiming the end of the day. Hundreds of pairs of feet ran to their lockers and the hallways were jam-packed with girls eager to get home. Alice-Miranda said goodbye to Ava and Quincy, who headed for the back door on their way to the subway station.

'I'd better not walk out with you,' said Lucinda, her gaze dropping to the floor.

'Don't you go out the back door?' Alice-Miranda

assumed that Lucinda must walk home, since she only lived opposite the Met. It wasn't far at all.

'No, Raymond picks me up out the front.' She looked embarrassed. 'I'm not allowed to walk.'

'Oh.' Alice-Miranda's mouth formed a perfect circle. Lucinda's situation was far more serious than she had first imagined.

'Anyway, I don't want Raymond to see us together,' Lucinda added.

'Why not?' Alice-Miranda asked. 'Surely you're not worried about that silly Highton-Smith – Finkelstein feud? And he won't have any idea who I am, will he?'

'No, I don't think so, but my father always asks him and Dolores who I'm with at the end of the day and if it's not the daughter of one of Mama's friends then Papa will ask me lots of questions until he gets to the bottom of things.'

'You know, you could tell him the truth: I'm a new friend from overseas and I'm only here for a short time,' Alice-Miranda reasoned.

'You don't know my father, Alice-Miranda. He won't stop until he knows your name. Once he's made up his mind about something there's no changing it,'

Lucinda replied. 'Please let's just keep our friendship a secret, for now.'

'If that's what you want.' Alice-Miranda reached out and held Lucinda's hands.

Lucinda gulped. 'We have to.'

'Oh, hello Lucinda.' Alethea had just spotted the two girls. 'You haven't had an argument already, have you?'

Alice-Miranda shook her head. 'Of course not.'

'Then why so sad?' Alethea asked in a baby voice as she stared at Lucinda.

'I'm not sad, Thea, but thank you for asking,' Lucinda smiled. 'It's nice to know that you care so much.'

'Of course I care, I wouldn't want my new friends to be in a fight now, would I?' her southern twang was as thick as pumpkin pie. 'Enjoy your afternoon, girls. Be careful in the traffic.' Here she glared at Alice-Miranda. 'Manhattan's a dangerous place for little girls.'

'Thanks for your advice, Thea,' Alice-Miranda replied.

Lucinda closed her locker door and headed for the front door.

Jilly Hobbs was standing in the foyer farewelling

her students. It was something she liked to do every day.

'Hello Alice-Miranda, how was it?' Miss Hobbs enquired.

'Wonderful,' Alice-Miranda fizzed. 'I've made three lovely friends and we went to the Met for art class and this afternoon Mr Underwood told us that we're having a Science fair soon.'

'I'm so glad you're enjoying yourself. Have a great afternoon.'

Alice-Miranda had arranged to meet her parents near the front steps. They had made plans to go to the Rockefeller Center and take the elevator to the viewing platform known as the Top of the Rock, providing that the weather was clear. She had given in to her mother's request to take the town car, but only so long as they could ride the subway later in the week.

Alice-Miranda spotted Whip Staples outside the front of the school wearing a brightly coloured vest. Traffic duties must have been another of his jobs.

'Good afternoon, Mr Whip,' Alice-Miranda called out.

'Good afternoon to you too, Miss Alice-Miranda,' he hollered back. 'So how did we do? Will you be coming back again tomorrow?'

Alice-Miranda hadn't noticed Alethea join the bus line behind her.

'I hope not,' the older girl hissed into Alice-Miranda's ear. 'That would make life better for everyone, wouldn't it?'

Alice-Miranda smiled at Whip and answered, 'Of course. I've had a wonderful day.' She turned around and looked at Alethea. 'I've told you. Your secret is safe with me.'

'Yes, but I really don't think I can trust you after what you did to me last time.'

'Alethea –' Alice-Miranda began.

'What did you call me?' Alethea's face was blood red.

'Thea,' Alice-Miranda corrected herself, 'you have nothing to worry about.'

A yellow school bus pulled up at the kerb. 'Save me a seat, Gretchen,' the older girl called out. 'At the front. You know I get bus sick if we're anything past the fourth row.'

Gretchen turned around and tried to smile, hoping that the ten or so girls in front of her all preferred the rear of the vehicle.

Alice-Miranda spied her mother standing on the other side of the street beside the town car.

'Stay there, darling, and I'll come and get you,' Cecelia Highton-Smith called out.

A fleet of black vehicles lined the far side of the one-way street while yellow bus after yellow bus pulled in nose to tail to collect their cargo outside the front door.

Alice-Miranda spotted Lucinda crossing the street holding hands with a stout woman in a maid's uniform. She decided that was probably Dolores, who Lucinda said had worked for their family for years and was one of the only people her father trusted to look after her.

'Hello Mummy.' Alice-Miranda embraced Cecelia who leaned down to kiss her daughter on the cheek.

'Come on, you can tell Daddy and me all about your day when we're in the car.' She held tightly to Alice-Miranda's hand and they walked towards Mr O'Leary, who was holding open the kerbside passenger door. Just as Alice-Miranda was about to hop into the vehicle, she couldn't help but give Lucinda a quick wave as she got into the car ahead.

Lucinda had no idea what came over her, because without thinking she raised her hand and waved right back.

On the way to the Rockefeller Center Alice-Miranda barely stopped to take a breath. She told her parents and Mr O'Leary everything about her day. Hugh and Cecelia were so pleased that she was enjoying herself and that she had already made some friends.

'You know I said that I want to go on the subway? Well, two of my friends, Ava and Quincy, catch the subway to and from school and they've both asked if I'd like to go home with them one afternoon, so may I?' Alice-Miranda asked.

'Darling, I just don't know if it's safe,' her father replied. 'It's all well and good for me to take you but I'm not so sure about two little girls on their own.'

'Ava and Quincy go every day on their own, although they're not really on their own because at the end of school there are loads of other children around. Please?' Alice-Miranda smiled up at her father, her eyes sparkling.

'Oh, all right, but I want to talk to their parents first before you go off on any of these excursions, young lady.' Hugh Kennington-Jones had come to the conclusion long ago that his little daughter was as capable as anyone he knew and once she'd made up her mind to do something there was really no point stopping her.

'Mummy, you know I will be absolutely fine.' Alice-Miranda intercepted her mother's protest before she had time to start. 'And can we invite Ava and Quincy and Lucinda and their parents to the opening of the store?' she added.

'Of course, darling, that's easy,' her mother replied. 'You'll have to tell us their full names and addresses so we can add them to the official guest list.'

'I'm not sure.' Alice-Miranda bit her lip. 'I'll find out tomorrow. Oh, except for Lucinda. Her surname is Finkelstein.'

Her father and mother exchanged quizzical looks.

'Finkelstein, you say?' said Hugh, frowning.

'Yes, her parents are Morrie and Gerda,' Alice-Miranda explained. 'The same ones you were telling me about this morning, Mummy, when we looking at their window displays.'

'And she's your friend?' her mother questioned.

'Oh yes, Mummy. Lucinda's lovely,' Alice-Miranda confirmed.

'I wonder what her parents will say about you two being friends,' said Hugh.

'Lucinda is worried about that too, so she's not going to tell them just yet. But I told her I was happy to go and speak to them as soon as she decides it's the right time,' said Alice-Miranda.

Cecelia touched Alice-Miranda gently on the cheek. 'Darling, if I know Morrie Finkelstein, he might never be happy about you being friends with his daughter.'

Chapter 15

Alice-Miranda and her parents rode the elevator to the Top of the Rock just as they had planned. While queuing for the lift, they had their photograph taken sitting on a steel girder, to replicate a famous picture of the workmen who built the Rockefeller Center back in the 1930s. The men were on a beam high over the city just eating their lunch as if they were sitting on a park bench. Alice-Miranda could hardly believe how brave they must have been, building skyscrapers with no safety harnesses at all. Her mother said that it made her feel queasy just looking at it.

A light breeze had blown the sky clear and in the afternoon sun, it was a dazzling blue. Even on a Monday there were plenty of people about, taking in the views of Manhattan and beyond.

'Ooh, look!' Alice-Miranda called to her parents, who were staring out towards the East River. 'I can see the store.'

'Stand there darling and I'll get a picture of you and Mummy with Highton's in the background.' Hugh zoomed in with his wife and daughter in focus. Through a gap between two skyscrapers he could see Highton's on Fifth opposite the park. Something moving on the rooftop garden caught his eye and he adjusted the zoom to see if he could make it out more clearly.

Hugh laughed when he realised what it was.

'What's the matter, Daddy?' Alice-Miranda asked.

'Surely we don't look that bad,' said Cecelia, with a quizzical frown.

'No, darling, it's not you two. Come and look at this,' he handed Cecelia the camera and she stared through the lens, stifling a laugh.

'Well, come on, Mummy, share,' Alice-Miranda instructed.

Her father grabbed Alice-Miranda around her waist and held her up so she could get the right angle on the camera. Her mother held the bulky equipment for her.

'Oh Daddy, its Mrs Oliver. And I think she's dancing,' Alice-Miranda giggled. 'We shouldn't be spying on her.'

'Sweetheart, she must realise that she's not doing it in private,' her father replied. 'I think she caught the Bollywood bug before your aunt's wedding. Wasn't she going to come out with us this afternoon?'

'Yes, but she said that she had some other things to do,' Cecelia smiled. 'I hadn't realised that dancing on the rooftop was one of them.'

'Well, I think she's gorgeous,' Alice-Miranda replied.

Hugh took several more photographs of his 'girls' standing at various points around the deck. A kindly old man, impeccably dressed in a suit and stylish trilby hat, asked if Hugh would like to stand in with Cecelia and Alice-Miranda and he would take a photograph. The trio lined up in front of the Empire State Building and grinned for the camera.

'I don't know about you two but I have to be getting back,' said Hugh. He was itching to spend some more time alone with Nanny Bedford's memories.

'Really, darling? We said that we'd have all of our work done by three pm each day so we could spend time with Alice-Miranda,' Cecelia reminded her husband.

'I know, but something unexpected has come up and I really should deal with it,' Hugh explained. 'Why don't I catch a cab uptown and you and Alice-Miranda can take a walk and Seamus will pick you up later.'

'All right.' Cecelia gave her husband a curious look. 'Is it anything I should be worried about?'

'No, no, of course not. Just some Kennington's business,' Hugh reassured her.

'Well, miss, where would you like to go?' Cecelia asked.

Alice-Miranda pulled her miniature map of the city from her blazer pocket and unfolded it in front of her. 'Looking at this –' She ran her finger along the streets – 'it's only a few blocks down and two across to get to Times Square,' she informed her parents. 'It will be dark in a little while and I'd love to see the lights.'

'That's do-able, darling,' her mother smiled.

In the gift shop, Hugh Kennington-Jones purchased their 'men on a beam photograph' and Alice-Miranda asked if she could buy some post-cards, which she intended to send to everyone back at Winchesterfield-Downsfordvale.

The family rode the lift down to street level and Hugh bade his wife and daughter farewell, heading off to hail a cab on Madison Avenue. Alice-Miranda and her mother set off down Sixth Avenue turning right into West 45th Street, onto Broadway and towards the famous lights of Times Square.

Chapter 16

'Mama, do we have to go to the salon on Saturday afternoon?' Lucinda Finkelstein was sitting under the covers in the middle of her enormous bed, her knees drawn up in front of her.

'I don't understand what you mean, Lucinda.' Gerda Finkelstein sat on the edge of the bed and looked at her daughter.

'Couldn't we do something else? Something different?' Lucinda had no idea how her mother would react, but meeting Alice-Miranda today had inspired her to at least ask the question.

'But we go every Saturday. Afternoon tea at the salon is part of life, Lucinda, like death and taxes,' Gerda replied.

'But that's just the point, Mama. Aren't you bored with the salon? I mean, we meet up with the same people every week and they talk about the same things and then afterwards you always seem uptight about something that someone has said. Like last week when Mrs Schwarzkopf was going on about her daughter Emily and coming home in the car you were cross, and said that Rita Schwarzkopf never has anything to talk about unless it's her own children who have apparently done something amazing each and every day of their lives.'

'Well.' Gerda looked at Lucinda. 'Rita Schwarzkopf is a pain in the neck. And I don't believe for one minute that Emily is going to be her school valedictorian. The girl is as dumb as a rock.'

Lucinda was shocked to hear her mother say such a thing. 'But she's meant to be your friend, Mama.'

'Of course Rita's my friend,' Gerda said, frowning. 'We've been friends since we were six years old.'

'But I thought friends were people that you actually liked and you enjoyed spending time with.' Lucinda was fiddling with a stray curl as she spoke.

'Lucinda, that's just life. Sometimes your friends drive you crazy, but they're still your friends.' Gerda was beginning to lose patience. She wasn't used to Lucinda questioning anything about their lives, let alone Saturday afternoons at the salon. 'Anyway, your father would be devastated if he heard you talking like this. You know that he had the whole place specially remodelled based on that photograph of the salon at the Palace of Versailles that you showed him. Sweetheart, he did it all for you.'

'I'd much rather see the real thing.' Lucinda knew she was pushing her luck.

'Well, that's just not possible,' her mother snapped. 'You know your father doesn't like to travel.'

'But we could go to France, Mama. Just you and me, and we could visit Paris and the Palace of Versailles.' Lucinda's eyes lit up.

Gerda tilted her head to one side and looked at Lucinda carefully.

The sixth floor at Finkelstein's had played host to a tea salon for years but recently Morrie had set about renovating the whole floor, relocating the menswear section and installing a massive ballroom which he had named The Grand Salon. The official opening was in a couple of weeks, the same day as the reopening of Highton's on Fifth.

'What has got into you, young lady?' Gerda reached over and stroked Lucinda's brow.

'I just want to have some adventures, Mama, that's all. Even in New York, if you'd let me,' Lucinda pouted.

'What are you talking about? You have plenty of adventures. Isn't your teacher taking you to the Met for your art classes? I can't imagine many girls get to do that every week.' Gerda Finkelstein leaned down and kissed her daughter's cheek.

'What about Sunday? Couldn't we go to the zoo?'

'You know your father is allergic to animals,' her mother replied.

'But that doesn't mean *we* can't do something,' Lucinda protested.

'Sundays are family days, Lucinda, at home. Why would we need to go anywhere else – you and your brothers have everything you could possibly want right here.' Gerda didn't understand her daughter's outburst at all. 'Goodnight Lucinda.' She walked towards to door.

Lucinda's room was more like her very own

apartment than a child's bedroom. As well as an ensuite bathroom, she had her own playroom and study. And what Gerda had said was true: the Finkelstein mansion had its own swimming pool and there was even a bowling alley in the basement. There was everything a person could ever want.

Gerda hesitated. 'Lucinda, is there someone you'd like to invite to the salon on Saturday?'

'Oh, Mama, yes.' Lucinda's mind was racing.

'I know we haven't had the McAlisters for a while and you and little Lilli always seem to get on so well,' Gerda suggested.

'It's not Lilli McAlister,' Lucinda said with a frown. 'Can I invite a new friend?'

'Well, you know that will take more than a few days to arrange. It wouldn't be for this week. Your father will have to make sure that they're suitable and then we can send an invitation.'

'I don't understand why father has to approve my friends, Mama. Why can't he trust me?'

Gerda Finkelstein drew in a sharp breath.

'What's the matter?' Lucinda asked.

'Lucinda, don't be too hard on your father. He just wants the best for you.' Gerda's eyes shone and she felt the sting of tears threatening.

'What's wrong, Mama?' Lucinda demanded.

'Nothing, Lucinda. Nothing at all. Goodnight.' She flicked off the light and beat a hasty retreat from the room.

Lucinda's face fell. How could she invite the one person she really wanted to? Her father would never allow it.

Chapter 17

Hugh Kennington-Jones had returned to the penthouse to find Mrs Oliver shimmying her way around the dining room, cutlery in hand as she set the table. He could just make out the tinny sound of sitars coming from the earphones jammed into both her ears. She twirled and shrugged her way around the table, laying place settings in time with the music, an enormous smile plastered across her face.

Off-loading the final knife and fork, Dolly raised her arms to the ceiling and engaged in some rather fancy hand movements and then spun around mid-shoulder shrug to see Hugh grinning at her from the doorway.

'Oh, sir.' Dolly grimaced, and then rolled her eyes. She pulled the earphones out and snapped off her player.

'Please don't stop on my account, Dolly,' Hugh chuckled.

'You could have given an old woman a heart attack,' Dolly admonished. 'Sneaking up on me like that.'

'I didn't sneak up at all,' Hugh protested. 'You couldn't hear a thing with that music in your ears. And did you know there's a direct line of sight from the Top of the Rock to the rooftop garden here at Highton's?' he teased.

'Really?' Dolly Oliver asked. 'I can't imagine there's anything interesting to see up there.'

'I don't know, Dolly. I think you might have been entertaining half the city this afternoon. Well, at least anyone on a floor higher than the rooftop – and perhaps a few pilots and passengers en route to JFK.'

'Well, I'm glad to be of service – and what better place to trot out my new talents than New York,

New York. I wonder if there were any Broadway producers watching.' Dolly raised her eyebrows. 'I might have a new calling. Cooking, inventing and Bollywood dancing. And you know I feel fitter than I have in years. I've been thinking about adding belly dancing to my repertoire, but Shilly's not so keen. I think she's afraid of the outfits – a little too reveal-ing for her taste.'

Hugh laughed.

'On a more serious note, sir, are you alone?' Dolly thought the apartment was much too quiet for Alice-Miranda to have returned with her father.

'Yes, I left the girls heading towards Times Square. I've got some work to do,' Hugh replied.

'Would you like me to bring you a drink?' Dolly enquired.

'What I'd really love is a strong cup of tea if you wouldn't mind?' Hugh asked.

'I'll get that now. Will you take it in the study?'

'Yes, please.' Hugh Kennington-Jones exited the dining room and strode along the hallway to the study. He pushed open the door and walked over to the huge mahogany desk. There, he took the key from where he'd placed it under the lamp base and opened the top drawer, removing Nanny Bedford's diary and laying it on the desktop.

Hugh opened the book and stared at the swirling script in front of him. Reading Nanny Bedford's diary was a little like being in possession of a time machine, he thought to himself.

It made him smile to read Nanny's account of his birth and how his mother just adored her newborn son. Hugh felt a twinge of sadness. She wasn't to know what lay ahead, that her life would be cut so unfairly short.

And then when Hugh was just eighteen, his father had suddenly died of a brain aneurysm while getting ready for work one morning at Pelham Park. Hugh was away at school in his final year. With no living siblings, Pelham Park had come to him, but it wasn't somewhere he wanted to live. He felt very little affection for the foreboding mansion with its hundred-plus rooms. Early on, he'd left it in the capable hands of their family butler and housekeeper but Hugh had had a gnawing feeling that a house like that, sitting idle, was extraordinarily wasteful. For a long time he simply didn't know what to do with it.

A lesser young man would have baulked at the thought of all that responsibility, not only for the house but the company as well. But Hugh, having inherited his mother's commonsense as well as his father's business brain, worked alongside his father's trusted aide and confidant, the positively ancient Archibald Button, to ensure that the business would continue to function while he took time doing all the regular things young men his age did, including travelling and going to university. It was true that he spent most of the holiday periods working at Kennington's but he allowed himself the luxury of not taking over the business until the age of twenty-six. Henry Kennington-Jones had died at sixty-seven and Hugh vowed the same fate would not befall him. He wanted some balance in his life.

When he met and finally married Cecelia Highton-Smith after nearly eight years of courtship, he had happily moved into her family home, Highton Hall. Much prettier than Pelham Park, it had a warmth and liveliness he'd never before known in a house. Just looking at the place made him smile and together they forged a life full of happy memories there. It was his wife who suggested Pelham Park be turned into a nursing home for the disadvantaged. She reasoned that Kennington's could afford to run it as another arm of the business, subsidised by the massive profits from the grocery stores. They certainly didn't need two monstrous family piles. With her new baby on her hip, Cecelia oversaw a massive renovation, removing the dark wallpapers and gloomy drapes. Over almost two years, new life was breathed into the Park's ancient walls. Cecelia was inordinately proud of the project and Pelham Park had been hailed as a model of philanthropic endeavour, and one of the loveliest aged-care facilities in the country. Cecelia's only regret was that they didn't get to visit more often. Alice-Miranda particularly loved her time there playing with the residents.

Hugh thought about what Hector had said to him earlier. Could it really be true that his brother was out there somewhere? Alive? Hector would be on his way home now, mid-flight, so there was no point telephoning him until the morning at the earliest.

Hugh found himself wondering how difficult it would be to have his brother's casket exhumed from the family crypt. He hadn't decided yet if he should pursue it. But if his brother wasn't dead, then where on earth was he, and why would Hugh have been allowed to believe for all these years that he was gone?

Hugh didn't hear Mrs Oliver come in.

'Looks intriguing.' She placed the teacup down on the edge of the desk and stared at the open diary.

Hugh was jolted back to the present. 'Oh! Dolly, thank you. 'I'm not really sure I want to know. He stared at the yellowed pages. 'It belonged to my Nanny.'

'Goodness, sir, wherever did you get that from?' Dolly smiled. 'Any deep dark family secrets?'

Hugh looked up at her. 'That's just what I'm afraid of.'

'Well, let's hope not, sir. Mr O'Leary telephoned to say that he was picking up Cecelia and Alice-Miranda in about half an hour. I'll serve dinner at 7.15 pm if that's all right with you?'

'What was that?' Hugh was lost in his thoughts.

'Dinner at 7.15 pm?' Dolly repeated.

'Yes, of course. Thank you. Oh and Dolly, if you wouldn't mind, please don't tell Cecelia about this old thing.' He nodded at the diary. 'It's nothing.'

But Dolly Oliver was unconvinced. She'd been with Hugh Kennington-Jones for long enough to see that something had him rattled.

Chapter 18

'Girls, please make sure that you're at the back doors on time today,' Mr Underwood grilled.

'Where are we going?' Alice-Miranda asked Lucinda, who was sitting beside her.

'The park. We go at least twice a week. We get to run around and have some fresh air – and the teachers get to buy coffee and hot dogs and pretzels,' Lucinda whispered. They were supposed to be finishing off their poetry.

'Is it just the fifth grade?' Alice-Miranda asked.

'No, sixth today as well,' said Lucinda.

Felix Underwood groaned.

'What's the matter, sir?' one of the girls asked.

'I just remembered that it's 5U's turn to look after Maisy. Any takers?' He glanced around the room at the girls, whose hands seemed glued to their desks.

Only Alice-Miranda's arm shot into the air. 'I will, sir,' she smiled.

'No.' Lucinda looked at Alice-Miranda and clutched her hands to her face. She was shaking her head.

'What?' asked Alice-Miranda. 'Is something the matter?'

'No, Lucinda's just being a drama queen, aren't you, Lucinda? I'm sure that you're going to love looking after Miss Maisy,' said Mr Underwood. 'Thank you for the offer. You'll have to go downstairs to reception and get her lead and accessories.'

'Accessories?' Alice-Miranda asked.

'The pooper scooper and the plastic bags,' Ava replied.

'Of course. What about Maisy? Where will I find her?' Alice-Miranda asked.

'Oh, believe me, she knows the routine. She'll be waiting at the back door. Park days are her favourites,' Felix Underwood informed her.

Alice-Miranda could hardly wait to look after Maisy. She reminded her of their gardener Mr Greening's labrador Betsy. They had the same lovely temperament.

Lucinda kept scowling at Alice-Miranda all through the rest of the lesson, which happened to involve a geometry quiz which meant the girls couldn't talk any more.

Alice-Miranda whizzed through the questions on triangles, and she loved finding the area and perimeter of a range of shapes, some of which required several different methods to achieve the solution. She handed her paper in to Mr Underwood a full fifteen minutes before the test time was up.

'Are you sure you don't want to go over this again?' he asked her as she placed the paper on his desk.

'No, sir,' she replied. 'Thank you for a lovely test. It was very enjoyable.'

Felix Underwood wondered if she was making a strange attempt at humour. Alice-Miranda sat back in her seat and pulled a book from her desk. She had recently become addicted to *Anne of Green Gables* and sat smiling to herself as she read Anne's adventures.

Felix Underwood hadn't planned to grade the papers until after school but Alice-Miranda's test sat there all alone, just begging for attention. Finally, curiosity got the better of him and he slid it across the desk. The first page involved some fairly straightforward questions about shapes so he wasn't surprised that she got them all correct. The second page was different – much more difficult – and he could hardly believe it when every answer received a tick. Alice-Miranda scored one hundred per cent on a paper that he thought would challenge some of his brightest students.

He scribbled the mark on the top, beside which he drew a big smiley face and wrote 'well done'. When Jilly Hobbs had told him last week that he was receiving a new student from overseas for a short period he was thrilled by the prospect. Broadening his girls' horizons was a wonderful opportunity for them all. When Jilly told him that the girl hadn't yet turned eight his enthusiasm waned. Babysitting a third-grader was not something he wanted to do for the next month. He had protested that she'd be better served in one of the younger grades but Jilly Hobbs just smiled and said, 'She'll be fine. I'm sure you'll be pleasantly surprised, Felix.' Not one to argue with the boss, he had hoped she was right.

From the moment he met Alice-Miranda, Felix Underwood knew there was something different about her. He'd never seen a child introduce herself so confidently and when she couldn't contain her excitement about their art lesson at the Met he knew she was something special.

The bell rang, rousing Alice-Miranda from her jaunt in Avonlea. Several girls were still finishing their tests and others were depositing them on Mr Underwood's desk.

'You shouldn't have offered to look after Maisy,' Lucinda groaned as she and Alice-Miranda made their way out of the classroom.

'Why not? She's adorable,' Alice-Miranda protested.

'Did you know that her nickname is Crazy Maisy? She didn't get that for nothing,' Lucinda grinned.

'So the new girl is about to find out the hard way, hey?' Ava joined Alice-Miranda and Lucinda as they walked towards their lockers.

Quincy caught up to her friends and began to giggle. 'Man, Alice-Miranda, you're in for something special.'

'What's the matter? Why do you think it's so amusing that I offered to look after Maisy? I thought you'd all love to do it,' Alice-Miranda said, frowning.

'It's okay, Alice-Miranda, we're just teasing,' said Ava.

'Not!' Lucinda and Quincy burst out laughing.

Alice-Miranda was beginning to wonder what on earth she'd let herself in for. But she knew she'd find out soon enough.

'Hurry up guys, we want to make sure we have time to eat lunch. Alice-Miranda, I'll get some extra for you,' Quincy offered.

'Oh, it's all right. I'm not that hungry,' she replied.

'Believe me, you'll need every ounce of strength you can get if that mutt gets up to her usual tricks,' said Quincy.

Alice-Miranda ducked into reception on her way to the cafeteria.

'Hello Miss Cleary.' Alice-Miranda appeared at the reception desk window.

'Hello to you too, Miss Alice-Miranda. How are you enjoying Mrs Kimmel's?' Miss Cleary leaned forward in her seat to get a better view of the tiny child.

'I love it,' Alice-Miranda replied. 'Everyone's so kind and the lessons are great fun.'

'That's good news,' Cynthia Cleary replied. 'What can I help you with?'

'I need to get Maisy's lead and her accessories, please.'

'Really?' Miss Cleary's brown eyes widened. 'Are you sure?'

'Of course. I volunteered to look after Maisy in the park,' Alice-Miranda replied.

'Good luck, sweetie pie.' Miss Cleary hopped off her chair and opened a cupboard behind her. She retrieved a lead with some small plastic bags. 'Here you go. Just don't mention the "s" word and you'll be fine.'

Cynthia Cleary handed Alice-Miranda the equipment.

'What's the "s" word Miss Cleary?' Alice-Miranda asked.

The telephone rang and Miss Cleary answered it. 'Good afternoon, Mrs Kimmel's School for Girls, this is Cynthia speaking . . . Oh yes, ma'am, I can help you with that.' She pointed at the receiver and mouthed to Alice-Miranda, 'I'm going to be a while.'

'I'll bring it back after playtime,' Alice-Miranda smiled. 'Well, not all of it, perhaps.'

Alice-Miranda waved and skipped off to the cafeteria to join her friends.

A few minutes later, Whip Staples opened the front door and walked into reception. He was clutching a pair of garden clippers and a small plastic bag full of geranium offcuts.

'Hey Whip, what are you doing in about half an hour?' Cynthia Cleary asked him.

'What do you need?' he asked.

'You know our new girl, the little one, Alice-Miranda? She just came and collected Maisy's lead. If you can spare the time, you might want to take a stroll over to the park and make sure that pooch behaves herself.'

'Happy to,' Whip Staples grinned. 'She's a cutie, that one.'

'Yeah, she sure is,' Cynthia Cleary smiled.

Alice-Miranda met Mr Underwood at the back door at exactly five minutes to one. Just as her teacher had predicted, Maisy was already there, her tail wagging like a windscreen wiper on high speed. Alice-Miranda reached down and clipped the lead onto her collar, and was rewarded with a slobbering smooch to the side of her face.

'Thanks Maisy. Yuck!' the child laughed as she took out a tissue and wiped her cheek.

Alice-Miranda spotted Alethea and Gretchen standing with the other sixth grade girls. She looked up and gave them a wave. Gretchen smiled and waved back but Alethea just sneered.

Mr Underwood called the roll for his class and Miss Patrick did the same for the sixth grade. At 1 pm two lines of girls meandered their way down East 76th Street towards Central Park, stopping at the lights at Madison Avenue and then again at Fifth. Alice-Miranda wondered what the girls had been talking about. Maisy wasn't the least bit difficult to control as she trotted alongside her, obeying every command. 'Sit' when they reached the lights, 'walk' when they got a green light and 'stay' when the girls needed to move to the side of the footpath to let other pedestrians through.

'You'd better hold on,' Lucinda advised Alice-Miranda as the group crossed Fifth Avenue and made their way through the gates towards the Alice in Wonderland statue and the model boat lake.

Alice-Miranda felt Maisy strain against her lead.

'Settle down, Miss Maisy, we can have a lovely run around once we're safely inside the park,' Alice-Miranda told her.

There was large patch of lawn for the girls to play on or they could just sit on the grass and chat.

Mr Underwood and Miss Patrick headed straight for the kiosk while the girls dispersed, some climbing onto the mushroom which formed part of the life-sized bronze Alice in Wonderland statue, others taking up residence on the park benches scattered around the edge of the grassed area, and a few walked over to watch the tourists navigating their model boats.

Lucinda, Ava and Quincy led Alice-Miranda and Maisy around the lake, pointing out some of the park's more famous landmarks.

Maisy trotted along beside her mistress, perfectly behaved. Alice-Miranda wondered what the others had been fussing about. Alethea and Gretchen were standing by the lake watching the boats when Alethea suddenly called out, 'Oh look, how cute, there's a squirrel!' apparently to no one in particular.

Maisy stiffened; she stopped in her tracks, her eyes darting from one side of the path to the other.

'Come on, Maisy,' Alice-Miranda urged her on. 'I can't see anyth-i-i-i-i-i-i-i-i-i-i-i-ng.'

The labrador took off at breakneck speed with the tiny child behind gripping tightly to the lead. Maisy raced into the bushes around a tree and shot back out again. Ahead of them a grey ball of fur darted in and out of the trees, at one stage racing straight up into the foliage overhead. Maisy leapt at the tree trunk, jumping up and down on the spot. Just as Alice-Miranda caught her breath the squirrel fled from its hiding spot and raced across open ground. In the distance, Alethea was watching and laughing so hard she thought her lungs would burst.

Maisy raced around the boat lake with the squirrel ahead. Alice-Miranda would never have believed that the dog could move so quickly, the way she lumbered around the hallways at Mrs Kimmel's.

'Maisy, STOP!' The tiny child strained on the dog's lead. Maisy ran around the edge of the lake, then across the grass and right through the middle of a picnic rug, where she sent the diners ducking for cover.

'I am so sorry.' Alice-Miranda's brown curls were flying as she strained to keep a hold on the wayward mutt.

'Why you!' One elderly picnicker shook his fist at Maisy. His wife was busy removing pasta salad from her hair.

The squirrel stopped. It twitched then stood up on its hind legs, as if daring its hunter to come closer. Alice-Miranda pulled as hard as she could and finally Maisy came to a halt.

Alice-Miranda was puffing and shaking and wanted to get back to the elderly couple and apologise properly. Lucinda, Ava and Quincy reached Alice-Miranda just as a voice from the edge of the pond shouted again: 'Oh, how cute, can you see it? There's another squirrel!'

The squirrel took off at top speed with Maisy after it. Alice-Miranda fumbled with the lead and realised to her horror that she'd let it go. Maisy was gone and the lead was bumping up and down behind her. The labrador raced along the edge of the lake with Alice-Miranda and her friends in hot pursuit. Maisy headed straight for Alethea and Gretchen, who squealed like piglets. Maisy's lead caught Alethea's ankles.

'Ah, ah, ah!' Alethea swayed wildly on the edge of the pond, her arms rotating like windmills.

A loud splash caught the attention of the sixth

grade teacher who had been busy chatting with the barista in the cafe.

'Thea Mackenzie, what on earth are you doing?' Miss Patrick yelled.

Alethea was sitting in the lake, wailing at the top of her lungs.

'Thea, get out of there.' Gretchen leaned over and offered her hand.

'Leave me alone,' Alethea screamed.

Andie Patrick ran towards the lake wondering what on earth had possessed an otherwise sensible child to launch herself into the pond.

'Thea, come on, you need to get out of there,' said the teacher, glaring.

'I didn't get in here. It was all *her* fault.' She pointed at Alice-Miranda and her friends as they disappeared over the hill after Maisy and her prey.

Girls began to gather at the edge of the pond and stare at Alethea, who finally managed to haul herself out of the water. She was covered in sludge and sobbing hysterically. Mr Underwood offered her his jacket, which she snatched from his outstretched hand.

Meanwhile, over on the East Green, Alice-Miranda and her friends were in hot pursuit of Maisy.

In the distance Alice-Miranda spotted someone that she recognised.

'Mr Gambino, HELP!' Alice-Miranda yelled at her hot dog vendor friend.

Lou Gambino looked up from his newspaper to see a golden labrador streaking across the open field. He couldn't be sure, as his eyesight wasn't as good as it once was, but he thought the dog was chasing a squirrel and behind the dog he saw a little girl with long curls and behind her three taller children. He scrambled to his feet and did the first thing that came to mind.

'Hey, doggie, would you like a hot dog?' he yelled and retrieved a freshly cooked frankfurt from the pot, flinging it as far as he could in the direction of the hound. 'Here have another one.' He hurled dog after dog and finally caught the labrador's attention. Maisy stopped in her tracks. She sniffed the air then raced towards the vendor, hoovering up the frankfurts as she went.

'Well, hello there.' Lou Gambino grabbed the pooch's lead and held tight. 'Ain't you a pretty girl?'

Alice-Miranda and her friends reached Lou's stand a few seconds later, all four of them huffing and puffing.

'Oh . . . Mr . . . Gambino . . . thank you,' Alice-Miranda threw herself on Maisy who was contentedly chomping on another of Lou's delicious dogs.

'You're very welcome,' he replied. 'I thought it was you, little miss.'

When the children had caught their breath, Alice-Miranda set about introducing her friends.

'Mr Gambino, this is Lucinda Finkelstein and Ava Lee and Quincy Armstrong. And that's Maisy.'

'And she's a really naughty dog,' Quincy added as she bent down and stared into the labrador's brown eyes.

Everyone, this is Mr Gambino.'

The girls all said hello.

'Where's Mr Geronimo?' Alice-Miranda asked, looking around the park.

'Harry takes Tuesdays off to look after his baby grandson,' Lou explained.

'Well, thank goodness you were here. You've saved me from a lot more trouble.' Alice-Miranda reached down and gave Maisy a pat. 'And you are a very determined dog. I'm just glad you never caught that poor –'

'Sh!' Lucinda put her finger to Alice-Miranda's lip. 'Don't say it.'

Maisy stared innocently at Alice-Miranda with her big brown puppy dog eyes.

'At least she's got good taste in hot dogs.' Lou Gambino grinned as he threw Maisy another one.

'I'm afraid someone set you up, Alice-Miranda. Everyone knows that the "s" word brings out Crazy Maisy. She doesn't even care about them unless someone points them out,' Ava explained.

'Have you done something to upset Thea?' Lucinda asked. 'I don't think she likes you very much.'

'I think she likes me a lot less now.' Alice-Miranda's mind flashed to the sight of Alethea sitting in the pond and shrieking like a banshee.

Chapter 19

Mr Staples strode down the path towards Lou Gambino's hot dog cart.

'Hello Whip,' Lou greeted his friend. 'If you've come for a dog, I think the best I can do is hand over that one.' He pointed at Maisy. 'Mutt's eaten me out of house and home.'

'Lou, good to see you.' Whip reached out and shook the other man's hand.

'Hello Mr Whip,' Alice-Miranda said. 'How did you know where to find us?'

'The girls by the lake said they'd seen you chasing Maisy down here. I should have known this morning that she was going to play up. She had that cheeky glint in her eye and I think the ladies in the library have been feeding her candy again. I know what too much sugar does to children – I should have known that it might have the same effect on dogs.'

Maisy looked up at her captors with her doleful eyes. She yawned loudly and it sounded for all the world as though she had apologised.

'Did Maisy just say "I'm sorry"?' Quincy asked with a grin. The group looked at the dog and laughed.

'Mr Gambino,' Alice-Miranda started, 'it's my fault that Maisy got loose and cost you all those hot dogs. I promise I'll come back after school and pay for them.'

'Don't you even think about it, miss. I was having a slow day anyway. Would've had to throw those dogs out, I'm sure, and now at least Maisy here has had a good feed and she can stop chasing those sq –'

'NO!' all of the girls yelled. 'Don't say it.'

Lou grimaced. 'Oops, I forgot.'

'Well, Maisy, we need to get you back to school.' Whip Staples took the lead from where it was wrapped tightly around the wheel of the hot dog cart. 'And I think your teachers will be looking for you four.'

Maisy stood up and gave herself a good shake. Then she lay down on her stomach and began to push herself along the grass.

'Have you got a tummy ache?' asked Alice-Miranda.

The group said goodbye to Lou, with Alice-Miranda promising to bring her parents and Mrs Oliver over to see him again as soon as she could.

'Goodbye girls,' Lou called and began to pack up his stand for the day. Truth be told, he was rather looking forward to getting home and having a quiet time reading the afternoon paper. He didn't enjoy Tuesdays nearly as much as the rest of the week, when he and Harry played chess and solved the problems of the world.

Whip Staples had a firm grip on Maisy's lead. She ambled along, stopping to scratch at her tummy.

'I hope frankfurts aren't poisonous for dogs,' said Lucinda as she studied Maisy's movements. She thought the pooch looked mighty uncomfortable.

'No, but if she had some candy earlier and all those frankfurts, she's probably got a mighty fine stomach-ache,' Whip Staples observed. 'I'll take her back to school.'

At the boat lake, the lady who ran the cafe had found an old towel so that Lucinda could dry off a little. The girl was wearing Mr Underwood's jacket and still crying about what had happened, although the racking sobs had been exchanged for a shuddering whimper.

Whip Staples appeared with Maisy firmly in hand and the girls beside him.

'There she is,' Alethea cried out when she saw Alice-Miranda. 'It's all her fault that I ended up in the lake. She let Maisy go on purpose.'

Alice-Miranda walked over to Alethea.

'I'm so sorry that you ended up in the lake, Thea. Maisy was just too strong and she got away from me. I didn't mean to let her go. I feel terrible. And I must find that elderly couple and apologise for ruining their picnic,' Alice-Miranda said.

'I saw you. You let her go on purpose just as she was close to me,' Alethea spat.

Alice-Miranda shook her head. 'Of course I didn't. I can't imagine how awful it is in that pond. I mean, there looks to be quite a lot of silt and mud. I wouldn't wish a dip in there on anyone.'

'Except me,' Alethea fumed. 'Gretchen saw you. She knows you let Maisy go on purpose, don't you Gretchen?' Alethea glared at her friend.

'Well, I, I'm not sure,' Gretchen replied.

'Are you my friend, Gretchen?' Alethea demanded.

'Of course,' Gretchen replied.

'Then you'd better tell Miss Patrick and Mr Underwood the truth, or I'll unfriend you this minute,' Alethea threatened.

Gretchen gulped. Her face fell.

'Mr Underwood.' Gretchen tapped the teacher on the shoulder. He and Miss Patrick were talking in hushed tones a few steps away from the girls. 'I saw what happened.'

Felix Underwood spun around. 'Excuse me, Gretchen, what are you talking about?'

'I saw what happened with Alice-Miranda and Maisy. She let go of the dog just as she was running past Alethea. And I think I heard her laugh as Alethea fell into the pond.'

Felix Underwood and Andie Patrick were shocked.

'Is that true, Alice-Miranda?' Miss Patrick asked the tiny child.

'Well, I did let go but I don't remember doing it and I certainly didn't mean to. And I'm sure that I didn't laugh at Thea falling into the pond. That would have been a terrible shock for her,' Alice-Miranda said.

Alethea began to sob. 'She pushed me.'

'What are you talking about, Thea?' Alice-Miranda eyes were wide.

'She reached out when she was running past and she pushed me into the pond. Maisy made me lose my balance and then it was easy for Alice-Miranda to push me in.'

'Are you sure, Thea? That's a very serious accusation you're making. I can't imagine that Alice-Miranda meant for you to end up in the pond. It was just an accident,' said Miss Patrick soothingly.

'Why don't you believe me? You weren't even there. You and Mr Underwood were too busy getting your coffee and talking. You didn't see it, did you?' Alethea accused her teacher. 'She pushed me!'

Andie Patrick and Felix Underwood exchanged glances. It was true. They weren't watching the girls – they were buying coffee and chatting with Frances, the girl in the cafe. They hadn't seen anything. It was Thea's word against Alice-Miranda's.

Andie indicated for Felix to walk away from Alethea so they could speak privately.

'What do you think?' Andie asked. 'Thea's really upset. And Gretchen said that she saw it too.'

'I just don't see Alice-Miranda pushing Thea in on purpose,' Felix Underwood replied. 'She's a really sweet kid.'

'I think we should tell Jilly. She might be able to get to the bottom of it. I met Thea's mother at the parent–teacher night and she's not a lady I'd like to upset,' Andie reasoned.

The two teachers walked back to Alethea.

'Well, what are you going to do about her?' Alethea glared at Alice-Miranda and pointed her finger.

'When we get back to school, you can both have a chat with Miss Hobbs and explain what happened – after you change into some dry clothes, Thea,' Mr Underwood informed the girls.

'I don't see why I should have to go and see the headmistress.' Thea began to sob again. 'She's the one who should be in trouble.'

Lucinda, Ava and Quincy were listening to Alethea. It was strange but the more upset she got the weirder her southern accent sounded. Quincy, whose father's family was from Alabama, was beginning to wonder about Alethea's southern origins.

'Mr Underwood, can we speak to you?' Lucinda asked her teacher.

'Certainly, girls.' Felix Underwood glanced at his watch. They were already late so another minute or two wouldn't matter.

'Alice-Miranda didn't push Thea. She's making it up,' Lucinda frowned. 'We were there. We saw everything because we were running after Alice-Miranda and Maisy, trying to help her. Thea just lost her balance, that's all.'

'Thanks girls,' Mr Underwood said. 'Maybe you can go and explain what you saw to Miss Hobbs too when we get back.'

Felix Underwood would have been quite happy to let the whole thing go, but he had a sinking feeling in the pit of his stomach that once she started something, Thea was fully prepared to see it through to the end.

Alethea confronted the girls as they walked away from the teacher. 'What did you say to Mr Underwood?'

He and Miss Patrick were busy rounding up the rest of the group.

'Alice-Miranda didn't push you,' said Ava, glaring at Alethea.

'She did so!' Alethea spat. 'You didn't see it.'

'We were right behind her,' Lucinda nodded her head. 'You just lost your balance because you were trying to get out of Maisy's way. And the only reason Maisy went crazy in the first place was because you pointed out the squirrel.'

'I did *not*! You're lying. You're all lying.' Alethea's southern drawl was sounding more clipped by the second.

'Thea, where did you say you were from?' Quincy asked.

'Um.' Alethea looked around. She hesitated, then replied, 'Alabama.'

'So where exactly in Alabama?' Quincy asked.

'Atlanta.'

Quincy was getting more and more suspicious. 'In Alabama?'

'What's it to you?' Alethea pulled a face.

'And you grew up there before you moved to New York?' Quincy continued.

'Yes, of course I did. Why are you asking?' Alethea demanded.

'I just think it's strange that someone from

Alabama would be from Atlanta, seeing as everyone knows Atlanta is in Georgia.'

Alethea looked as though she might explode.

'I never said I was from Alabama. Gretchen said that. And she's dumb, really dumb. Of course I am from Atlanta in Georgia,' Alethea fumed.

Gretchen stared up at her so-called friend. Her green eyes were like wet pools. 'Dumb, you think I'm dumb?'

Alethea was cornered. 'You're just not very good at geography, Gretchen, that's all. I didn't mean dumb at everything. Just Geography.'

'I'm perfectly fine at Geography,' Gretchen retorted. 'And you're just, just . . .' Gretchen was searching for the right word. 'Mean!'

'Miss Patrick,' Gretchen called to the teacher who was leading the two lines the girls had fallen into. 'I need to tell you something.'

'Don't you dare,' gasped Alethea, her steely eyes threatening.

'Or what? You'll unfriend me?' Gretchen turned around and stood tall, her hands on her hips. 'Don't worry. I've just unfriended myself.'

Alethea began to wail. 'It's all your fault,'

she screamed at Alice-Miranda. 'See what you've done.'

'Thea, please stop that noise,' Alice-Miranda reached out and touched the hysterical girl on the shoulder.

Alethea recoiled as though she'd been hit with a high-voltage wire. 'Don't touch me!'

'Just tell Gretchen the truth,' Alice-Miranda whispered. 'If she's really your friend she won't care about any of it.'

'That's easy for you to say,' Alethea growled. 'Everyone loves you!'

Chapter 20

'Morrie, darling, what's worrying you?' Gerda Finkelstein looked at her husband across the divide that was their dining room table. Lucinda and her brother Toby were sitting on Gerda's left and Zeke was sitting on the right.

Morrie Finkelstein chewed on the same mouthful of food, over and over again, like a distracted cow.

'Is it work?' Gerda tried again. 'You just seem so preoccupied.'

'It's nothing that we need to talk about

now, Gerda. Let's just enjoy our dinner,' he replied, glancing up at his wife before returning his attention to the plump fillet steak in front of him.

Gerda sighed. Morrie had been in a dark mood for weeks now. When she asked him if everything was all right he told her that it was nothing to worry about. He'd always been difficult but Gerda was beginning to think that growing older was making him downright impossible.

'How was your day?' Gerda asked, glancing around at her children.

Toby looked smug. 'I got an A for my history paper.'

'Don't you mean *we* got at an A?' Zeke raised his eyebrows.

'What do you mean, Ezekiel?' Gerda frowned.

'He used my notes,' Zeke replied. 'From when I wrote the exact same paper last year.'

'Toby, you need to do your own work,' Gerda chastised. 'You know your brother won't be there to sit your SATs for you.'

Morrie looked up at his sons. 'Don't ever do that again!'

'But Papa –' Toby began to protest.

'No.' Morrie pointed his fork at his son. 'You're a Finkelstein. We make our own way in this world and we do our best because we are the best.'

Lucinda watched her father and wondered what he was talking about.

'But Papa, you copy things too. The salon is an exact reproduction of the rooms at the Palace of Versailles,' she said.

'We did not copy them,' her father began. 'We improved them. We made them more beautiful. Our salon is better than Versailles.'

Lucinda didn't comment. There was no point. Her father was clearly in a very strange mood.

'What about you, Lucinda, did you have a good day?' Her mother tried to lift the weight that had descended on the dinner table and only seemed to be getting heavier.

'Yes, Mama,' she replied and loaded her fork with potato and beans.

Her mother was persistent. 'Well, what did you do? You must have done some interesting things.'

'The exact same thing I do every Thursday. I was driven to school, I went to school and I was driven home again. I did my homework and now I'm at dinner,' Lucinda said, deadpan.

'What has got into you, young lady?' asked Gerda. She was rapidly losing her patience.

'I'm bored, Mama. Why can't I go out in the afternoons with my friends?' Lucinda's thoughts spewed from her mouth before she had time to think.

'What are you talking about?' Morrie's head shifted slightly to the right and he stared at his daughter. 'Of course you can go out with your friends.'

'No, I can't, Papa. I can go out with the friends that you and Mama approve of. I don't like Bethany Barrington and I can't stand Carissa Dayton. They're rude and mean and they spend all their time being nasty about the other girls at school. I want to go out with my real friends.'

'Of course they're your real friends.' Gerda's dark look at Lucinda was like a warning shot over the bow of a ship.

'No, they're not. They're your friends' daughters and I can't stand them. I want to go out with *my* friends!' Lucinda clamped her hand to her mouth but it was too late. The words had already escaped.

'*Your* friends?' Her father looked her full in the face now. 'And who exactly are *your* friends, Lucinda?'

Zeke and Toby exchanged glances. Their little sister wasn't prone to outbursts at the dinner table. Lucinda hesitated a moment before she spoke up. Then she remembered what Alice-Miranda had said about making the most of every day.

'Ava and Quincy.'

'Ava, the girl from East Harlem and Quincy, the daughter of those rowdy jazz musicians?' her father replied.

'Yes, Papa,' Lucinda nodded.

'Out of the question.' Morrie tensed his grip on his cutlery.

'But they're my best friends in the world. They're kind and fun and they like me in spite of everything.'

'They like you in spite of *what*?' her father demanded with a sharp look.

'All this.' Lucinda waved her knife and fork around in the air. 'Our money and our home and the store and everything.'

'Lucinda, that is exactly why it is your mother's and my job to protect you. You don't understand. They like you *because* of all this. Her father's brows knitted together. 'When you're a Finkelstein everyone wants a piece of you.'

'That's not true. They like me because I'm funny and silly and we laugh together. They feel sorry for me.' Lucinda's stomach lurched. She had already said too much.

Gerda intervened. 'They're not like us, Lucinda. Those girls, their lives are different to yours.'

'Yes, much more exciting.' Lucinda pouted. She had a sick feeling rising in the back of her throat. The mere fact that her father knew as much as he did about Ava and Quincy worried her.

'Ava – she is on a scholarship, right?' Her father raised his eyebrows. 'What good would it do her, you two being friends? Imagine if you invited her here. There is no point in raising a person's expectations if you can't see them through. And I can't stand jazz music – it's an abomination – an assault upon the ears.'

Toby and Zeke had no idea where this conversation was heading.

Zeke finally spoke up. 'But Papa, you let Toby and me choose our own friends.'

'That's not relevant to this conversation,' Morrie reproached his son.

'But of course it is. Why shouldn't Lucinda be allowed to have her own friends? She's right, you know, about that whining Dayton child. She's foul. Last time she was here I caught her putting handfuls of Mother's best chocolates into her pockets. Snivelling little thief,' Toby added.

'When I want your opinion, boys, I will ask for it.' Morrie silenced his sons, glaring from one to the other.

'Ava and Quincy are my friends and there's nothing you can do about it,' Lucinda challenged her father.

'What has got into you?' Her father's grey eyes drilled right through his daughter. 'I forbid you to have any contact with either of those girls. You must not speak to them. Clearly they have put all sorts of nonsensical ideas into your head.'

'But –' Lucinda began.

'Lucinda, you heard me. You will not say another word on this topic.' He faced his wife. 'Gerda, have Bethany Barrington and her mother stop by tomorrow afternoon. Lucinda will feel much better when she understands who her real friends are.'

Lucinda's lip began to quiver. 'But Papa!'

'Lucinda! Go to your room. You can come out when you feel ready to apologise,' Morrie ordered.

Lucinda pushed back her chair, knocking carrots over the edge of her plate as she threw her cutlery down. She fled from the dining room and down the hallway to her room, where she slammed her bedroom door as hard as she possibly could.

Gerda Finkelstein stared at her husband. 'Morrie,' she began, 'don't you think you're being a little hard on . . .' She stopped mid-sentence.

Morrie looked up from his plate and arched his left eyebrow. 'No,' he replied firmly. 'Pass me the salt, Ezekiel.'

His wife knew better than to continue with her question. When Morrie Finkelstein made up his mind about something he rarely changed it. Lucinda would have to fall into line, just as Gerda herself had done these past twenty years.

Chapter 21

'I'm so excited Mummy.' Alice-Miranda was positively bursting. It was the end of her second week at school and she was having a wonderful time, except for being worried about Lucinda. The day after the argument with her father, Lucinda had told her friends all about what had happened. She even threatened to run away and live in the zoo if she had to. Alice-Miranda offered to speak with Mr Finkelstein immediately but Lucinda had begged her not too. It was clearly a situation Alice-Miranda had to keep a close eye on.

The lessons were excellent and Alice-Miranda couldn't wait to go to the Met again. They'd had to skip their art class this week to attend a fascinating talk by a visiting scientist, so she was hoping to go on the weekend with her parents to finish her picture.

She'd hardly seen Alethea either, as the sixth grade girls had been away on camp all week. Although her mother was trying hard to limit her working hours, most of Alice-Miranda's after school excursions had taken place with her father. So far, they had visited the Natural History Museum, the Stock Exchange and the Statue of Liberty, but there were some things she was still very eager to do.

'Oh, darling, I'm really not sure about this,' her mother sighed. 'Your father and Mr Gruber both tell me that you'll be perfectly safe and of course I'd rather believe them than think about the alternative.'

'We'll be fine.' Alice-Miranda stood up from her seat at the kitchen table, walked around to where her mother was sitting and wrapped her arms around her neck. 'Please don't worry.'

'All right, sweetheart, but just promise that you'll go straight to Quincy's and not take any detours on your way home.'

'Of course we will, Mummy,' Alice-Miranda

said, leaning around to stare at her mother. 'We're very sensible, you know, and it's not as if I'm on my own. Ava and Quincy will be there too. I just wish Lucinda could come. It's not fair that she was too scared to even ask.'

'You mustn't interfere. The Finkelsteins have their reasons. I'm sure Morrie wouldn't appreciate anyone telling him how to raise his daughter.' Cecelia rested her head gently against Alice-Miranda's shoulder.

Cecelia Highton-Smith had grown more and more concerned about Morrie Finkelstein's behaviour since their arrival in New York.

When Gilbert Gruber had announced at dinner that the Finkelsteins were planning to open the Grand Salon on the same day as the Highton's launch party, Cecelia had telephoned the next afternoon to let Morrie know about the clash. The Highton's invitations had been out for at least a month and Morrie had only just issued his. He was terribly apologetic and said that he hadn't realised, which seemed very strange given that he and Gerda had already replied to the Highton's event, saying that they would love to attend. She wondered if he was planning to abandon his own party – it seemed highly unlikely.

Then when she and Alice-Miranda had seen the

roses in the Finkelstein's window display, Cecelia discovered that the suppliers had been stripped bare. It did seem a strange coincidence that they were the exact same variety that she had been planning to use at her opening. Fortunately, the discovery had been made early enough to source another floral contractor.

Cecelia had kept on hoping that these things were all just silly misunderstandings until one of her long-standing designers had called and said that she was withdrawing her clothing line and wouldn't be with Highton's at all any more. Cecelia couldn't even convince the woman to come in for a meeting. But the designer let slip that Morrie Finkelstein had made her an offer that was just too good to refuse. Cecelia and Hugh decided they would invite Morrie over to the store for a private tour and to see if they couldn't at least get him to reschedule the salon event, even just to an earlier time in the day. Cecelia hoped that if they made Morrie feel important, he might reconsider. New York City was more than big enough for both stores – in fact it was big enough for more than a dozen stores – and this Finkelstein feud was really starting to get her down.

Cecelia was staring off into the distance, wondering whether the store would ever be ready in time for the opening.

'Isn't it exciting, Mummy, that Quincy's father is a famous trumpet player?' Alice-Miranda bubbled.

Cecelia started. 'Sorry darling?'

'Mr Armstrong. I wish we could see him play. Do you know that their jazz club is one of the oldest and most respected in the whole city? It says so here in my guidebook.' Alice-Miranda ran her finger down the page and stopped at Armstrong's. 'And apparently the food is delicious too. Quincy's great-grandmother is in charge of the kitchen and her mother greets people at the door. How exciting to have the whole family involved! Quincy's older brother has just started playing in the band too.'

'Well, don't get in the way, sweetheart. The Armstrongs are a very busy family,' her mother warned.

'And what time will you and Daddy come and pick me up?'

'When I spoke with Quincy's mother she suggested we come at seven,' Cecelia replied.

Alice-Miranda had been thrilled when Mrs Armstrong had telephoned her parents earlier in the week and asked if she wanted to go home with Quincy on Friday afternoon.

'All right, young lady. I'm sorry, but your father and I have meetings this morning so Dolly will take you to school. Have a wonderful day and we'll see you later at the Armstrongs'. Now run along and brush your teeth,' Cecelia instructed.

Alice-Miranda kissed her mother's cheek and scurried out of the kitchen.

'I'll meet you at the lift in a couple of minutes, dear,' Dolly Oliver called after her.

✷

'I can't wait until this afternoon,' Alice-Miranda told Quincy, who was sitting opposite her in the cafeteria. Ava and Lucinda had just hopped up to get some drinks.

'It'll be fun,' Quincy grinned.

Ava was going to Quincy's too – her mother was picking her up at the end of her shift downtown – but Lucinda wasn't formally invited. She'd told Quincy there was no point asking her and it would only make her father even madder than he already was.

Lucinda and Ava reappeared balancing a tray of hot chocolates between them.

'What's with the long face, Finkelstein?' Quincy asked as the two girls passed out the steaming mugs.

'You know.' Lucinda frowned and slid into the booth beside Alice-Miranda. 'You're all going on this great adventure after school and I'm going . . . to a play date with Carissa Dayton. Maybe I should just come, but then you might have to keep me, because I don't think I'd be welcome back home again.'

'I could speak with your parents,' Alice-Miranda offered for at least the eighth time.

'No!' Lucinda protested. 'That will never work. Mama wouldn't understand and Papa, well, he's crazy these days. I don't understand what's got into him.'

'It is rather silly,' Alice-Miranda said. 'I mean, one day you'll be grown up and he won't be able to control your life any more.'

'I wish. You know, when we had that argument last week he said that he *forbade* me to talk to Ava and Quincy. Seriously, who does he think he is? He wants me to spend all my time with girls I can't stand. Doesn't he understand that you can't force people to be friends if they don't want to be?'

'You mean like Thea and the way she seems to hate you, Alice-Miranda, even though you're perfectly kind to her?' Quincy said, glancing across at her friend.

'Don't worry about Thea,' Alice-Miranda replied. 'I think her life is just a little bit complicated, that's all.'

'Hmph. I think she's a first-class fake. Anyone who says they're from Atlanta in Alabama is either really stupid or has something to hide,' Quincy said.

'Thea's all right,' Alice-Miranda said gently.

'Well, I'm just glad that Gretchen told the truth about what happened at the park last week or you could have been in big trouble,' said Ava seriously.

Lucinda was deep in thought. 'You know, I'm surprised my father hasn't planted some spies inside the school to tell on me. Oh!' she whispered. 'Maybe he has. He seemed to know a lot about you two.' She looked at Ava and Quincy. 'It's a miracle that he hasn't found out we're friends, Alice-Miranda. I can't imagine what he'd do. I don't know why but he seems to dislike your mother an awful lot.'

'That's just ridiculous,' Alice-Miranda was firm. 'Mummy's never said a bad word about your father. Whatever imaginary thing he thinks she has done to him is plain nonsense and I've got a good mind to –'

'Please Alice-Miranda,' Lucinda interrupted her. 'Don't do anything. It will only make it worse.'

Alice-Miranda tapped her finger against her cheek. She had a very strange feeling about Morrie Finkelstein, but at the moment she had no idea what to do about it.

'We'd better get moving,' said Ava, looking at the clock on the wall.

Quincy slurped the last of her hot chocolate and Lucinda gathered the empty mugs and offered to take them back to the counter.

'Mr Underwood said we can have some extra time to research our Science projects,' Alice-Miranda informed her friends.

'I don't think an hour's going to make much difference for us,' said Ava, rolling her eyes, 'unless there's an astronaut hiding out in the library.'

Alice-Miranda grinned. 'Come on.'

Chapter 22

Alice-Miranda, Ava and Quincy said goodbye to Lucinda and headed for the back door. Lucinda raced out the front. She didn't dare be late as her mother was picking her up so they could go to the Daytons' for afternoon tea. The week before, just as her father had ordered, her mother had invited bossy Bernadette Barrington and her ghastly daughter Bethany over to the house. And as always Bethany spent the whole time nosing her way through Lucinda's bedroom, moving her collection of miniature animals all over the shelf, riding her rocking horse so hard that Lucinda thought at any minute she might launch it through the window, and insisting on playing hide and seek (which Lucinda worried gave Bethany way too much time on her own).

This afternoon would be just as torturous but for a whole other set of reasons. Carissa Dayton didn't speak. She just nodded and stared. Lucinda always wondered what was going on in her head. Her mother Fifi spent her whole life telling everyone about how clever Carissa was. She was always coming first in this and that and giving recitals on the violin and piano and more recently the harp. Lucinda thought it was a pity that no one had ever taught her how to talk.

Lucinda made her way across the street and disappeared into the back of the town car where her mother was waiting for her.

Alice-Miranda, Ava and Quincy bounced along towards the 77th Street subway entrance on Lexington Avenue. As they descended the stairway, Alice-Miranda stopped and raised her nose in the air. She took in a deep breath.

'What on earth are you doing?' Quincy called back to her.

'Taking it all in,' Alice-Miranda replied. 'I want to savour all of the smells and the sounds of the subway, seeing as this is my first time on it.'

'You know, sometimes you foreign people are a little on the weird side,' Ava giggled. 'The subway smells like the subway.'

'Oh no, it smells like cold concrete compressed with the scent of millions of travellers and the seasons and food. It's like nothing I've ever come across before,' Alice-Miranda bubbled.

'Like I said, sometimes I just don't understand you people from other countries. Anyway, hurry up or we'll miss the next train,' Ava urged her little friend.

Quincy and Ava both had metro passes because they travelled on the subway every day. Alice-Miranda's mother wanted to pre-purchase her daughter's ticket too but Alice-Miranda insisted that she buy her own. Ava and Quincy guided her over to the ticket machine where they quickly worked out what to do and then helped another man, who was on holiday from Sweden, work out how to buy his pass too.

The girls then proceeded through the turnstile and descended another flight of stairs to the platform below.

'It's rather lovely for a subway,' Alice-Miranda remarked.

'There ain't nothing lovely about the subway,' Quincy said, frowning.

'But look at all those mosaic tiles. Someone spent a lot of time creating that 77th Street sign,' Alice-Miranda observed. 'And the columns give the whole place a sense of grandeur.'

'I think you're crazy.' Quincy looked up. 'But you know, I've never really noticed either of those things.'

'And those mosaics *are* pretty,' Ava added. 'I like that blue.'

'Hey, this isn't fair,' Quincy remarked.

'What's not fair?' Alice-Miranda asked.

'You're coming home with me and I'm supposed to be showing you things you've never seen in New York and you've just pointed out things I've never paid any attention to in my life,' Quincy grinned.

A rattling hum far off in the distance grew to a soft howl as the train approached through the tunnel. Metal on metal screeched as the carriages ground to a halt in front of the three girls. The doors slid back and they hopped on board. Quincy guided Alice-Miranda and Ava to sit together. Two rows of seats faced inwards along the exterior walls, with stainless steel handrails attached to the ceiling for commuters to hold onto when all the seats were taken. At this time of day the carriage was only about half full.

An electronic sign indicating where they were and which stations were coming up blinked its messages from above the doors. Alice-Miranda thought this was terribly clever. They would be alighting at 42nd Street, Grand Central Station, and then catching another train across to Times Square before walking three blocks to Quincy's place.

Alice-Miranda looked around the carriage at all of the people who were going about their daily business. Some gripped shopping bags, there was a young couple holding hands, and three tourists with day packs and cameras were studying a small map. She noticed a young man sitting along from her at the end of the row, wearing far more clothing than would seem necessary for the day and clutching a flat black bag, a bit like a skinny suitcase. He wore a battered pork-pie hat and seemed to be shivering.

Quincy and Ava were chatting and didn't notice Alice-Miranda stand up and walk towards him.

'Excuse me, sir, are you all right?' she asked.

The man looked up. Frown lines like railway tracks ran from the top of his forehead to the tip of his nose.

'You're shivering and I thought perhaps you might not be feeling well,' Alice-Miranda tried again.

The man seemed unable to speak.

Quincy looked over at her friend. 'Hey, Alice-Miranda. What are you doing?'

Alice-Miranda turned to face her. 'I'm just checking to see if this gentleman is all right. He's got an awful lot of clothing on and he's shivering.'

'Leave him alone,' Quincy urged, barely louder than a whisper. 'He's been here every day this week.'

'Well then, if he's always on the train, why don't you know him?' Alice-Miranda asked.

'Because unlike you I don't go around talking to homeless strangers.' Quincy had stood up and was now standing close behind Alice-Miranda, tugging at her blazer sleeve.

'That's silly. If you travel together on the same train every day, you should at least know the man's name.'

Alice-Miranda turned back around and stepped closer to the man. She looked into his grey eyes.

'My name is Alice-Miranda Highton-Smith-Kennington-Jones.' The tiny child held out her hand. 'And I'm very pleased to meet you, Mr . . .'

The man stared at her. He gulped and ran his tongue around the inside of his mouth.

'Come on, Alice-Miranda,' Ava hissed. 'You don't know anything about him.'

The man's hand, half-covered by a grubby fingerless glove, reached up and made contact with Alice-Miranda's. Finally he spoke. 'I'm Callum, Callum Preston.'

'It's very nice to meet you, Mr Preston.' Alice-Miranda smiled at him. 'Are you feeling okay?'

'A little cold,' he replied.

'I hope you haven't caught a fever.' The child reached out and placed the back of her hand on Callum's forehead.

He flinched and she withdrew her hand. 'I don't think you're running a temperature,' Alice-Miranda concluded. 'Would you like a drink?' She pulled a bottle from her backpack and offered it to him. 'I'm afraid it's only water.'

He nodded, hurriedly unscrewed the cap and proceeded to gulp the entire contents.

'It looks like you needed that.'

He offered the bottle back to Alice-Miranda.

'Why don't you keep it?' she suggested. 'You can fill it up again.'

'Thank . . . thank you, miss,' Callum replied. 'That's very kind.'

'This is my first time travelling on the subway,' Alice-Miranda blurted, 'and it's wonderful.'

'I'm glad you're enjoying yourself,' Callum nodded.

'Do you catch the train often yourself, Mr Preston?' Alice-Miranda asked.

Ava had shuffled as close as she could and together with Quincy she was intently watching Alice-Miranda's interaction with the man.

'I'm here so often lately, it feels a bit like home,' the man replied.

'Really? You must be very busy then, travelling all over the place.' Alice-Miranda sat down beside him. 'What do you do?'

Callum Preston fingered the handle of the expensive-looking black folio he was holding onto. 'I'm, I'm an artist.'

'Is that your work in there?' Alice-Miranda looked at the case.

Callum nodded.

'I'd love to see it. May I, please?' she asked.

Callum Preston slowly began to unzip the bag. He flapped it open across his lap revealing two watercolour paintings, one of a polar bear and the other of the Alice in Wonderland statue in Central Park, covered in children.

Quincy and Ava had both stood up to get a better look and were now standing right in front of Callum, staring.

'Wow!' Quincy gasped. 'Those are awesome.'

Callum Preston looked up at the girl with the black plaits. 'Thanks,' he whispered.

'Mr Preston, these paintings are extraordinary. Is that Gus from the zoo?' Alice-Miranda pointed at the polar bear.

Callum Preston nodded. He shuffled through several more paintings that were hidden behind the larger works, pulling out a smaller pencil drawing of a small child with long curls gazing up at a strange-looking creature.

Alice-Miranda studied it. 'Oh, that's that funny old lazy tamandua that Daddy told me lets off rather nasty smells.'

Ava leaned over and took a closer look. 'Hey, Alice-Miranda, look at that girl in the picture!'

'Mr Preston, do you remember when you drew this?' Alice-Miranda asked.

'Sunday, a couple of weeks back, I think,' he whispered.

Callum Preston held the picture up so that all three girls could see. Other passengers in the carriage were watching this rough-looking young man and the three school girls, wondering what to make of it all.

'Mr Preston, do you know, I think that child there might be me,' Alice-Miranda smiled.

He turned the page around and looked at it, then glanced back at Alice-Miranda. 'Would you spin around for a second, miss,' he asked her.

He held the picture aloft and looked at Alice-Miranda's back.

'I think you're right,' he replied.

'That's just the funniest coincidence, isn't it?' Alice-Miranda giggled. 'Mummy and Daddy took me to the zoo on the first Sunday we were in town and that tamandua was my favourite animal. And fancy that you drew a picture of her and me.'

Quincy glanced up at the electronic notice-board.

'Come on, we've got to go. Our stop's next,' she told Ava and Alice-Miranda.

'It's been very nice to meet you, Mr Preston,' Alice-Miranda smiled. 'Perhaps I'll see you again soon.'

'Here.' He handed her the picture of the tamandua. 'Please take it. It was meant to be.'

'That's awfully kind. Are you sure?'

The train ground to a halt at Grand Central Station. Quincy and Ava had picked up their backpacks and were already heading for the door.

'Alice-Miranda, hurry up,' Quincy called as a crowd began to push into the carriage.

'You'd better go,' Callum urged as he pressed the picture into Alice-Miranda's hand.

'Thank you, Mr Preston.' The tiny child turned and swung her satchel over her shoulder. 'See you again soon.' Holding tightly to the sketch, Alice-Miranda raced through the crowd and onto the platform where the girls were waiting.

Ava hugged her friend. 'Thank goodness. We thought we'd lost you in there.'

'I'm fine,' Alice-Miranda replied. 'And look, Mr Preston insisted that I have this.' She held up the picture, which both girls admired.

'He's really talented.' Quincy spoke first. 'I thought he was just some random homeless guy but he's clever. I wonder why he's always on the train.'

'Of course he's homeless,' Ava observed. 'He looked as though he hadn't eaten for days and I bet he was wearing every piece of clothing he owned.'

'Do you really think that he has nowhere to live?' Alice-Miranda was shocked. 'But he's an artist. Surely he doesn't live on the streets.'

'It doesn't take much to become homeless in New York City, Alice-Miranda. Who knows what happened to him but I'd guess that he's riding the trains to stay off the streets. Although he had a lot of pictures of the park – maybe he sleeps there,' Quincy added.

'That's terrible.' Alice-Miranda looked closely at her picture. The level of detail was quite extraordinary, right down to the spots on her skirt. 'I wish I could help him.'

'You can't save everyone, you know,' Ava frowned.

Alice-Miranda opened her satchel and carefully placed the sketch inside her favourite notebook for safekeeping.

'Come on, we've got to get to the other platform,' said Quincy. She took Alice-Miranda by the hand and together the three girls scurried to meet their connecting train.

Chapter 23

Alice-Miranda had never felt quite so instantly at home as she did when she arrived at the Armstrongs' that afternoon. Granma Clarrie, a tiny round woman who was dwarfed by her great-granddaughter Quincy, had greeted Alice-Miranda as if she were long-lost family.

'Why, you must be Quincy's little friend that we been hearing so much about. Ain't you the cutest little miss? Come here and give Granma Clarrie a hug,' she had commanded.

Alice-Miranda adored her from the minute she locked eyes with the silver-haired woman whose hug was as warm as hot buttered toast on a frosty morning.

Ava and Quincy were greeted with similar enthusiasm.

'Your mama's downstairs, Quincy,' said Granma Clarrie, 'so I'm on duty for now. I already been down there once this afternoon to check on Harry – make sure he's cooking my recipes the way the good Lord intended.'

Harry Poke was in charge of the kitchen in the club. But everyone knew that Granma Clarrie was there every night on 'quality control'. Everything on the club's menu came from her family and she was very proud of their authentic Southern cuisine.

Alice-Miranda raised her nose in the air and drew in a deep breath. 'Well, something up here smells delicious,' the child observed.

Granma Clarrie opened the oven door and removed an enormous pie. 'Apple and rhubarb and I've got a key lime in the refrigerator,' she informed the girls.

'Yes, please!' Alice-Miranda bubbled.

'Yes, please – which one?' Ava asked.

'May I try a small slice of both?' Alice-Miranda asked.

'Alice-Miranda, I'd be positively offended if you didn't.' Granma Clarrie removed the second pie from the fridge and placed it beside the steaming pastry mound on the island bench in the middle of the kitchen. She pulled a knife from the block by the sink and began to cut into the sweet confections.

Quincy's family lived above their jazz club in a large apartment set over three floors. An eat-in kitchen, living room and Granma Clarrie's quarters occupied the first floor while Quincy's parents had a bedroom, ensuite and office on the second. Quincy and her brother Isaac's rooms and bathroom were on the third floor. The club occupied the street level and a basement below. Quincy's father Eldred had played jazz trumpet since he was a boy when his father owned the club and his father before that. Armstrong's was part of New York City history. It had operated from the same building in Hell's Kitchen for over fifty years and before that it was in another building just down the street.

After the girls had consumed their afternoon feast, Quincy took Alice-Miranda and Ava on a tour of the house and then the club downstairs.

Of course Ava had been there before but she loved watching Alice-Miranda's reactions as they explored the dressing rooms, the kitchen and even the cellar.

Alice-Miranda adored the burr walnut panelling that enveloped the club like a wooden cocoon. The luxurious furnishings harked back to a time when men in tuxedos and women in cocktail gowns ventured out every evening and glamour was a way of life. She could imagine what it must have been like: full to the brim with celebrities, many of whose signed photographs hung along the wall in the entrance.

'Look at all the stars up there. Ella Fitzgerald and Marilyn Monroe and President Kennedy and there's Mohammed Ali and Elizabeth Taylor. Your family has hosted some very famous people,' Alice-Miranda said excitedly to Quincy.

'I've never paid much attention to those old photos. Granma's always saying this and that about those people but they don't mean much to me,' Quincy said with a shrug. 'She knows everyone.'

Alice-Miranda leaned in close to get a better look at one of the photographs. Two men and an extraordinarily beautiful woman between them stood shoulder to shoulder, smiling broadly.

'Goodness!' she exclaimed. 'Do you see who that is?'

'No,' Ava and Quincy replied together.

Each of the photographs was signed or had small engraved plaques at the bottom, identifying the patrons.

'Look, it says *Mr Horace Highton, Miss Ruby Winters and Mr Abe Finkelstein*. That's my great-great-grandfather – the one who started Highton's. Goodness, that must be Lucinda's great-great-grandfather with him,' Alice-Miranda declared.

'I wonder who that lady is.' Ava peered at the photo. 'She sure is pretty.'

'They all look so happy. I wonder what happened. Mummy said that they were meant to start a store together and at the last minute they went their separate ways. Something came between them.'

'Or someone?' Quincy raised her eyebrows.

'Do you think so?' Alice-Miranda asked. 'Maybe that would make sense. But I don't think my great-great grandmother was ever called Ruby. I'll have to ask Mummy.'

'Come on,' Quincy beckoned. 'Come and meet everyone.'

Quincy introduced Alice-Miranda to her parents

Eldred and Maryanne and their white-haired bartender Alfie, who had been at Armstrong's as long as anyone could remember. He whipped up three raspberry ice-cream spiders and the girls sat at the bar like three little ladies to drink them. Alice-Miranda and Ava were thrilled to learn that they weren't being picked up at 7 pm after all. Their parents had been invited to the club for dinner and the early show. The girls finished their frosty treats then headed back upstairs to play games.

Granma Clarrie had long gone down to the club to supervise the kitchen. As it was a family affair, Quincy's parents and her brother were downstairs too, getting ready for the Friday night crowd. During the week, Armstrong's played host to a variety of guest performers, but Friday nights belonged to Eldred and his band, which now included Isaac on the drums.

Just before 6.45 pm, as a long queue formed on the pavement outside the club, Quincy led her friends downstairs. Their table was front and centre and they were soon joined by Hugh and Cecelia and Ava's mum Dee Dee.

The group was now sitting enjoying the music and an array of Southern dishes that had been delivered to the table. Quincy and her mother had joined them and there were three spare seats awaiting the arrival of Granma Clarrie, Eldred and Isaac.

Alice-Miranda's chocolate curls bounced up and down in time with the beat of the snare drum as she wiggled in her seat. Quincy's father licked his lips, and then raised his trumpet in the air, making contact with the mouthpiece and blasting a noisy tune. A ginger-haired man on piano joined in and finally the saxophone player added his own smooth sounds to the quartet. Alice-Miranda stared at the group, wondering what was going to happen next. They had been playing non-stop for almost half an hour, taking it in turns to have solo spots. Three final notes exploded from the stage and the audience erupted into applause.

'Thank you very much, folks,' Eldred Armstrong's deep voice oozed into the microphone, as smooth and rich as golden syrup. 'We're going to take a short break and be back with you in just a little while. In the meantime, you enjoy that Southern fried chicken, young lady.' He pointed towards Alice-Miranda as a huge plate of food was deposited in front of her. 'Or you'll be in a mess of trouble with Granma Clarrie.'

Alice-Miranda beamed. 'Mr Armstrong is so talented, Daddy.'

'He sure is, sweetheart,' Hugh Kennington-Jones replied.

'That's why I was thinking, Daddy . . .' Alice-Miranda began.

'Uh oh.' Her father used a toothpick to pry out a piece of Louisiana crab cake that was stuck in his teeth. 'Should I be worried?'

'Of course not. I just thought perhaps Mr Armstrong and his band could play at the opening of the store. Wouldn't that be wonderful?' Alice-Miranda enthused.

Cecelia looked up from her buffalo wings. 'Darling, I think that would be amazing but we'll have to see what's already been arranged. And it's rather short notice for Mr Armstrong, too.'

Eldred Armstrong arrived at the table with Granma Clarrie and Isaac in tow.

'Mr Armstrong, that was wonderful,' Alice-Miranda enthused. 'And Mummy says that you might be able to play at the store opening next Saturday night, if you wanted to, of course.'

'Thank you, little lady.' Eldred's dark eyes shone.

'We'll talk,' Cecelia mouthed at Eldred with a smile.

'Yes, ma'am,' Eldred nodded.

'And Granma Clarrie, this meal is delicious. I know Mrs Oliver would love to get her hands on your recipes.' The tiny child licked her lips and wiped her hands on her napkin.

'It is a pleasure to cook for someone with such a fine appreciation of my food.' Granma Clarrie blew Alice-Miranda a kiss, which she promptly caught and blew right back.

The rest of the evening flew by. Alice-Miranda had a long chat with Ava's mother about her work as a police detective.

'It sounds very exciting,' Alice-Miranda said. 'Are you working on any interesting cases?'

'There is one that's pretty big,' Dee Dee replied. 'I suspect it might go all the way to City Hall.'

'Perhaps I might be a detective when I grow up,' Alice-Miranda said.

'I think your parents could have some other ideas,' Dee Dee laughed. 'Maybe you can take over the business?'

'Oh, I don't know about that,' Alice-Miranda

replied. 'I'm sure that Mummy and Daddy would be happy for me to choose my own career.'

Dee Dee smiled. She didn't argue but couldn't imagine that the daughter of an empire like Highton's would be allowed to do anything as ordinary as become a member of the police force. But the child *did* seem rather determined.

'How are things coming along at the store?' Dee Dee asked.

'It's going to be amazing but I can't believe there's only a week to go. It's still a big mess – but don't tell Mummy I said that. She's a bit upset about things,' Alice-Miranda explained.

'Really?' Dee Dee enquired, frowning.

'There have been lots of little mix-ups and delays but I'm sure that if anyone can work it out, Mummy can, and Tony and George.'

'Who are they?' Dee Dee asked.

Tony's the builder in charge and George is his foreman. He's quite young but he's very helpful and he works really long hours,' Alice-Miranda nodded.

'Oh really?' Dee Dee smiled at her. 'Don't worry. I'm sure everything will work out just fine. And Ava and I are looking forward to the party.'

'Me too,' Alice-Miranda grinned.

After another musical set, the show was over and there was a short space of time before the second seating.

'Thank you for the most wonderful evening,' said Alice-Miranda as she hugged Granma Clarrie. She reached out to shake hands with Eldred Armstrong, who instead leaned in and gave her a hug too, as did Quincy's mother Maryanne.

Alice-Miranda hugged Quincy and Ava.

'Oh, I almost forgot!' Alice-Miranda exclaimed. 'Mummy, you have to come and see this' She slipped her hand into her mother's and tugged her in the direction of the club's foyer.

Her father and the rest of the group followed.

'There.' Alice-Miranda pointed. 'Up on the wall. Look.'

Cecelia Highton-Smith leaned in to get a better look.

'Oh, goodness me, it seems we're not the first members of this family to have discovered the joys of Armstrong's,' she said, smiling.

'Is that your great-grandfather, Cee?' Her husband leaned in to take a closer look.

'Yes, it's dear old Horace,' she said.

'But Mummy, look who great-great-grandfather Horace is with,' Alice-Miranda urged.

Her mother leaned in again and re-read the plaque at the bottom of the photograph.

'Oh, Abe Finkelstein,' she whispered. 'Morrie's great-grandfather.'

'But who's the lady Mummy? It says her name is Ruby Winters. Was that great-great-grandpa Horace's wife?' Alice-Miranda asked.

'No. Your great-great grandmother was Eleanor Goodchild.'

Granma Clarrie was standing at the back of the group, craning her neck to get a better view.

'Which photo y'all looking at?'

'That one.' Alice-Miranda pointed up on the wall as Granma Clarrie pushed her way to the front.

'I remember that woman,' Granma Clarrie nodded.

'Oh Granma, don't you be going on now.' Eldred Armstrong shook his head. 'You couldn't have been more than five years old when that picture was taken. If you were born at all according to what age you're always telling us you are.'

'I may be a little more mature than I let on, Eldred, but I'm not lying. It was opening night, my papa's first club over on 42nd Street. I was just a little girl but she was the most beautiful creature I ever laid eyes on. I was poking my head around the corner of the office door to get a better look. She right near took the breath from my lungs.'

'But Granma Clarrie, that's ninety-one years ago, and you can't possibly be, well at least ninety-six,' Alice-Miranda gasped.

'The truth might as well come out now, child. I am as near to ninety-seven as I will ever be.' Granma Clarrie threw back her shoulders and stood as straight as she could.

'But you're amazing!' Alice-Miranda smiled at her.

'Thank you, dear. Being busy is what makes me so. And one more thing I never forgot. You see that man there holding the hat, he left just after that picture was taken and that other man there, he asked her to marry him that same night. I was supposed to be sleeping in the cot on the floor in the office but I was poking my head out and I saw him put a ring on her finger.'

'Goodness me, Granma Clarrie, thank you for that wonderful story,' Cecelia smiled.

'You pay no mind to that grandmother of mine,' Eldred Armstrong tutted. 'She thinks she knows half of America, and the other half, well they just the ones she says ain't worth knowing. And I'm absolutely positive her storytelling is getting better with age.'

The group finally bade one another farewell. Alice-Miranda collected her schoolbag and with her parents headed for their town car, which was parked outside the entrance to the club.

'So darling, did you enjoy today's adventures?' Cecelia asked as Seamus O'Leary closed the back door.

'Oh Mummy, it was amazing. Isn't Granma Clarrie wonderful – and I can't believe she saw Great-Great-Grandpa Horace in the flesh. I wonder if Mr Finkelstein married that beautiful woman. And I almost forgot. When we were on the subway this afternoon we met the most remarkable man. I was a little worried about him at first because he was wearing an awful lot of clothes and he seemed to be shivering but I checked his forehead and I was fairly sure that he didn't have a temperature,' Alice-Miranda babbled.

Her mother gasped and drew her hand to her mouth.

'Darling, you really mustn't talk to complete strangers, let alone check their temperatures,' Cecelia warned. 'Hugh, I told you that it wasn't a good idea allowing Alice-Miranda to travel on the subway.'

Her father shrugged. 'Too late now, Cee. And as far as I can tell she's still in one piece.' He winked at Alice-Miranda.

'It turns out that Mr Preston is the most talented artist,' Alice-Miranda began.

'You've lost me, sweetheart. Who's Mr Preston?' her mother enquired.

'The man on the subway, Mummy – with all the clothes. He was carrying an enormous flat satchel and it turns out that he's a terribly clever artist and guess what?'

Alice-Miranda opened her backpack and pulled out her notebook.

'Oh dear, you didn't ask for one of his paintings, did you, young lady?' her father frowned.

'No, Daddy. He insisted that I have this.' Alice-Miranda passed the pencil drawing across the back of the car to her father.

Hugh Kennington-Jones nodded. 'Jolly good, indeed.'

'And can you see what it is?' his daughter asked.

Hugh stared. His brow wrinkled.

'It's the zoo isn't it?' he asked.

'Yes, Daddy. It's that tamandua I liked so much – and look carefully.' She leaned forward. 'Can you see the little girl in the picture?'

'Yes, well only the back of her,' her father replied.

'But who does she look like?' Alice-Miranda swivelled further around in her seat.

Hugh Kennington-Jones stared at his daughter and then at his wife sitting beside her. Cecelia frowned.

'What is it, darling?' she asked her husband.

Hugh handed her the picture.

'Take a look for yourself,' he sighed.

'Heavens, it's not,' Cecelia frowned.

'Yes Mummy, it's me!' Alice-Miranda exclaimed. 'Imagine that. Mr Preston was in the zoo on the very same morning that we were and he was drawing the tamandua right when we were there and that's me in the picture. And fancy, in a city of over a million people, that I met him on the subway.'

Hugh Kennington-Jones and Cecelia Highton-Smith stared at each other.

'What's the matter, Mummy?' Alice-Miranda looked from her mother to her father. 'Daddy, why are you looking like that?' She thought her parents would be as excited as she was that she had met such a clever fellow.

'Darling, don't you think it's just a little bit too strange?' her mother began.

'What do you mean?' Alice-Miranda asked.

'Well, you said it yourself, sweetheart. In a city of over one million people, fancy that Mr Preston drew a picture with you in it and then he met you completely by chance on the subway.'

'It is fortunate, isn't it,' Alice-Miranda said eagerly.

'Hugh, you don't think this fellow orchestrated the whole thing, do you?' Cecelia asked.

'Of course not, darling,' he replied, trying to convince himself as much as his wife.

'Oh Daddy, Mr Preston isn't dangerous or anything, if that's what you're worried about,' Alice-Miranda assured her parents.

But Cecelia and Hugh both had strange feelings about this man and his chance meeting with their daughter on the subway. And Morrie Finkelstein had seemed to know *quite* a lot about the problems they were having at the store when Cecelia called to invite him for tea earlier in the afternoon.

It was all very strange indeed.

Chapter 24

The next morning, Cecelia Highton-Smith sat at the breakfast table drinking her tea and nibbling on a piece of toast spread with strawberry jam.

'Is everything all right, ma'am?' Dolly Oliver looked up from the stove where she was stirring a small pot of porridge.

'Oh, I don't know, Dolly,' Cecelia sighed. 'I can't help wondering what Morrie Finkelstein might do next. And that man Alice-Miranda met on the subway! It does seem rather a coincidence that he had made a drawing of her at the zoo. I hate to think the worst of people but . . .' Her voice trailed off.

'Well, if there's one thing I know about your daughter, she knows people and she's nobody's fool.' Dolly took the pot from the stove and poured the porridge into a cereal bowl. 'Is there anything else worrying you?' Dolly asked, wondering if Hugh had yet shared his own mysterious secret.

'No, although I am curious what sort of business associate of my husband's makes breakfast appointments at the crack of dawn on a Saturday. We promised Alice-Miranda we'd have all of our work done during the week, and now I feel terrible because I have a couple of meetings later today myself and I've been caught up so many times already. Dolly, if it's not too much bother, would you mind keeping an eye on her?'

'Mind? Of course I don't mind. In fact I'm looking forward to some time with her. She can show me around the park and I know she wants to go back to the Met and finish the drawing she had started for her art class.' Dolly sat down opposite Cecelia and poured a drizzle of honey onto her steaming porridge.

Cecelia glanced up and smiled. 'Thank you, Dolly. I don't know what we'd ever do without you.' She stood up and walked to the sink where she rinsed her cup and saucer and popped them into the dishwasher.

'Leave that, ma'am,' Dolly instructed. 'Go and see to your work. I'll wake Alice-Miranda shortly.'

It was almost nine o'clock but given their late night at the jazz club Cecelia was glad that her daughter was still sleeping. Her mind was abuzz. That photograph at Armstrong's had got her thinking. Surely someone in this town had to know why Abe Finkelstein and Horace Highton had fallen out so spectacularly. Maybe there would be some record of Ruby Winters. She would see what she could find out. If only there were more hours in the day.

*

Alice-Miranda pulled her sketchbook from her satchel and sat down on the little stool in front of the painting of *The Dance Class*. Dolly Oliver peered over the child's shoulder.

'Oh my dear, that's wonderful,' she complimented, looking from Alice-Miranda's sketchbook to the painting in front of them.

'Thank you, Mrs Oliver. I'm so glad we could come today. I really want to work on my dog. He looks a little odd, especially as I've erased half of his head. Please don't stand here waiting for me,' the child requested. 'I'm sure that you'd much rather have a look around and I'll be perfectly fine on my own for half an hour or so.'

Dolly Oliver glanced around the gallery. There were several older women milling about together and a couple of students sitting on the floor with their sketchbooks. Truth be told, she was rather keen to have a peek at the Egyptian exhibit.

'Well dear, I might pop along and see some of those treasures from Ancient Egypt, if that's all right with you,' she replied.

'Of course.' Alice-Miranda had already started working on repositioning the dog's face. When she looked up a moment later, Mrs Oliver was chatting with the security man standing at the far entrance to the room, no doubt asking that he keep an eye on her. She wished her family wouldn't worry so much. Where would be safer than the Metropolitan Museum of Art with its hundreds of security cameras and guards in every room?

'Goodbye dear. I won't be long,' Dolly called and scurried away, aware that the Egyptian exhibit was quite a trek downstairs and across to the other side of the vast building.

Alice-Miranda spent time perfecting her work. Her fluffy dog, which didn't appear in the original painting at all, now looked quite at home among her dancers in their frothy white tutus.

She was concentrating hard on adjusting the ribbons on one of the ballerina's shoes when a deep voice commented, 'You've done a mighty fine job of that.'

Alice-Miranda looked up to see a man studying her picture.

'Oh, thank you,' she said. Then she looked at him more closely. 'Didn't I see you last time I was here?'

'Yes,' he said with a smile back at her. 'That's right.'

'You suggested that I make the dog look as if he was dancing and so that's what I've done,' Alice-Miranda replied.

'It looks very good,' the man nodded. 'As though it should have always been there.'

'Do you come here often?' Alice-Miranda stood up and placed her sketchbook on the fold-out stool.

'Mmm, yes, I suppose I do,' the man replied.

'And do you have a favourite?' Alice-Miranda asked.

The man nodded. Alice-Miranda noticed that he was very well dressed and had quite the loveliest hands. His fingers were long and elegant, with the most perfectly manicured nails.

'Which one?' Alice-Miranda looked up at him.

He nodded again.

'Oh, silly me. That one there, just next to us,' she said, pointing. 'It's lovely.'

Alice-Miranda considered the small painting of a mother and her young son. He was resting his head in her lap. She was dressed in clothes from a more genteel time and the boy was wearing suspenders and a cap.

'That's a beautiful picture,' Alice-Miranda commented. 'I think it captures perfectly just how much they love each other.'

The man's brown eyes twinkled. 'Yes, I've always thought that too,' he replied.

'And what about you? Do you have a favourite?' he asked.

'Well, I love this Degas of course, but there's another painting in the gallery next door. It's terribly clever with all sorts of creatures entwined in it. It looks medieval, I think.'

He smiled. 'I think I know the one.'

'I am so sorry,' Alice-Miranda said. 'I've completely forgotten my manners.'

The man frowned.

'I should have introduced myself. My name is Alice-Miranda . . .'

Her voice was drowned out by a message over the intercom system requesting security at the front entrance.

'. . . Jones,' she finished.

She held out her tiny hand and he smiled.

'It's lovely to meet you, Alice-Miranda. I'm Ed.' He held onto her hand for just a moment but long enough for Alice-Miranda to know that his hands were as soft as they were lovely to look at.

'Do you have a surname?' she enquired.

'No, Ed's just fine,' he replied.

'Well, Mr Ed, it's lovely to meet you too.'

The man began to laugh. 'Please, just Ed is fine. You're far too young to know this but there was once a television show about a talking horse called Mr Ed.'

Alice-Miranda bit her lip and giggled. 'I'm terribly sorry. I had no idea. But I'd love to see it. I'm sure my pony Bonaparte would love it too. On second thoughts, he'd probably want to be the star and he'd be awfully mean to Mr Ed,' she babbled.

'Well, all the best with finishing your picture.' Ed leaned down and picked up the sketchbook. 'Perhaps you could redefine that man's face a little. At the moment he looks, ah . . . too happy.' He handed the book to Alice-Miranda.

'Oh yes, I see what you mean. Faces aren't really my strong point,' she said, frowning as she studied the picture.

'Well, just let your hand draw what your mind sees. You'll be fine.'

Alice-Miranda wondered what he meant. She turned to ask but just like the first time she'd met him, he'd completely disappeared.

'Goodness, Ed must be a magician. He's certainly good at vanishing,' Alice-Miranda said to no one in particular.

'Hello dear, who are you talking to?' Dolly Oliver asked.

'Myself actually. I met a lovely man and he was helping me with my picture, but he's gone,' Alice-Miranda replied.

Dolly studied Alice-Miranda's drawing. She

looked at the Degas on the wall and back to the sketchbook.

'I think I prefer yours my dear,' she smiled. 'That dog just adds something Mr Degas missed. He's got far too much white space down there in the front.'

'Thank you,' Alice-Miranda grinned. 'But Mr Degas was one of the world's best artists and I'm just a little girl learning to draw. How was the exhibition?'

'Dusty and delightful,' Dolly replied. 'Now don't rush, dear, I'll just have a wander around in here and then I think we should grab a bite of lunch. I'm rather peckish.'

'Me too. I'm almost finished,' Alice-Miranda replied.

Dolly Oliver wandered around the room spending mere seconds glancing at some of the artworks but lingering longer on the things that caught her eye. After lapping the gallery she arrived at the small painting beside *The Dance Class*.

Alice-Miranda was packing up her pencils and sketchbook. She folded her stool ready to return it to the lady at the education desk.

'I've seen that painting before,' Dolly mused, pointing at the mother and son, 'but not here.' She shook her head as a vague memory scratched at the back of her mind. 'I can't for the life of me think where it was but it's certainly familiar.'

'The man I met, Ed, said it's his favourite painting in the whole gallery,' Alice-Miranda announced.

'Well, it is especially lovely and I do like the light on the mother's face. She looks as though she adores that child,' Dolly said. 'There's something a little mesmerising about it.'

And right then and there Dolly remembered exactly where she had seen it.

'Oh, my goodness me!' she exclaimed. 'That painting.' She waggled her finger.

'What is it, Mrs Oliver?' Alice-Miranda's eyes widened.

'My dear girl, you'll hardly believe this but many years ago, not long after I started working for your newly married grandmother, she insisted I accompany her to a house party. You see, I commenced my employ with your family as your grandmother's maid.'

'But *you're* not a maid,' Alice-Miranda protested. 'You're part of the family.'

'Yes, well, things were different back then, dear,' Dolly smiled. 'At the house party I met your father for the first time. He was just a tiny lad, not yet four years old.'

'Where was the party? Was the painting there?' Alice-Miranda was practically bursting.

'My dear, it was at Pelham Park,' Dolly replied.

'But Pelham Park is where Daddy's family lived.'

'Yes, and that painting, I'm sure of it, it was hanging in the guest bedroom where your Granny Valentina stayed. I remember commenting that it was such a lovely piece,' Dolly remarked, 'and thinking what a pity that it was closeted away in a bedroom and not in a more public part of the house.'

'I wonder how it came to be here,' Alice-Miranda murmured. 'Did Grandpa Kennington-Jones give away his collection?'

'Goodness, no. I'm sorry to say, dear, but Henry Kennington-Jones had a reputation for being . . . well, not exactly the most generous of souls, especially after his wife and their eldest son were killed in that terrible motor accident. Your poor father, it's a credit to himself that he turned out to be such a wonderful man. They all said that he was just like his mother. She was a real beauty, your grandmother

Arabella; apparently she'd been an artist's model before she married your grandfather. I only met her on that one occasion and a warmer woman you'd be hard-pressed to find. But Henry was a hard fellow. For him life was all about the business.'

'What a delicious mystery!' Alice-Miranda exclaimed. 'We must find out how the painting came to be here. I wonder if Daddy gave it away when he inherited the estate.'

'Mmm, that's a possibility.' Dolly peered in closer to read the citation beside the painting. Then she shook her head. 'No dear, I don't think so.'

Alice-Miranda leaned in too and read the words aloud. '"An anonymous gift to the museum, 1971." Daddy would have been a little boy then and Grandpa was still alive, wasn't he?'

'This is a mystery, indeed!' Dolly Oliver declared before her stomach let out a gurgly whine. 'Oh dear, I think that tummy of mine is telling me that our detective work will just have to wait. Where would you like to have lunch?'

Alice-Miranda giggled as Mrs Oliver's stomach registered another high-pitched complaint. 'I know exactly what I want. Let's go and see Mr Gambino and Mr Geronimo.'

The tiny child slipped her hand into Dolly's. She glanced back at the painting. She had a strange feeling about that picture and one way or another she was going to find out how it came to be in the Metropolitan Museum of Art in New York City, so very far from home.

Chapter 25

Hugh Kennington-Jones stared out of the open window at the skyline on the other side of the park. Down below, the streets thrummed to the sound of the Monday morning traffic but he was blissfully unaware, lost in his own thoughts. He didn't hear the knock at the door either and was still gazing into the distance when Mrs Oliver placed the tea tray on the corner of his desk.

'Sir?' she asked.

'Oh Dolly, I didn't even hear you come in,' Hugh apologised.

'If you don't mind me saying, Mr Hugh, whatever is in that diary seems to be causing you some nasty frown lines.'

'It's like a jigsaw puzzle that's missing several critical pieces. And I don't want to bother Cee with any of it. She's got enough on her plate. Morrie Finkelstein is coming over for a private tour of the store this morning and I know she's anxious to see if she can't put this feud behind them.'

Dolly set about pouring Hugh a strong cup of black tea.

'Is there anything I can do?' she asked. 'You know I have some time on my hands. One can't spend all day dancing and cooking,' she smiled.

The mystery of Nanny Bedford's diary had deepened over the weekend. Hector phoned to tell Hugh that the coroner's report into the accident which claimed Hugh's mother's and brother's lives was missing. There was no proof that his brother had been with his mother that terrible night.

'Oh Dolly. I have a feeling that there has been a terrible injustice.' He shook his head slightly before lifting the china cup to his lips.

'How do you mean, sir?'

Hugh hesitated. 'You must promise not to tell a

soul. Cee has enough to worry about at the moment and I really don't want to get anyone's hopes up.'

'Of course, sir. I think you should know me well enough by now,' she replied.

Hugh nodded. 'I don't think my brother died in that car accident with my mother.'

'What makes you say that?' Dolly gasped.

'Nanny's diary. She writes about the blazing rows my father and Xavier were having just before the accident. I think my brother wanted to make his own way in the world and my father would have none of it.'

'If you don't mind me asking, sir, how did you come to have Nanny Bedford's diary?'

'Do you remember when Cee found my father's old desk in the attic at Pelham Park? It was when she was overseeing the renovations.'

Dolly nodded. 'Yes, she was thrilled to bits but I wasn't sure what happened to it after that.'

'Cee had it sent to the office and I've been using it ever since. I thought it was a fitting link to Father. Well, a few months ago, I knocked over a steaming cup of tea and it burned a mark into the top of it. I sent it away to be restored and asked that they give the whole thing a proper clean-up while they were at it. When it was returned several weeks ago there was a letter taped inside the top drawer and a note from the cabinet-maker saying that he had found it in a hidden compartment.'

'And the letter?'

'It was to my father from Nanny Bedford, written just before he died – when I was eighteen. She said that I should know the truth. Well, when I saw that letter I looked her up, but she had passed away just a month before. Then my man Hector found this.' He pointed at the diary. 'Clearly the poor woman was sufficiently terrified of my father and his reach that she never revealed the full extent of his secrets.'

'I'm not sure if Alice-Miranda has mentioned this, sir, but when we were in the Met on Saturday, I came across a painting that I was sure I'd seen somewhere else, a long time ago. It took a moment for me to remember, but I'm just about certain that it was at Pelham Park the time I accompanied your mother-in-law there.'

'No, Alice-Miranda didn't mention it. You're sure, Dolly, that it was from Pelham Park?'

'Well, sir, I am getting old but it's a lovely painting and I remember commenting to your mother-in-law that it was a pity it wasn't on display in a public part of the house. But then again, your father's art collection was extensive, as I recall.'

'Perhaps Father donated it,' Hugh suggested.

Dolly arched her left eyebrow. 'Really, sir? Your father?'

Hugh frowned. Dolly was right. His father wasn't renowned for his philanthropic endeavours. 'But Mother was a generous soul. Perhaps she gave it away without Father knowing.'

'Sir, I don't think so. The citation says that it was donated anonymously in 1971. Your mother died in 1970, didn't she?' Dolly replied.

Hugh took another sip of his tea. He gulped loudly and set the cup back onto the saucer.

'Take a look for yourself, Dolly.' Hugh motioned towards the diary. 'If my brother is alive, then where is he? And why did he just disappear?'

Dolly picked up the weathered book and looked thoughtfully at its burnished leather cover and yellowed pages.

'I have to go and meet Cee downstairs. Morrie will be here shortly,' Hugh informed her. 'But you might as well read it properly. See if there's anything I've missed.'

'I'll just clear the tray,' she said.

'No, I'll take it to the kitchen,' said Hugh. 'You stay here. And when you're finished please just lock it in the top drawer.'

★

Downstairs on the ground floor, Cecelia Highton-Smith was pacing. She had walked the length and breadth of the cosmetics counters and checked and rechecked product placements, signage, and even the colour of the paint on the feature walls.

'Cecelia, dear, you're going to wear a furrow in that marble floor,' Gilbert Gruber called from the mezzanine above, where he had been watching her.

Cecelia stopped and looked up at him. 'Oh Gilbert, I'm wound up like a top. Morrie Finkelstein is due any minute and I don't know how this meeting is going to go.'

'I've just taken a call that's not going to give you any more confidence, I'm afraid. I'll be right down.' Gilbert scurried away to the stairs.

'What is it?' Cecelia asked as he approached her.

'It seems that several more of our suppliers have entered into exclusive arrangements with

Finkelstein's in the past few days. I don't know what Morrie is promising them but this is getting out of hand.'

'I don't understand. Everyone knows we're about to reopen,' Cecelia fumed.

'Perhaps Hugh can help,' Gilbert soothed.

'I don't know, Gilbert. He's been terribly preoccupied the past couple of weeks – disappearing here and there to secret meetings. Whenever I ask, he says that it's just Kennington's business and nothing to worry about, but I've never seen him so distracted.'

Gilbert's telephone rang in his pocket. It was security to let him know that Morrie Finkelstein had arrived and was on his way up from the parking garage.

'Hello darling.' Hugh slid in beside his wife and kissed her cheek.

'Oh there you are, thank heavens. He's here.' Cecelia managed a tight smile.

'I thought you might like to give him the grand tour and then I've arranged for you to have lunch in the corporate dining room, Cecelia,' said Gilbert, placing a calming hand on her shoulder. 'Don't worry about Morrie. You've known him for a very long time. And these bullyboy tactics of his – well,

I'd suggest you give as good as you get and he'll likely back down completely.'

'Gilbert's right, darling. Morrie has no right to steal our suppliers and we need to let him know that it's not on. We've never approached anyone he has an exclusive agreement with and he needs to pay you the same courtesy,' said Hugh firmly.

'Yes, you're absolutely right.' Cecelia smoothed her skirt and adjusted her blazer lapels.

The lift bell chimed and out marched Morrie Finkelstein, dressed from head to toe in black and wearing a smile that would scare spiders from their webs.

'Here we go,' Cecelia whispered, before saying loudly, 'Morrie, how lovely to see you.'

Chapter 26

On Monday morning, Alice-Miranda met Quincy, Ava and Lucinda at the fifth grade lockers before class. She told them all about her day with Mrs Oliver at the Met, and Sunday when her parents took her to Yankee Stadium to watch a baseball game. Alice-Miranda fizzed with excitement about the crowd and the action and said that the best part was when the man in front of her caught a fly ball and the whole place erupted with cheers.

'Did you have a good weekend, Lucinda?'

Alice-Miranda noticed that her friend was unusually subdued.

'Same as always,' Lucinda replied. 'It's not fair. You get to have so much fun and all I do is go to the stupid salon with Mother and her horrible friends and their awful daughters.'

'Surely it can't be that bad,' Alice-Miranda soothed. 'There must be a couple of girls you get along with.'

'It's worse than that bad.' Lucinda looked as if she might cry. 'Papa picked a dress that was way too tight – it felt like a sausage skin and Bethany Barrington called me a giant wiener all afternoon.'

'Why didn't you wear another dress?' Alice-Miranda asked.

'Because I have to wear the dress Papa picks out for me. It's always been that way,' Lucinda sighed.

'Couldn't you have got a bigger size?' Ava asked.

'No, he prides himself on knowing exactly my size, or so he thinks.'

'That's just stupid,' Ava said.

'Come on, Finkelstein, being an Upper East Side princess must have *some* good bits,' Quincy said, with a little smile at her.

'I'd trade it all in a second to know what real life is like,' said Lucinda as she foraged around in her locker.

'We had some real-life action on the subway on Friday when Alice-Miranda befriended this random homeless guy and Quincy and I thought we'd all end up . . .' Ava gulped and ran her finger across her throat.

Alice-Miranda defended him. 'Mr Preston was lovely and very talented too. I didn't think for one second that he was going to hurt us and I hope he's not really homeless because that would be too terrible for words.'

The bell rang, scattering girls this way and that. Alice-Miranda grabbed her books and closed her locker.

'Come on, Lucinda,' she said as she slipped her hand into the taller child's. 'And you're never going to believe who we saw a photograph of on the wall at the Armstrongs' club . . .' Alice-Miranda told her friend all about their great-great grandfathers and the lady called Ruby Winters.

The girls hadn't noticed Alethea standing at the end of the corridor. Having spent all week at camp getting the cold shoulder from Gretchen, she was as miserable as ever. But her mother refused to move her to yet another school.

'She's going to pay for what she's done,' Alethea breathed, before turning on her heel and scurrying upstairs to class.

✳

The morning lessons flew by and Alice-Miranda was looking forward to the afternoon art class at the Met. Mr Underwood explained that today they were having a tutorial from a renowned artist. Alice-Miranda was hoping to stop by the information desk and see if she could find out any more about that painting hanging next to *The Dance Class*. The rest of the weekend had been so busy she'd quite forgotten to tell her parents about Mrs Oliver's discovery.

During the lesson before lunch, the girls were working on their projects for the Science Fair. Lucinda had been paired up with Alice-Miranda and they were creating a sculpture of icebergs in the Arctic, to demonstrate the effects of global warming. There was plaster of Paris all over the desk, and about as much covering the floor.

Ava and Quincy were surrounded by styrofoam, which they were cutting up to make a model of the solar system.

'Now, girls, you'll need to take your projects down to the storeroom,' Mr Underwood instructed.

Just as he finished his sentence the bell rang. 'But before you go, you have to get this place spick and span. And I hear there are burgers for lunch today as a special treat, but no one's leaving before this room is cleaned up.'

The class sprang into action. Felix hoped the girls wouldn't be too disappointed to find that they were vegie burgers.

'And be on time this afternoon. I'll meet you at the back doors.'

Alice-Miranda and Lucinda balanced their construction on a sheet of plywood and teetered towards the storeroom at the end of the hall.

'It's starting to look like the Arctic, I think,' Alice-Miranda commented.

'Sort of,' Lucinda replied. 'We need to get more chicken wire and build up some of those icebergs a little more.'

Alethea appeared and blocked the hall. 'What's that rubbish?'

'Hello Thea. It's our Science project,' Alice-Miranda replied.

'It's the Arctic,' Lucinda added, 'and we're going to show how the polar cap is melting and the polar bears are getting stuck out in the ocean on chunks of ice.'

'Who cares about smelly old polar bears? I think it's stupid,' Alethea spat. 'Like you!'

'Thea, there's no need to be nasty. I've apologised to you about the park and you know I didn't let go of Maisy on purpose,' said Alice-Miranda.

'Yes, you did.' Alethea narrowed her eyes. 'And one day you're going to pay for what you've done.' She pushed her hand into the wet plaster and caused the side of the construction to cave in.

'What did you do that for?' Lucinda shouted.

Alethea shrugged her shoulders and stalked off down the hallway.

Lucinda wrinkled her nose. 'I can't believe I thought she was nice when we first met her. She's awful.'

'She's lonely,' Alice-Miranda replied.

'Well, she doesn't deserve to have any friends with an attitude like that.'

'Everyone needs a friend, Lucinda,' Alice-Miranda smiled.

The girls deposited their model onto a shelf and tried to push the side back into place.

'Come on, let's get some lunch,' Lucinda said as they headed off to the bathroom to wash their hands.

'I'll meet you there in a little while,' Alice-Miranda replied. 'There's someone I want to see first.'

Alice-Miranda raced upstairs to the sixth grade lockers. She was hoping to find Gretchen. Alone.

Chapter 27

Cynthia Cleary had just popped out to the kitchen-ette to make herself a cup of coffee when the front door buzzer went off. It sounded like a mosquito tapping out morse code. Whoever was on the other side was in a hurry to be heard.

She balanced her cup and rushed back to her desk, where she hit the intercom button.

'Good afternoon, may I help you?' she asked.

'So you are there. Open this door immediately,' the voice on the other side demanded.

'I am sorry, sir, but you will need to identify yourself.' Miss Cleary peered into the monitor to see if she could recognise the man.

'What! You don't know me? I'm Morrie Finkelstein,' the man hissed through gritted teeth.

Cynthia Cleary looked again. Of course it was Mr Finkelstein. She recognised him from those dreadful advertisements for his store.

'I'm sorry, Mr Finkelstein, please come in.' Cynthia released the door lock.

Morrie Finkelstein stomped into the reception with a sneer from ear to ear.

'How may I help you, sir?' Cynthia pushed the visitors' sign-in book in front of Morrie, who ignored it completely.

'Jilly Hobbs,' he demanded.

'Yes, sir, what about Miss Hobbs?' Cynthia Cleary gulped. Morrie's eyes darted around the room like a squirrel in the park.

'Get her for me, you idiotic woman,' he ordered.

'I'm sorry, Mr Finkelstein, but Miss Hobbs is in a meeting right now and she has asked not to be disturbed.' Miss Cleary clasped her hands together tightly, wondering what he was going to say next.

'I don't care if Miss Hobbs is taking tea with the President of the United States, you tell her that I want to see her and I want to see her NOW!' he roared at the young woman.

Miss Cleary jumped as Morrie's hand slammed down onto the counter top, causing Miss Cleary's coffee to slosh all over the papers piled neatly on her desk.

'Yes, sir, I'll see if she's available,' Cynthia stood up from her seat. She was trembling like a jelly as she made her way out from behind the reception desk and across the foyer to the headmistress's study.

Morrie Finkelstein's eyes followed her the whole way.

She was about to knock on the door when he pushed past her and slammed his hand against the timber frame.

'So that's where she is. Good grief, the woman doesn't know the first thing about running a business, does she? Everyone can see her in there,' he growled as he turned the handle and marched straight into the study.

Jilly Hobbs was entertaining one of the school's most generous benefactors. Between tea and finger sandwiches, the woman, now close to ninety, was telling Jilly that she intended to leave a significant portion of her vast estate to Mrs Kimmel's, seeing that she had no children of her own and wasn't at all fond of her only nephew.

Maisy was lying on the floor near the old woman's feet, her nose dangerously close to the sandwich tray.

Cynthia Cleary raced around in front of Morrie Finkelstein. 'I am sorry, Miss Hobbs. I tried to stop him but Mr Finkelstein insisted that he see you right now.'

The frightened look on the receptionist's face told Jilly Hobbs as much as she needed to know.

'Good afternoon, Mr Finkelstein. How lovely of you to come.' Jilly oozed charm as thick as cold custard. 'Now, sir, I've just been having a wonderful meeting with Miss Heloise Horowitz.' The old woman stood up and turned around. Morrie gulped loudly. His shoulders slumped as though someone had just stuck a pin in him and let out all the hot air.

'Aunt Heloise,' he twitched. 'How lovely to see you.' Morrie shuffled forward and, with quivering lips, brushed the old woman's heavily powdered cheek.

'I hope everything's all right, Morrie. Barging in here as if you own the place,' she tutted. 'I'd have expected more of you – oh, except that it's *you*.'

Morrie's face fell and at that moment he was again nine years old, being told off for some or other misdemeanour.

'And how is your mother, Morrie? I haven't seen her for a week or so but I'm having tea with her tomorrow.'

'Mother is fine, thank you for asking.' Morrie hadn't spoken with his mother in over a week either but he wasn't about to let his aunt know that.

'Well, Miss Hobbs, it has been a most marvellous luncheon. I must be getting home and I will send those papers via my attorney next week.' Heloise Horowitz gathered her walking stick and handbag and tottered towards the door.

'My pleasure, Miss Horowitz. And thank you for your extraordinary generosity. I'll see you to the car,' Jilly Hobbs offered.

'No, no, my dear, you've been too kind. My nephew will escort me. It's not far. My driver is just outside.'

Morrie Finkelstein sighed loudly and let out a shallow growling sound.

'Is there a problem, Morrie?' Heloise enquired, raising a drawn-on eyebrow.

'Of course not. It's my pleasure, Aunt Heloise,' he gulped.

He spent the next ten minutes escorting his aunt the short distance from Jilly Hobbs's office door to the pavement in front of the school. Morrie made sure that the front door didn't click shut on his way out, suspecting that the receptionist might not be so keen to let him in again. His lip curled as his aunt told him a story he'd heard at least a hundred times before, and he couldn't help wondering what the old bat was doing there and how much of his family's money she was giving away.

Morrie deposited Aunt Heloise into her car and sped back inside.

This time Jilly Hobbs was ready for him.

'Come in, Mr Finkelstein,' she instructed. 'Wasn't it a charming coincidence that your mother's sister was here today? Heloise is such a sweet and extraordinarily generous woman.'

Jilly motioned for Morrie to take a seat on one of her plump armchairs, and she sat down opposite.

'She's a gold-digging man-eater,' Morrie retorted. 'Six dead husbands, all of them billionaires and a fortune she's done nothing to earn. And you, Miss Hobbs, you're completely reprehensible.'

'I'm sorry,' Jilly replied and pushed herself further back into her chair. 'I have no idea what you're talking about.'

'Oh yes, you do. Allowing Cecelia Highton-Smith's daughter to come here and corrupt my child's mind. You're a disgrace. I'm pulling Lucinda out of school effective immediately,' Morrie erupted.

'I don't understand.' Jilly was using her very best soothing tones.

'Well, understand this. I have long given *my* financial support to this institution but no more. I am withdrawing my child and my money – unless you remove that brat today.'

'What on earth are you talking about?' Jilly Hobbs was fast losing patience. 'Alice-Miranda is no brat I can assure you, and I'm quite certain that Lucinda can decide for herself who she wants to be friends with.'

'No, she can't!' Morrie stood up and stamped his foot. His nostrils flared in and out like sheets flapping in a breeze.

'It's bad enough that my daughter has taken up with two other most unsuitable girls, but to find out today, from Cecelia Highton-Smith herself, that my Lucinda has befriended her daughter . . . I am in utter disbelief! I can only imagine that she's as beguiling as her mother, with the same sinister undertones,' Morrie ranted.

Jilly Hobbs was beginning to think that Morrie Finkelstein had completely lost the plot. Nothing he was saying made any sense at all. She knew he had a reputation for being a rather controlling and jealous fellow but, judging by the display in front of her just now, she thought that was a very mild assessment of his personality to say the least.

'Mr Finkelstein, sit.' Jilly's voice now had a sharp edge to it, one not often heard. She stood up and walked to her telephone. 'Miss Cleary, please bring us some tea. Chamomile, please.'

She walked back around to the other side of her desk and sat down opposite Morrie. Maisy was helping herself to the last of the sandwiches on the plate beside Morrie's chair.

'Mr Finkelstein, I can hear that you're upset. Why don't you start at the beginning and tell me what's really troubling you.'

'You can stop all that psychobabble, Miss Hobbs. I know what you're trying to do and it won't work.

I'm Morrie Finkelstein. I'm rich and I'm important and I run the best darn department store this
town has ever known. Now get my daughter. We're
leaving!'

'I'm sorry, Mr Finkelstein, but the girls are at
lunch so it will be difficult to locate her until the
bell goes.'

'That's fine.' Morrie stood up. 'I know where the
cafeteria is. I paid for it.' He barged past Jilly and
stormed through reception towards the back stairs.

'Lucinda Finkelstein, where are you?' he shouted,
sending little girls scattering this way and that.

'Miss Cleary, call Mr Staples and ask him to go
to the cafeteria, immediately,' Jilly shouted as she
raced after him.

Chapter 28

Alice-Miranda took the last bite of her vegie burger. 'That was delicious.' She wiped the crumbs from her lips, folded her paper napkin and placed it on her empty plate.

'Yeah, it was okay, but next time we have burgers I hope they use meat,' said Ava, wrinkling her nose.

'I need to take some books back to the library before the end of lunch,' Quincy informed her friends. 'Who's coming with me?'

Ava, Alice-Miranda and Lucinda all agreed to go.

The girls were finishing their hot chocolates when, from the far end of the hallway, came a roaring voice.

'Lucinda Finkelstein, where are you?' it bellowed.

Lucinda froze. 'That's my father. If he sees me with all of you, I'm done for.'

'I wonder what he's doing here,' Alice-Miranda said.

Before anyone had time to answer, Morrie Finkelstein arrived in the cafeteria. His face was red and he was snorting and blowing like a raging bull. Silence descended on the room. Girls chewed and swallowed but no one said a word.

Lucinda slumped down in the booth, willing herself to be invisible.

'Where is my daughter?' Morrie demanded as he searched the room. 'Lucinda Finkelstein, you come out here NOW!'

Alice-Miranda leaned across the table and patted Lucinda's arm.

'Don't worry,' she whispered. 'I can't imagine what's upset your father so badly, but I'll talk to him.'

'No!' Lucinda objected, but before she had time to say anything more, Alice-Miranda leapt up from the booth and walked across the open floor to meet Mr Finkelstein.

'Hello Mr Finkelstein.' She looked up at him and smiled. 'My name's Alice-Miranda Highton-Smith-Kennington-Jones and I'm very pleased to meet you.' She offered her tiny hand.

'You! What have you done with my Lucinda?' he demanded.

'Nothing, Mr Finkelstein, but you do seem rather upset.'

'Really? Do you think so? Why, you impertinent little brat!' he roared.

'Now, Mr Finkelstein, with all due respect, you don't even know me. I can't imagine you could make your mind up about someone when you've not spent more than a minute in their company,' Alice-Miranda replied.

The rest of the girls and staff in the cafeteria stared.

Lucinda stood up. She smoothed her skirt, gathered all her courage and emerged from the booth to face her father.

Her father's eyebrows furrowed together like a pair of knitting needles, but this time his voice was calm. 'Lucinda.'

She walked towards him.

'Hello Papa. Why are you here?' she asked.

'We are leaving, Lucinda. You have lied to me about your friends. I forbade you to continue any contact with those two –' He pointed at Ava and Quincy as they walked up behind his daughter – 'and now I find that you have fallen under the spell of this child. A sworn enemy of the Finkelsteins!'

'But Papa, Alice-Miranda is not my enemy. She's my friend, a very good friend.' Lucinda looked at Alice-Miranda, who reached out and slipped her hand into Lucinda's.

'Stop that nonsense.' Morrie leaned forward and tore the children's hands apart. 'Get your things, Lucinda. This is not negotiable and you will not speak back to me. You are leaving Mrs Kimmel's right now and I am hiring a tutor this afternoon.'

'No! That's not fair!' Lucinda screamed and ran past her father into the hallway and up the stairs.

Morrie turned on his heel and took off after her with Alice-Miranda and a stampede of girls and staff behind.

'Mr Finkelstein, please wait,' the tiny child called.

Morrie stopped in his tracks. He turned around and held out his hand, like a policeman on traffic duty.

'Enough of this nonsense. Do not follow us. Lucinda is my daughter and she will do as she is told. I will not have any of you interfering.'

Miss Hobbs and Mr Staples arrived on the scene. Morrie directed his rage at the headmistress.

'Miss Hobbs, if you want this school's reputation to remain intact then I advise you to tell these people to leave me and my daughter alone. I am taking Lucinda with me and there is nothing you or anyone else can do about it.' Morrie's eyes drilled right through the headmistress.

'All right, Mr Finkelstein,' Jilly conceded. 'Children, staff, please return to the cafeteria or whatever else you were doing. Do not try to stop Mr Finkelstein. I am sure that he and I will speak later and sort out this small problem.'

Morrie rolled his eyes.

'Mr Finkelstein, please, I think you're being awfully unfair,' Alice-Miranda spoke.

'Unfair? Oh, that is rich coming from a Highton, but then I suppose your family knows all about being unfair,' he spat.

Alice-Miranda remained calm. 'I don't know what you're talking about Mr Finkelstein, but I'm sure that it's all just a dreadful misunderstanding.'

'There is no misunderstanding. I'm taking my daughter and she will never ever see you again. You can stop pretending to be her friend.' Morrie looked at Miss Hobbs. 'Now get Lucinda and bring her to reception within the next five minutes.'

Morrie stalked off towards the front of the school.

'Poor Lucinda,' Quincy sighed. 'What can we do?'

Jilly Hobbs surveyed the forlorn group. 'Girls, I'm afraid there is nothing you can do at the moment. Mr Finkelstein needs some time to calm down and I need to get Lucinda. You three, come with me. I'm sure you'd like to say goodbye.' Jilly looked up and raised her voice ever so slightly. 'Everyone else, please go back to what you were doing.'

The group found Lucinda clearing out her locker. Her face was streaked with tears.

'There's no point making things any worse,' she sniffed. 'He's not going to change his mind.'

'Lucinda, you're right about your father being a bully.' Quincy patted her shoulder.

'You know I asked you all not to give up on me,' Lucinda said. 'Well, you might as well. I can't ever escape.'

'Lucinda.' Alice-Miranda grabbed her friend's

hands. 'There has to be a reason why your father doesn't like my family. If I can find out what it is, then surely we can put this silly feud behind us and your father will realise that whatever our great-great-grandfathers did to each other, it doesn't have anything to do with the rest of the family.'

Lucinda leaned forward and hugged Alice-Miranda tightly. 'I wish you were right. But I don't think anything you say will ever change his mind.'

'Come along, Lucinda.' Jilly Hobbs picked up the girl's backpack. Tears welled in the corner of the headmistress's eyes too.

Quincy and Ava embraced Lucinda.

'Don't forget to look across the road when you visit the Met. I'll be in the window, like a canary in a gilded cage.' Tears now streamed down Lucinda's cheeks.

'Lucinda, we'll find a way to make your father see sense,' said Alice-Miranda and hugged her again. 'I promise.'

Chapter 29

The bell rang not long after Lucinda left Mrs Kimmel's with her father. Mr Underwood's class gathered at the back door, but instead of the usual chatter there was an uneasy silence weighing the group down.

In two straight lines the girls walked the usual route to the Metropolitan Museum of Art. Alice-Miranda, Quincy and Ava searched the upstairs windows of the Finkelstein mansion opposite, behind its ornate masonry and ironwork fence, but there was no sign of Lucinda.

'Come on,' Alice-Miranda smiled. 'Things will work out. You'll see.'

But Quincy and Ava weren't so sure. It seemed that Morrie Finkelstein was a champion at holding a grudge.

Once inside the building, the class followed their teacher to a small lecture theatre, with tiered rows of seating and a small stage.

'Girls, it's important that you give our guest your full attention. I know you're upset about what happened earlier, but I'm sure that Lucinda wouldn't want you all moping around on her behalf.'

Alice-Miranda was busy retrieving her notepad from her bag when a tall man with salt-and-pepper coloured hair entered the room.

'Girls, I'd like to introduce you to our very special lecturer, renowned artist Mr Ed Clifton.' Felix Underwood grinned and began clapping vigorously.

Alice-Miranda looked up. 'Well, that explains a lot,' she whispered to her friends.

'What do you mean?' Quincy asked.

'Mr Clifton helped me with my picture the other day. I hadn't realised he was a famous artist. No wonder he had such good suggestions.'

The class listened as Mr Clifton explained a range of techniques and ideas. He showed some slides of different paintings in the museum and the styles the artists had used.

'And this is one of mine. It's here in the museum if you'd like to take a closer look at some stage,' Ed said with a smile.

'Look Ava, it's that painting we were admiring the other week. I told Mr Clifton it was one of my favourites and he didn't even mention he painted it. I thought it was from the fifteenth century or something.'

'Oh yeah. If I painted something like that I'd tell everyone,' she confirmed.

The class listened quietly to the rest of Mr Clifton's talk and at the end Mr Underwood stepped forward. 'Girls, please thank our special guest.'

'Well, that was boring,' Quincy complained as Mr Clifton received a stirring round of applause.

'I thought he was great,' Alice-Miranda buzzed. 'I had no idea there were so many different ways to paint a picture.'

'I had no idea what he was on about most of the time. Scraping, polishing, feathering; I thought he was talking about cleaning the house,' Ava complained.

Alice-Miranda giggled.

'Okay, girls, please head out to the main foyer and I'll meet you there in a minute,' Felix Underwood instructed. 'I've just got to find someone to shut off this projector.'

The class made their way to the giant entrance hall. Alice-Miranda was thinking about the painting Mrs Oliver had recognised, next to the Degas, and wondering who she could ask about it when she spotted Mr Clifton outside the museum on the top of the steps. He was talking to someone.

Alice-Miranda squinted into the light. 'Hey.' She nudged Quincy. 'Can you see that man talking to Mr Clifton out there, the one with all the bags?'

'Yeah, some homeless guy,' Quincy said, pulling a face.

'No, he's not. Isn't that . . . I'm sure it's Mr Preston, from the train.' Alice-Miranda scurried towards the doors.

'Hey, Alice-Miranda, come back. We're supposed to wait in here,' Ava called after her.

Alice-Miranda ran up to the unlikely pair.

'Mr Preston!' she exclaimed. 'I thought it was you. Well, this is the funniest coincidence.'

Callum Preston stared at the child, wondering where he'd seen her before.

'You don't remember, do you? On the train, last Friday. You gave me that drawing of the tamandua at the zoo – and I was in it,' she reminded him.

'Oh, of course. I beg your pardon, miss,' he apologised.

'And I enjoyed your lecture very much, Mr Clifton,' said Alice-Miranda, staring up at the taller man.

'You're Alice . . .' Ed began. He scratched the top of his head.

'Miranda,' she finished.

'Of course, Alice-Miranda. The Degas girl,' Ed nodded.

'You didn't tell me you painted that other picture I said I liked so much,' Alice-Miranda chided.

He looked sheepish. 'You didn't ask who painted it.'

Alice-Miranda grinned. 'How do you two know each other?' Alice-Miranda asked.

'Callum here was one of my best students.' Ed Clifton patted the young man on the back.

'Doesn't say much at the moment, does it?' Callum cast his eyes downward, staring at the stone steps.

'I wish you'd come sooner. How long has it been?' Ed asked.

'Just a couple of weeks. But hey, there have got to be some advantages. I reckon there's nothing I couldn't tell you about the subway system. And there are some great spots in the park too,' he joked.

'So you really *are* homeless,' Alice-Miranda whispered.

'Yeah, not exactly proud of it.' Callum's hands tensed on the handle of his folio.

'But that's terrible,' she said.

'No, that's life in New York City when you're a struggling artist,' Ed replied. 'But I think we can work something out.'

Callum swallowed hard. He wondered what his friend meant.

'I think it must be fate, running into you today. My assistant's just decided she's going to spend the rest of the year in Paris so I need someone to start – today,' Ed said happily. 'And there's an empty flat at the back of my studio.'

Callum looked at him in shock. 'Ed, wow. Really? That's amazing.'

'That's fantastic,' Alice-Miranda said, and grinned. 'Where is your studio, Mr Clifton?'

'Just across the street. Not far,' he replied.

'Oh, I almost forgot. Mr Clifton, you know that painting you love so much, next to the Degas? When I was here on the weekend, Mrs Oliver, who is our cook but she's really a part of our family, well, she was over at the Egyptian exhibit while I was finishing my picture and so you didn't get to meet her. But when she came back and you had gone – I think you really must be called Ed Houdini because you're so terribly good at disappearing – well, Mrs Oliver looked at that painting and it took her a little while but she remembered that she had seen it somewhere before.'

'Really?' He looked at her, wondering where this was heading.

'Yes, and can you believe that the place she saw it was my grandparents' house?' Alice-Miranda breathed.

'Your grandparents?' He tilted his head.

'Yes, Granny and Grandpa Kennington-Jones. Of course, they died before I was born but they were Daddy's parents and they lived in a huge place called Pelham Park, which Daddy never liked very much because he said that it was far too sad, but Mummy had it all done up and now it's a wonderful place

273

where old people live.' Alice-Miranda finally drew a breath.

'So you're Alice-Miranda Kennington-Jones?' Ed asked.

'No, I'm Alice-Miranda Highton-Smith-Kennington-Jones.'

He frowned.

Callum Preston turned his head in the direction of the store. 'You mean like Highton's on Fifth Avenue?' he asked.

'Yes, Mr Preston. Mummy and Daddy are here at the moment because they're reopening the store next week and I've been going to school at Mrs Kimmel's. But I was wondering, Mr Clifton; you adore that painting and I was hoping you might know how it came to be here. Mrs Oliver said that Grandpa Kennington-Jones wasn't known for his generosity and Granny was killed in a terrible motor accident with my father's older brother the year before the painting was donated.'

Ed Clifton drew in a sharp breath but Alice-Miranda didn't notice. She'd just seen her class lined up inside the foyer. Quincy and Ava were making extravagant hand gestures telling her to hurry up.

'It looks like I have to go,' she said. 'Goodbye, see you again soon, and good luck with your job,

Mr Preston.' She waved at the two men and scampered away to rejoin her class.

Ed Clifton stared at the tiny child as she disappeared through the doorway. 'Xavier died,' he murmured under his breath.

'What did you say, Ed?' Callum Preston asked.

'Oh, nothing, Callum. Let's get you over to the studio.'

Chapter 30

That afternoon, Mrs Oliver was waiting outside the school to walk Alice-Miranda home. Impeccable as always, her trademark brown curls were set in place against a rather stiff city breeze.

Dolly greeted the child with a hug. 'I'm sorry, dear, but your mother has had a very difficult day and your father has some worries of his own, so you're stuck with me.'

'I don't mind being stuck with you one bit. I gather Mummy's meeting with Mr Finkelstein didn't go well,' Alice-Miranda said thoughtfully.

'How did you know?' Dolly asked.

Alice-Miranda explained about Morrie Finkelstein arriving at the school and removing Lucinda.

'Oh dear me, your mother will be devastated.' Dolly shook her head. 'The man's a beast.'

'We must find out what happened all those years ago between Great-Great-Grandpa Horace and Abe Finkelstein. It's so silly.' Alice-Miranda shook her head. 'You know, there's a photograph of the two of them with a lady called Ruby Winters on the wall at the Armstrongs' club. Granma Clarrie says that she remembers them – it was opening night and Miss Winters was the most beautiful woman she'd ever seen. Isn't that amazing!'

'Astonishing. Granma Clarrie must be almost a hundred,' Dolly Oliver replied.

'Not quite, but close, though you'd never know it,' Alice-Miranda said.

'She must be a remarkable woman to still be running a kitchen at her age,' Dolly marvelled. 'Now, your mother and father have given me instructions to entertain you for the afternoon. They're both caught up for a couple of hours. Is there anywhere you'd like to go?' Mrs Oliver asked.

'As a matter of fact, I was rather hoping to spend some time at the New York City Library.' Alice-Miranda winked at Mrs Oliver.

'Oh dear, what are you up to, young lady?' Dolly smiled.

'I'm sure there must be loads of archived newspapers there and I wonder if we might be able to find out about Miss Winters,' Alice-Miranda explained.

'Shall we call Mr O'Leary?' Dolly asked.

'No, I know a much faster way to get there.' Alice-Miranda took Dolly by the hand and the pair headed towards Lexington Avenue and the 77th Street subway station.

✳

Alice-Miranda and Mrs Oliver arrived at the New York City Public Library not really knowing where to start their search. A kindly young woman at the desk called Miriam asked what it was they were looking for. Alice-Miranda introduced herself in the usual way and explained that they were trying to find out about a lady called Ruby Winters who they thought may have been engaged to a man called Abe Finkelstein.

Miriam said that it sounded like they should be looking at newspaper articles and if that was the case they would have to search the microfilm, which could take quite some time.

'Do you know what year you're looking at?' she asked. 'That would narrow things down.'

'I think 1920 is the best year to start,' Alice-Miranda replied. 'Isn't that when the Armstrongs' club was opened?' She looked at Mrs Oliver, who shrugged her shoulders.

'I don't know, dear,' the older lady added.

Miriam bit her lip. 'We've just transferred a whole lot of the records into the database. I'm not sure if we'll find it there but I could have a look. It might save a lot of time,' she offered.

'That would be wonderful,' Alice-Miranda smiled. 'I can't tell you how exciting it would be to solve this mystery. You see, the Finkelsteins have had a grudge against the Hightons for so long and nobody seems to remember what it's about at all. Great-Great-Grandpa Horace and Abe Finkelstein were meant to go into business together but something came between them and since then the Finkelsteins have hated us.'

'Alice-Miranda, dear, not everyone's as intrigued by this story as you are.' Dolly Oliver smiled apologetically at the young woman.

Miriam grinned. 'It sounds intriguing to me, and I'm all for a bit of detective work. Until now the most exciting thing that's happened to me today was discovering my husband had packed a cream cheese bagel for my lunch.' The young woman turned to her computer and punched *Miss Ruby Winters* into the search field. She hit enter and the program began scanning thousands of documents.

Alice-Miranda folded her arms on the countertop and rested her chin there.

'Goodness!' the young woman exclaimed. 'This is a stroke of luck.'

'What is it?' Alice-Miranda asked eagerly.

'Perhaps I should rephrase that. It's a stroke of luck finding something but I'm afraid your Miss Winters wasn't very lucky at all,' said Miriam as she scanned the document.

She turned the monitor around so that Mrs Oliver and Alice-Miranda could see the results.

Emblazoned across the front page of the *New York Times* was the headline '38 Killed in Wall Street Bombing'. Further down, in the body of the text, the name Miss Ruby Winters was highlighted on the screen.

'It seems your Miss Winters was one of the unfortunate souls who lost her life that day,' Miriam said, frowning.

'That's terrible.' Alice-Miranda was wide-eyed. 'Does it say anything else about her?'

'Hold on a minute. There are nine articles here with her name in them.' Miriam was glad no one was queuing behind these visitors. There was something about this tiny child with her cascading chocolate curls and brown eyes as big as saucers that made Miriam feel terribly daring. 'I'm not supposed to do this but I'll print them off for you and then you can have a proper read,' she said with a quiet giggle.

Miriam glanced around the room to check that no one was watching before she hit the print button. The machine behind her whirred into life, spitting out a pile of paper, which she promptly handed to Alice-Miranda.

'Thank you so much,' said Alice-Miranda.

'You will come and tell me what you discover, before you leave?' Miriam asked.

'Of course,' Alice-Miranda grinned.

'Thank you, dear,' Dolly added. 'You've been very helpful.'

The old woman followed Alice-Miranda as she skipped through the giant reading room in search of a vacant desk.

Chapter 31

Morrie Finkelstein sat at his desk. A triumphant smile was plastered across his face. This was going to be his year, Finkelstein's year. The year that he proved he could make more money than any other store in the city. He would finally be number one, exactly where he belonged.

Everything was falling into place. He'd enjoyed seeing Cecelia Highton-Smith begging him to leave her suppliers alone. Not likely. Morrie had revelled in his game of Chinese Whispers. The Highton's renovation had only ever been a couple of weeks behind but Morrie couldn't help spreading some rumours that he thought they had 'problems'. Highton's couldn't keep people locked into contracts for ever, could they? He'd made some interesting contacts in the past few months at City Hall too, and he couldn't believe how easy it had been to convince that stupid builders' foreman to make some extra cash. Morrie frowned as he recalled an uncomfortable moment earlier in the day; when he met Cecelia Highton-Smith at the store, that young idiot walked right up and said hello. The man was getting a little above his station, Morrie thought to himself. He needed to terminate that arrangement – and soon.

Framed photographs of Morrie's forebears lined the walls of his office. Abe Finkelstein would have had it all if Horace Highton hadn't reneged on their deal at the last minute. Morrie unlocked his desk drawer and pulled out a small tin box with charred corners. He sat it on the desk and turned the tiny key. A faded scrap of paper was all that remained of Abe Finkelstein's worldly goods. Morrie's father and grandfather had passed it down through the family, their proof that the Hightons were never to be trusted.

Morrie scanned the paper. Half of a letter, horribly smudged and torn down the middle. But Morrie knew what it meant.

> *I cannot believe*
> *the events that have unfolded*
> *To have all that I have cared*
> *snatched away from me*
> *It is the ultimate act of betrayal*
> *and cannot be forgiven*
> *Horace . . . my trusted aide*
> *my friend and confidant*
> *never again . . . such evil*

It was Finkelstein family folklore that Horace Highton had signed the papers at the bank on his own, cutting Abe out of the deal. Morrie's great-grandfather had been caught completely off guard and the poor man had a breakdown and spent a couple of months in a mental asylum. When he got out of the hospital, Abe found the land on Park Avenue and a wealthy backer, and started his own store. He had married a sturdy lass called Marjory Tannenbaum, had two children, and then died in a mysterious fire that tore through the store one evening. Rumours circulated that Horace Highton might have had something to do with it, but it was never proven. Of course, that just added fuel to the already bitter feud. The Hightons would always be the Finkelsteins' enemies, no matter how many stunts Cecelia and her little daughter pulled.

Despite what his own daughter thought, Morrie hadn't enjoyed pulling her out of school. But she had to understand what it meant to be a Finkelstein. He was protecting her. She'd only be hurt. Everyone knew that the Hightons hated the Finkelsteins. It was a fact of life, like breathing.

Chapter 32

Alice-Miranda and Dolly Oliver arrived home armed with some remarkable findings.

'Mummy, are you here?' Alice-Miranda called as the lift opened into the hallway. 'Daddy, are you home?'

But the apartment was silent.

'Come along, dear, why don't you go and have a bath and hop into your pyjamas and I'll make us something to eat. I'm sure your parents will be home soon enough.'

'I wish I had Lucinda's telephone number.' Alice-Miranda looked at Dolly. 'I have to tell her what we found out.'

'I don't think Morrie Finkelstein would appreciate your call, dear, and I suspect the Finkelsteins would have a private number anyway. Perhaps you could write to her instead.'

Alice-Miranda nodded. 'That's exactly what I'll do. And then I'll write some more postcards to Millie and Jacinta and everyone back at school as well.'

'After your bath, all right?' Dolly instructed.

Alice-Miranda nodded and ran to her room.

Dolly walked through the hall and into the kitchen where she saw the light on the telephone blinking. She pressed the button to listen to the messages.

'Hello Dolly, hello darling, Mummy here. I'm so sorry but I've got to entertain some important suppliers tonight. Morrie Finkelstein has done some serious damage this afternoon. He's very cross with me. I think I made a big mistake telling him that you and Lucinda were friends and now he's even more determined to ruin us. But don't worry – Mummy's made of sterner stock than that. I hope you had a lovely afternoon with Dolly. Now run a bath and hop into your PJs and I'm sure that Dolly will make you something yummy to eat. Love you. Oh, and Daddy's joining me a little later. He had some business back at the store so he won't need any supper either.'

Dolly opened the refrigerator and pulled out four eggs.

'Boiled eggs and toasty soldiers will do us just fine this evening,' she said to herself.

She took a saucepan from the drawer and was filling it with water when the telephone rang.

'Hello, Dolly Oliver speaking,' she answered. 'Hello Ambrose, dear, how wonderful to hear from you. Yes, yes, all going well. Keeping very busy. And what about you?' Dolly pulled up a stool and settled in for a long chat.

Alice-Miranda decided against a bath and instead hopped into the shower for a quick scrub. She dried herself off, pulled on her pyjamas and shoved her feet into her slippers. Outside her bedroom she saw that there was a light on in her father's study and wondered if he had arrived home while she was in the shower.

She skipped to the end of the corridor and knocked gently on the door.

'Daddy,' she called. 'Are you there?' Alice-Miranda

turned the handle and poked her head inside. Her father was nowhere to be seen. She was about to leave when something caught her eye. It looked like a letter and it was lying untidily in the middle of the floor as if perhaps her father had dropped it on his way out. She opened the door and walked inside, scooped the letter up and placed it carefully on the vast desk beside an ancient leather-bound book. She couldn't help noticing a couple of notes, in her father's own handwriting, hastily scrawled onto a notepad.

Painting in Met – how did it get there?
Xavier alive?
Where is he?

And there was a newspaper cutting too. Alice-Miranda picked it up. It was a death notice for Arabella Grace Kennington-Jones and Xavier Edward Kennington-Jones. Her grandmother and uncle.

Her mind buzzed. Xavier had been killed in the same accident that had claimed her granny, hadn't he? But why did her father write *Xavier alive?* She wondered if it was possible that her father's brother wasn't dead after all these years.

Alice-Miranda ran her fingers over the leather-bound book beside her father's note. She opened the cover. Tucked inside was another much smaller book.

'Wow!' Alice-Miranda exclaimed to herself. 'That's beautiful.' She studied the illustrations closely, smiling at the surprising details.

Something tugged at Alice-Miranda's memory.

'Oh my goodness!'

It was no wonder her father had been so distracted these past few days. Alice-Miranda bit her lip. It seemed that everyone had a mystery to be solved.

Chapter 33

The next morning, after a dream-filled sleep, Alice-Miranda awoke to find her mother had already left the apartment for work and her father had apparently flown home on some urgent Kennington's business.

'Your mother's quite beside herself,' Dolly Oliver announced as she placed a mountain of scrambled eggs and crispy bacon on Alice-Miranda's plate. 'And who knows if your father will even get back in time for the opening?'

'Poor Mummy,' the tiny child sighed. 'It's not fair that Mr Finkelstein should make her life so complicated.'

'Well, your mother feels terrible that she's not here for you either, my dear. She was wondering if you might be better off going back to Winchesterfield-Downsfordvale.'

Alice-Miranda shook her head. 'That's silly. I love Mrs Kimmel's and there's still so much of the city I haven't seen and we've only got another week or so. You don't mind keeping me company in the afternoons, do you?'

'Good heavens, dear, not at all, although you must remember that even with my new Bollywood fitness regime, I'm still not as young as I once was,' said Dolly Oliver, smiling down at her young charge.

'Besides, I've got to help Lucinda. Hopefully what we found out yesterday about Ruby Winters might make Mr Finkelstein see that there's absolutely no point at all to his feud with Mummy. I mean, it's really too stupid for words,' Alice-Miranda babbled.

'Well, your mother will be pleased that you're not upset with her,' said Dolly as she buttered some toast.

Alice-Miranda couldn't imagine there was a reason to be upset with her mother at all.

'Come along, dear, stop talking and start eating or you'll be late for school,' Dolly instructed.

⋆

Lucinda Finkelstein was tired of crying. Her face was a patchwork of red and she shuddered with every breath. When she and her father had arrived home yesterday he locked her in her room and told her that she was a traitor.

Morrie had forbidden Gerda from spending any time with Lucinda either, telling his wife that 'the child needs to understand what it means to be loyal'.

Gerda had begged Morrie to at least let her take Lucinda her evening meal but he wouldn't allow it, instead timing Dolores's visits in and out to deposit a plate of goulash and some bread, both of which were returned uneaten to the kitchen.

Morrie had arranged for his personal assistant to interview several tutors this morning.

Lucinda dragged herself out of bed and shuffled to the window, peering through the drapes as her father's car disappeared into the traffic on Fifth Avenue.

Almost at the same time, a key turned in the lock and her mother entered the room.

'Lucinda,' Gerda spoke gently from the doorway.

Lucinda didn't reply.

'I'm sorry, Lucinda. I wanted to come last night but your father wouldn't allow it,' Gerda sniffed.

'I don't care, Mama,' Lucinda snapped.

Gerda walked over to where Lucinda was standing at the window. She put her hand on her daughter's shoulder.

Lucinda recoiled. 'Don't touch me!'

Gerda withdrew her hand and hovered behind her. 'Your father is . . .'

'Insane,' Lucinda whispered.

'Lucinda! He just wants the best for you.'

'No, he doesn't. He doesn't know anything about me. He treats me like I'm a possession, not a person. He might as well sell me at the store. And you never stick up for me. What sort of a mother allows her daughter to be treated like . . . goods?' Lucinda turned and faced her mother.

Gerda's lips quivered. 'The same mother who can't even stick up for herself.'

'I'm going back to school, Mama,' Lucinda announced.

'No! You mustn't. Lucinda, I will do my best to speak to your father, I promise, but please don't do anything to make the situation worse. I beg you.' Gerda's face was now streaked with tears. 'He'll calm down in a week or two and then I'm sure you can go back. When is the Highton child leaving?'

'What's that got to do with anything? Alice-Miranda is my friend and, yes, she is leaving soon but what about Quincy and Ava? Father forbids me to have anything to do with them too,' Lucinda said.

'Yes, but I'm sure things can go back to the way they used to be. Your father didn't make such a fuss about them. I've known for a long time that you played with Ava and Quincy at school and I did my best to keep it from him. It's just that yesterday when Cecelia Highton-Smith told him that you and her daughter had become such good friends, he was so mad. I've never seen him like that before. Well, not for a long time,' Gerda explained. 'I don't understand him either, at times.'

'Alice-Miranda is the kindest person I've ever met, Mama. I don't understand why we can't be friends.

She said herself that we probably have more in common than anyone. Father might be able to keep me locked up now, but just wait, as soon as I'm old enough I'm leaving and then I will never, ever be back. Is that what he wants?' Lucinda threw herself onto her bed.

'Of course not, darling,' said Gerda, sitting down beside her.

'Please leave me alone, Mama,' Lucinda breathed into her pillow. 'Just go!'

Gerda Finkelstein stood up. How did she ever let it all get this far? Things had to change and fast, for everyone's sakes.

Chapter 34

Alice-Miranda barely saw her mother over the next few days. And when she did, Cecelia was so busy on the telephone and running up and down to the store that there never seemed a right time to tell her about their discovery at the library. Her father still wasn't back, either. And school was different too. There should have been four friends and now there were only three. It was all a little off balance. Alice-Miranda enjoyed Mr Underwood's lessons and she had fun with Quincy and Ava, but Lucinda should have been there.

Alice-Miranda had written to her every day, but so far there was no reply. She wondered if the letters were even getting to Lucinda at all. She had asked Mrs Oliver for some plain paper and envelopes rather than her usual embossed stationery. Ava and Quincy didn't have Lucinda's telephone number and when Alice-Miranda asked Miss Cleary, the receptionist told her that she wasn't allowed to hand over private information.

Mrs Oliver met Alice-Miranda every afternoon after school and together they explored the city. They'd been to Staten Island and Ground Zero, across the Brooklyn Bridge and to tea with the storybook character Eloise from *Eloise at the Plaza*. Alice-Miranda loved their adventures and she was pretty sure Mrs Oliver was going to relent sooner or later and take a ride in a pedicab.

★

Alice-Miranda was finishing off her and Lucinda's Science project.

'That's looking good,' Felix Underwood commented.

'Thank you, Mr Underwood. I just wish Lucinda was here,' Alice-Miranda replied.

Felix sighed. 'Sometimes rich people are really hard to figure out.'

'Why do you say rich people?' Alice-Miranda asked. 'I'd have thought all people can be a little perplexing at times.'

'I suppose I look at someone like Morrie Finkelstein: he has everything a man could possibly want and more, and he's so bitter and angry. He doesn't appreciate that he has a great daughter and more money and opportunities than anyone has a right to. I just don't understand. If I had heaps of money, I'd rather use it to help other people than keep it all hoarded away for me.'

'I see what you mean, Mr Underwood. Mummy and Daddy say that being wealthy is a huge responsibility and we should never take anything for granted,' said Alice-Miranda, nodding her head.

'It sounds like your parents have their heads screwed on exactly the right way.' Felix grinned at his youngest student. 'So,' he said, 'are you game to look after Maisy again at the park today?'

Alice-Miranda glanced over at Ava and Quincy who were arguing over whether Jupiter or Saturn was closest to the sun.

'Why not? I'm pretty sure I've got that dog's measure now,' Alice-Miranda smiled.

The bell rang for the start of lunch and Alice-Miranda trotted downstairs to get Maisy's lead and accessories.

'You're not really taking her out again, are you?' said Miss Cleary, as she reluctantly handed over the goods.

'I'll be fine, Miss Cleary. Truly. I know what sets her off and I'm almost certain I won't have the same problem again this time.'

Ava and Quincy were horrified when Alice-Miranda met them at the cafeteria and told them her plans.

'But what about Thea?' Ava asked. 'She's got it in for you, Alice-Miranda, and one "s" word and Crazy Maisy will be off.'

'I don't think I have to worry about Thea,' Alice-Miranda replied.

'Why? Is she away?' Quincy asked.

'No, she's here,' Alice-Miranda said.

As always, Maisy was at the back door with her tail on high speed dusting the walls and everything else in her path. Alice-Miranda clipped the lead onto her collar.

'Now, Miss Maisy, are we going to have a good time at the park today?' Alice-Miranda bent down and looked into the labrador's big brown eyes.

Maisy frowned.

'I think you know exactly what I just said.'

Maisy's tongue shot out and she slobbered on Alice-Miranda's cheek.

'Yuck.' She wiped her face with a tissue.

'Hi there.' Gretchen walked over and scratched Maisy between the ears.

'Hi Gretchen. You know, if you keep doing that, she'll be your friend for life,' Alice-Miranda said as Maisy began to drool all over the floor. 'Where's Thea?'

'She's just gone to get her sweater,' Gretchen replied. 'Thanks for telling me all that stuff the other day. It explained a lot and well, you know, she's not all bad.'

'I know that,' Alice-Miranda grinned. 'Nobody is.'

Thea appeared and the two girls split apart.

'What are you doing with that dog?' Thea narrowed her eyes. 'She'd better not come anywhere near me.'

'Well, I'm sure that nobody is going to do anything to upset her,' said Gretchen, glaring at Alethea. 'Are they?'

'No, and why are you looking at me like that, Gretchen? I thought we were friends,' Alethea said.

Gretchen was stern. 'We *are* friends, Thea. I'd say I'm your best friend. And I'd really like it to stay that way.'

Alice-Miranda laughed as Gretchen and Alethea squabbled the whole way to the park.

Chapter 35

Lucinda had been imprisoned at home for four days. Her father had employed a tutor, Miss Hinkley, who arrived each morning at nine and departed by three. Lessons were taken in the study attached to Lucinda's bedroom and while Miss Hinkley was nice enough, Lucinda had no desire to befriend the young woman, in case she might think the job was permanent.

Each afternoon, Lucinda's mother would appear and insist that she put on a dress so they could go and visit one or another of her awful friends and their hideous daughters. Lucinda despised those outings but her mother insisted that they may make her father feel better about sending her back to school.

Gerda poked her head into the room. 'Lucinda, please meet me downstairs in five minutes.'

Lucinda didn't answer. She walked into her wardrobe and put on the dress Dolores had selected earlier in the day. She scraped her hair into a ponytail, cursing the springy curls that escaped around her face, and went downstairs.

Her mother was already in the car. Gerda leaned forward and spoke to their driver, Raymond, in hushed tones.

'Are you sure, ma'am?' Lucinda heard him reply.

'Very,' Gerda replied.

'As you wish.' Raymond looked at Gerda in the rear-vision mirror.

Lucinda's eyes were fixed on the street outside the gates. She watched the children bounding along with their friends on the way home from school.

Most of her mother's friends lived uptown, so Lucinda was surprised when Raymond didn't make a left turn into one of the cross-streets but instead headed downtown, past East 75th and further down past Highton's. But she didn't ask. Her mother likely had some errand to run.

She looked out the window at all the people in the city going about their business. It was strange to live in such a big place and not really know it.

The car continued through Midtown and into the lower part of Manhattan. Lucinda had really begun to wonder about their destination; she couldn't remember travelling this far downtown in her life.

'Mama,' she said finally, 'where are we going?'

Gerda Finkelstein looked at her daughter. 'To see a friend.'

'Who?' Lucinda asked as the limousine headed towards the Brooklyn Bridge.

'Just someone I need to see,' Gerda replied.

Lucinda wasn't accustomed to her mother behaving so mysteriously. Her tummy began to flutter.

'It's all right. You don't need to come in with me,' said Gerda, sensing her daughter's unease.

The limousine weaved its way off the Brooklyn Bridge and into the suburbs before pulling up outside a row of brownstone buildings. A curtain moved slightly and Lucinda wondered who was looking at them. Her mother gathered her handbag and moved to the door, which Raymond opened for her.

'I won't be long.' Gerda patted her daughter on the knee.

'Can I come?' Lucinda blurted. 'I don't want to stay out here on my own.'

'Raymond will be here,' her mother replied. 'But if you want to, yes, you can come.'

Lucinda followed her mother out of the car and onto the street. Gerda walked up the short flight of steps and rang the buzzer. The door opened. A rail-thin woman wearing a headscarf stepped out onto the porch. Lucinda stayed behind on the pavement.

'Oh my heavens, is it really you?' It sounded like the woman had something caught in her throat.

'Yes. It's me, Louisa,' Gerda replied. 'May we come in?' Gerda motioned for Lucinda to join her.

'You must be Lucinda,' the woman said. 'Last time I saw you, you were so small. I nursed you in my arms.'

'Lucinda, this is Louisa,' Gerda said.

'Hello,' said Lucinda.

'Please come, come in. I'll make us some tea.'

Lucinda noticed that Louisa walked with a

limp. She and her mother were led down a hallway and into a small sitting room.

'I hoped you'd come.' Louisa glanced at a tea tray laden with cups and saucers and a small plate of cakes sitting in the middle of the coffee table. 'I'll just boil the kettle and fill the pot.'

Louisa hurried off to the kitchen. Gerda motioned for Lucinda to sit down on one of the floral sofas.

'How do you know each other, Mummy?' Lucinda looked at her mother, who was studying some photographs on the wall.

'We were friends a long time ago,' said Gerda.

'But why haven't I met Louisa before?' Lucinda asked.

Gerda opened her mouth to reply when Louisa re-entered the sitting room. She busied herself making two cups of tea and then asked Lucinda if she would like one too.

Lucinda shook her head. 'No, thank you.'

'I wasn't sure if children drank tea so I've got some juice. Would you like that?' Louisa asked.

'Yes, please,' Lucinda replied.

Louisa handed Lucinda a glass of orange juice

and sat down beside the child on the sofa opposite Gerda.

The two women sipped their tea. Lucinda grew increasingly aware of the uneasy silence between them.

Finally, it was Gerda who spoke first.

'How are you, really?' she asked.

'Well,' said Louisa, the corners of her mouth turning up just a little, 'apart from losing my hair and feeling as though my mind has gone with it most days, I'm okay.'

'I didn't know you were so ill,' Gerda started. 'I would have come.'

'I know you would have but I didn't want you to get into trouble. Knowing how he feels about me, that last time at the house with Lucinda . . . He was so mad. I just didn't want to put you in that position again. I can't really believe that you're here now.' Louisa placed her teacup back onto the saucer with a sharp chink.

Lucinda watched this exchange, not knowing what to make of it.

'But there's not much time left and I didn't want to go without saying goodbye.' Louisa's blue eyes filled with tears.

Gerda Finkelstein stifled a sob. She put down her

teacup, walked over to Louisa and put her arms around her. Louisa stood and the two women embraced as though their very being depended on it.

Lucinda didn't quite know what to do. She felt like an intruder. This was a part of her mother's life she knew nothing about and now she was watching something unfold that she felt she had no right to see.

'Mama,' Lucinda whispered. 'Would you like me to go and wait in the car?'

It was Louisa who spoke first. She looked up at Lucinda, her mascara tracking down her face.

'Please, Lucinda, I'd like to spend a little bit of time with you, if I may. It would make me very happy.'

Lucinda nodded.

Her mother sat back down and Louisa patted the seat beside her, beckoning for Lucinda to move closer. The gangly child did as she was asked.

'You're going to be a very tall girl,' Louisa observed. 'And I see you've inherited your father's lovely curls.'

Lucinda pulled a face and a handful of hair. 'Believe me, there is nothing lovely about this hair. My brothers are so lucky. They take after

Mummy and I've just got this terrible frizz,' Lucinda griped.

Louisa smiled. 'Well I can remember when you were just a wee little thing and you had the most delicious curls. They flopped in your face and you were forever pulling them. I gave you some hairclips with stars on them and you used to wear them all the time.'

Lucinda frowned. 'I've still got them. I've got this long piece of ribbon with all my hairclips attached and the stars are right at the top. I love them.'

'Oh, I am glad. So I've been part of your life all along and you haven't even known it,' Louisa said, and reached for her teacup.

'But why haven't we seen you?' Lucinda asked.

Gerda Finkelstein sighed. 'Because your mother has been a stupid fool and I've let your father tell me what to do for more years than I care to remember.'

Lucinda wondered if she had heard her mother correctly.

'Lucinda, Louisa was my best friend in the world before I married your father,' Gerda began.

Chapter 36

On Friday afternoon, Dolly Oliver met Alice-Miranda after school as she had done every day that week.

'Hello Mrs Oliver.' Alice-Miranda ran down the steps and onto the pavement.

'Good afternoon, my darling girl.' Dolly enveloped the tiny child in her arms. 'It seems Millie has finally got around to writing to you.' She retrieved a letter from her handbag and gave it to Alice-Miranda.

'Oh, thank you for bringing it. I thought they'd forgotten about me.'

Alice-Miranda opened the envelope and unfolded the paper. She scanned its contents, laughing and smiling.

'It sounds like Millie and Jacinta are getting along *most* of the time,' Alice-Miranda informed Mrs Oliver. 'Miss Hephzibah and Miss Henrietta are well and the renovations are coming along at Caledonia Manor. Oh no, Bonaparte bit Mr Walt on the bottom when he was leading him out to the paddock. He's a naughty boy,' Alice-Miranda tutted.

She folded the letter and placed it back into the envelope, then stuffed it into her school satchel. She looked up at Dolly and said seriously, 'I've been thinking about something today.'

Dolly bit her lip. 'Oh dear, that sounds ominous.'

'I promise it's not. I was just thinking that I've been so bossy all week telling you where I wanted to go and all the things that I wanted to see and it's been awfully selfish of me not to ask if there's anything you'd like to do,' Alice-Miranda offered.

Dolly smiled down at her young charge. 'Well, that's very thoughtful, my dear.'

'Is there?' Alice-Miranda looked at her expectantly. 'Anything you'd like to do?'

'Well, as a matter of fact, there is,' Dolly replied. 'And I think you might like to go there too.'

'What is it?' Alice-Miranda bubbled.

'I think I might keep this one a secret until we get there.' Dolly Oliver arched her eyebrow at the child and gave a mysterious smile. Dolly took Alice-Miranda by the hand and the pair headed towards Park Avenue.

'Are we walking there?' Alice-Miranda asked.

'No dear, it's a little too far for these old legs of mine. I walked from the store to school and that's just about done me in,' Dolly replied. 'Keep your eyes open for a taxi.'

Standing on the corner of Park and East 75th, Alice-Miranda scanned the oncoming traffic but for once there didn't seem to be a yellow vehicle in sight.

A doorman wearing tails and a top hat stepped out from the awning of the apartment block he stood sentry in front of.

'Excuse me, miss, ma'am, are you looking for transportation?' he asked.

Alice-Miranda pulled Dolly towards him.

'Yes, sir,' the child replied.

'I'm afraid that you might have to wait a while. It's just on shift change time for the drivers,' the man informed them.

Mrs Oliver frowned.

'But look,' Alice-Miranda grinned and pointed. 'There's someone who can take us.'

'You wanna lift?' The man weaved across two lanes of traffic and pulled up beside the kerb.

Mrs Oliver shook her head. 'Oh, I don't think so.'

'Please, Mrs Oliver. Think of it as an adventure,' said Alice-Miranda, tugging on her arm.

'I don't know.' Dolly's brow puckered and she frowned fiercely.

'I'm sure that it's perfectly safe – and there's hardly any traffic at the moment – well, for New York, anyway,' Alice-Miranda pointed out. 'Please.'

Mrs Oliver consulted the silver-haired doorman.

'What do you think?' she asked.

The man nodded. 'I've been known to use them every now and then,' he replied.

Alice-Miranda ran towards the contraption and leapt into the carriage. The young man on the bicycle, aware of his elderly passenger's uncertainty, hopped off and assisted Mrs Oliver into the seat.

'Thank you, young man,' she nodded at him. 'Now, please take the greatest of care. No lane-changing and watch your speed.'

Alice-Miranda grabbed hold of Dolly's hand. The pedicab pulled out from the kerb.

'Ma'am, where would you like to go?' the young man called back.

'Serendipity 3,' Dolly replied. 'I believe it's on East . . .'

'Sixtieth, ma'am between Second and Third. You're in for a treat, little lady,' he said, glancing around at Alice-Miranda, who beamed back at him.

'Please, keep your eyes on the road, for heaven's sake.' Dolly gripped the edge of the carriage and held on as though her very life depended on it.

✳

'Scrambled eggs and bacon?' Dolly asked as Alice-Miranda wandered into the kitchen just after 8 am on Saturday morning.

'Yes please, although I think my tummy is still full from that delicious food yesterday afternoon. I couldn't believe that's where you wanted to go in the whole of the city.' Alice-Miranda walked up behind the older woman and put her arms around her waist.

'Well dear, you know food and inventing are my passions so I was keen to see what all that fuss about frozen hot chocolate was,' Dolly replied. 'And now I know.'

'Has Mummy gone downstairs?' Alice-Miranda opened the refrigerator and retrieved a carton of juice.

'Yes dear, she's been up for ages. I know there are still a few things worrying her about the opening this evening.'

Alice-Miranda poured herself a glass of orange juice and returned the carton to the fridge.

'Has she heard from Daddy?' she asked as she sat down at the table.

'Yes, he should be in sometime early this afternoon, which is a blessed relief.' Dolly Oliver placed a small mound of scrambled eggs alongside two strips of crispy bacon.

'I think I might see if Mummy and Mr Gruber need any help downstairs,' Alice-Miranda decided. 'I can't wait to see how everything looks.'

'Well, dear,' Dolly instructed, 'just don't get in anyone's way, that's all.'

'I won't,' Alice-Miranda smiled.

Alice-Miranda rode the lift down from the apartment to the ground floor, where the extravagant cosmetics counters and perfumeries were now stocked with their myriad wares. Several staff members were adding the finishing touches to the displays and Alice-Miranda smiled at them and said hello as she made her way around the floor. She had no idea where her mother would be but decided that if she started at the bottom and made her way up one level at a time she'd probably run into her somewhere. Through a marble archway, Alice-Miranda admired the beauty salon and then through another archway to the left was the handbag department. It all looked perfect, even without the floral arrangements her mother had planned.

The lift bell dinged and Alice-Miranda saw her mother walking out of the carriage. 'Hello Mummy.'

'Oh, hello darling,' Cecelia smiled and waved.

Alice-Miranda skipped over to meet her. 'The store looks amazing.'

'Yes, I think everything will be fine.' Cecelia ran the fingers of her left hand through her hair. 'Have you had a proper look around yet?

'No, I've only seen the ground floor but I was planning to take it one level at a time,' Alice-Miranda replied. 'Is there anything I can do to help?'

Her mother's telephone rang. Cecelia smiled apologetically at Alice-Miranda before answering it. 'What's that? No. I explained about that before. I'll be there in a minute.' She rang off. 'Sorry sweetheart, there's a problem with the change rooms on five. I have to go.' She pushed the button for the lift and the doors slid open. 'I'll see you later on.' And with that, Cecelia disappeared from sight.

Alice-Miranda trotted up the grand central staircase to the mezzanine level where three men were screwing a fascia board onto the temporary stage area which would play host to the formal celebrations.

She recognised their foreman. 'Hello Mr George,' Alice-Miranda said as his drill shuddered and whirled.

'Take that upstairs to five, will you?' George said to the other men, while pointing at a long piece of timber lying on the ground beside the stage. 'See what she's bleating about this time.' The men nodded and quickly disappeared.

'The store looks beautiful,' Alice-Miranda said,

wondering if he hadn't heard her say hello. 'I'm so glad that everything has come together for Mummy. She's been terribly worried, you know.'

'She's had good reason to be,' George smirked. 'All those little hiccups, driving her crazy.'

Over the past few weeks, Alice-Miranda had seen George working in the store on several occasions and had always given him a wave or a smile but she realised that up until now she'd never actually had a proper conversation with him.

'Well, there have been a lot of strange things happening,' Alice-Miranda commented.

'Right under her nose,' George said.

Alice-Miranda studied his face, searching for clues. 'Do you know something?'

'No. Why would I?' he snapped.

'I wasn't accusing,' Alice-Miranda replied. 'I know you've had so many problems to sort out and you've been working such long hours.'

'You don't know the half of it,' George mumbled to himself. 'But the pay's been good.'

'What did you say, Mr George?' Alice-Miranda asked.

'Nothing.' He shook his head.

'Well, I'll see you tonight at the gala,' Alice-Miranda smiled.

'Yeah, I wouldn't want to miss it. I think it's really gonna *go off*.' He stared past her as if lost in his thoughts.

Alice-Miranda hadn't enjoyed her conversation with Mr George at all. In fact there was something about him and what he said that gave her a very strange feeling indeed.

Chapter 37

'I'm not going to the stupid salon today, Mama, or any other day.' Lucinda refused to budge from her bed.

'Please Lucinda,' Gerda begged. 'If not for your father, for me.'

'Not until you tell Papa about Louisa.' Lucinda rolled over and looked her mother in the eye.

'But Lucinda, what's the point. Louisa is sick and your father will be so mad that we went to visit her.'

'I hope I'm never as weak as you,' Lucinda spat.

Gerda felt hot with shame.

She walked to Lucinda's wardrobe and pulled out the particularly beautiful white dress her father had brought home the evening before.

Lucinda sat up in bed. She watched her mother hang the dress on the handle of the tall chest. Gerda was a proud woman but at that moment she looked utterly defeated.

'Lucinda, today is the opening of the new salon. We must be there together as a family. Your brothers are dressed. Your father is ready. We cannot leave you at home,' her mother begged.

'All right, I'll go, as long as you tell Papa that I am going back to school on Monday and you are going to see Louisa as often as you want.' Lucinda hopped out of bed and walked across the floor towards her mother.

Gerda was tired of the fighting. 'I will,' she said, pulling her daughter in close and stroking the top of her head.

'He's a horrible person, Mama.' Lucinda stared up at her mother's brown eyes.

'No, he's just a proud man,' Gerda replied.

'He's been making trouble for the Hightons.' Lucinda took a step away.

'That's a terrible thing to say, Lucinda. Why do you think that?'

Lucinda shrugged. 'Because he has.'

'Don't tell lies about your father – he's not a bad man.' Gerda turned and left the room.

But Lucinda had proof. That morning, knowing her father had gone out, Lucinda had crept into his study. She didn't know what she was looking for or if she would find anything at all but it didn't take long to uncover her father's dirty secrets. In a notebook was a list of names and lots of large numbers with dollar signs. She was sure that her father was paying people to make trouble for Alice-Miranda's family. Lucinda had to get to Alice-Miranda and tell her what was going on. She just had to work out how.

*

The limousine ride from Fifth Avenue to Park may as well have been from Manhattan to the moon. Minutes passed like hours. Zeke and Toby would usually have been teasing their sister and joking around but this afternoon even they weren't in the mood. As the car pulled up in front of the store, paparazzi surrounded the vehicle.

'Here we are, family. Smile for the cameras. Remember, we are Finkelsteins and proud of that fact.' Morrie reached over and grabbed Gerda's hand and together they led the way through the crowd.

The salon was magnificent. In the tradition of the Palace of Versailles, Morrie had flown in the finest European craftsmen to complete his vision. The smaller rooms would play host to their usual tea parties but Morrie was certain that the grand ballroom would be the venue of choice for weddings, birthdays, anniversaries and any other significant occasions this side of the Hudson River.

'I just want to say thank you, friends, for being here this afternoon to celebrate this milestone in Finkelstein history. Our Grand Salon is without doubt the finest establishment in New York City and I suspect in the whole of the United States of America,' declared Morrie. He stood in front of the microphone like a peacock.

'My apologies for moving the party forward a few hours. It is in deference to our good friends over on Fifth Avenue; I was horrified to think that we might clash with their grand reopening. And you know I hate to miss a party.'

Lucinda couldn't believe what she'd just heard. Her father was making the most awful spectacle of himself.

'So please, everyone, make yourselves at home.' Morrie smiled like a fox with a free pass to the hen house.

Lucinda watched her father leave the stage and move from group to group. The Barringtons, the Daytons, the Schwarzkopfs, they were all there, lapping up his charm.

'Excuse me, Papa.' Lucinda tapped Morrie on the shoulder. 'Did you really say that you and Mama are going to the opening of Highton's this evening?'

'Of course, darling, we always support our friends in this city.' Morrie smiled at his daughter and at Bernadette and Bob Barrington, who were standing beside him.

'But you hate Cecelia Highton-Smith,' Lucinda spat. She could feel a flame-red rash creeping up her neck, setting fire to her cheeks.

'Lucinda, don't be ridiculous. Morrie Finkelstein doesn't hate anyone,' her father scoffed.

'Yes, you do. You pulled me out of school because I made friends with Alice-Miranda Highton-Smith-Kennington-Jones, you caused so much trouble for them and now you're going to the opening. How dare you?' Lucinda accused.

Gerda Finkelstein had been watching the exchange from a distance while Rita Schwarzkopf told her about her daughter's latest astonishing achievements.

'Excuse me, Rita, I've got to go.' Gerda raced across the floor and stood between her husband and daughter.

'Tell him, Mama. Tell Papa where we went this week,' Lucinda demanded.

'Lucinda, please calm down. This is not the time or place.' Gerda's forehead puckered like rows of cross-stitch.

Morrie frowned.

'Of course it's not the time or place. It never will be. You're a hypocrite, Papa, you're disgusting and I'm ashamed to be related to you,' Lucinda shouted. Everyone in the ballroom froze.

Even the orchestra fell silent.

'Lucinda Finkelstein, I will not be spoken to in that manner,' Morrie whispered. 'I think you need to come with me, young lady.' He grabbed her by the wrist.

Morrie led Lucinda from the ballroom to a small office where he directed her to sit down.

'Don't you ever speak to me like that again,' he fumed.

'Or what? You'll send me to boarding school? I'd love that,' Lucinda retaliated.

A telephone rang in Morrie's pocket.

He pulled the device out and stared at the screen.

'Oh, for goodness sakes, what now?' He stormed out of the room and slammed the door.

Lucinda watched her father through a glass panel as he stood in the hallway. His face was red and whoever was on the telephone only seemed to be adding to his already foul mood. She stood up and opened the door to listen.

'You can't do that,' Morrie whispered savagely. 'It wasn't part of the plan and I'm not paying you any more money. You've done your job. No more.'

Lucinda wondered who he was speaking to.

'But that would make me a monster.' Morrie rubbed the side of his face. 'Don't threaten me. You don't know who you're dealing with. There will be no bomb, you idiot.'

Lucinda's heart pounded. She closed the door and retreated back inside the office. Her father terminated the call and stormed off down the hallway.

Lucinda waited a minute, then checked to see that he had really gone. She needed to get to Highton's and fast – if someone was planting a bomb then hundreds of lives were in danger, including her best friend's.

Chapter 38

Alice-Miranda adored the cream silk dress with the drop waist and giant teal-green bow she had chosen to wear to the opening. A pair of matching teal ballet flats completed her outfit perfectly.

Cecelia had been ready for hours and was back downstairs with Mr Gruber doing a final check of the store. There were hordes of people running this way and that, delivering flowers and food and setting up entertainment. Her father had returned to New York after lunch but he had disappeared almost immediately and when he finally arrived back at the apartment he had gone straight into the study and asked not to be disturbed. Every time Alice-Miranda had tried to have some time alone with him, the phone rang, or someone summoned him to look at something important, or he simply vanished.

Alice-Miranda was in the kitchen pouring herself a glass of water when Dolly Oliver appeared.

'Mrs Oliver, is that you?' she gasped. Dolly had selected a figure-hugging gold Chantilly lace gown and matching bolero jacket to wear for the evening.

'Yes, just me, dear. I was a bit worried I might look like a piece of old mutton trying to pass for spring lamb,' the older woman laughed.

'No, not at all. I think that dress is perfect on you. And your hair is amazing,' Alice-Miranda replied.

Dolly Oliver's trademark impenetrable brown curls had been straightened into a very becoming short bob.

'You know, dear, I thought I'd just throw caution to the wind. Have some fun. Apart from the family nobody knows me in this city so why shouldn't I mix things up a little?' Dolly raised her eyebrows.

Alice-Miranda glanced at the clock on the

kitchen wall. 'We should head downstairs soon. I'll go and find Daddy.'

'Well, dear, I'll meet you in the hall. I'm sure your mother will be after as much moral support as she can get. I still can't believe that Morrie Finkelstein has the gall to turn up tonight. That man has a cheek and a half.' Dolly fished about in her purse and pulled out a small compact. She delicately powdered her nose then snapped the case closed. 'Not bad for an old bird,' she said to herself.

Alice-Miranda met her father as he emerged from the study.

'Hello Daddy,' she said as Hugh scooped her into his arms. 'There's something I really need to talk to you about.'

Hugh kissed Alice-Miranda on the cheek. 'I'm sorry, darling. I've been so distracted. Tomorrow, I promise. Just you and me and Mummy. We'll spend the day together and you can tell me everything.'

Alice-Miranda tried again. 'But Daddy –'

'Is it life or death? I think your mother really needs us downstairs.'

Alice-Miranda smiled and shook her head. Her discovery would just have to wait.

'My goodness, who's that?' Hugh peered down the hallway at Dolly tottering towards them on her heels.

He wolf-whistled cheekily.

Dolly's cheeks were aflame. 'Oh, get off with you,' she protested.

'Gee, if I wasn't married, Dolly,' Hugh teased.

'Then you'd be the most eligible bachelor I know.' Dolly turned her cheek towards Hugh, which he dutifully kissed.

The lift arrived and transported the trio to the ground floor, where they had been given strict instructions on where to stand to greet the arrivals. The official business would take place early in the evening on a specially built stage on the first floor mezzanine. Afterwards, the entire staff would be on hand to take small groups of guests on tours of the whole store where they could sample the different themed food and entertainment on each floor. Alice-Miranda couldn't wait to take her friends up to the see the toy emporium.

'Hello Mummy, Mr Gruber.' Alice-Miranda skipped towards her mother and Gilbert, who were standing by the front doors. 'The store looks gorgeous and so do both of you.' Alice-Miranda particularly admired Mr Gruber's sequinned black bow tie.

'Thank you, darling,' Cecelia cooed. 'You look pretty gorgeous yourself.'

Gilbert Gruber winked at Alice-Miranda.

After the fiasco with the rose suppliers, Cecelia had a change of heart and decided to go with an entirely white theme of lilies, tulips, hydrangeas and lily of the valley. Huge floral arrangements were now peppered among the cosmetics counters and perfume displays.

Hugh greeted his wife with a kiss. 'Darling, you've outdone yourself.'

'Thank you, sweetheart,' she said, and then frowned. 'But are you sure everything is all right?'

'Perfect, I'd say. I can't see what else you could have done,' Hugh replied, looking about the lavish room.

'No, I didn't mean with the store. With you.' She searched her husband's face for clues. He'd been very mysterious about his unscheduled trip back home and Cecelia couldn't help thinking there was something dreadful that he hadn't told her.

'As soon as this is over, I promise I'll tell you everything,' Hugh whispered. 'But tonight you enjoy yourself. Heaven's knows you've worked hard enough to bring it all together and I'm so proud of you.'

Cecelia smiled. Hugh had never disappointed her before. She didn't like to think he'd start now.

The first guests began to arrive. Onto the red carpet sauntered the mayor of New York, always keen for a photo opportunity, followed at close call by several movie stars, important business people, models, designers and celebrities.

Alice-Miranda smiled and said hello to everyone as she stood alongside her parents and Mr Gruber at the end of the red carpet.

'Look Mummy, there's Ava and her mother.' Alice-Miranda waved furiously as her friend alighted from the Highton's limousine, which had been sent to pick them up.

Flashes surrounded the pair as they walked the length of the red carpet, stopping to pose for the paparazzi.

When they reached Alice-Miranda, Ava squealed.

'That was awesome! Now I know what it feels like to be a star – and I think I kinda liked it.' She grinned from ear to ear and executed a couple of interesting dance moves.

'Why don't you and your mother go and take a look around. I won't be too long,' Alice-Miranda suggested.

Another fleet of limousines arrived and out hopped Granma Clarrie, Maryanne and Quincy. Eldred and Isaac were already upstairs on the fifth floor among the menswear, setting up to play later in the evening.

Granma Clarrie was wearing heels and a figure-hugging black beaded gown that must have weighed almost as much as she did.

Quincy and her mother giggled as Granma Clarrie stopped and posed for every single camera along the carpet.

'I'm ninety-six years of age young man, almost ninety-seven, in fact, and I'm hotter than a sizzling barbecue plate.' She blew kisses to everyone.

'Granma Clarrie, you look incredible,' Alice-Miranda exclaimed and hugged the old woman.

'I know,' she said. 'Thank you very much for having us tonight. And who do we have here?' She looked Gilbert Gruber up and down. 'If you were twenty years older, young man . . .'

Alice-Miranda giggled, then formally introduced them.

'Well, Mr Gilbert Gruber, I hope you've worn your dancing shoes,' Granma Clarrie said with a wink. 'Now where's that champagne?'

Quincy put her face in her hands and shook her head. 'Mama, can you please try to keep Granma Clarrie under control?'

'I'll do my best, honey, but I can't promise.'

'Good luck, Maryanne.' Hugh Kennington-Jones grinned and raised his eyebrows.

Within half an hour most of the guests had arrived and the family had retreated inside to mingle. Alice-Miranda was about to head off and find her friends when another limousine pulled up.

Morrie and Gerda Finkelstein emerged from the car. Morrie stormed towards the entrance with Alice-Miranda firmly in his sights.

'Where's my daughter?' he demanded.

'I'm sorry, Mr Finkelstein, but I don't know what you're talking about,' Alice-Miranda replied.

'Where are you hiding her?' She has to be in there somewhere,' he snapped.

Gerda Finkelstein's eyes were red and she looked as though she'd been crying.

'Alice-Miranda, are you sure she isn't here?' Gerda begged.

'I haven't seen her,' Alice-Miranda replied.

'You're lying,' Morrie spat. 'You're a Highton, you're always lying.' He pushed his way inside, snatched a glass of champagne from the nearest waiter and stalked off, scanning the crowd.

'Mrs Finkelstein, why do you think Lucinda came here?' Alice-Miranda asked.

'Because she told me that you're the only person who truly understands her. And she's not at home and I can't imagine where else she would have gone,' Gerda sniffed.

'How long has she been missing?' Alice-Miranda asked.

'She and her father had an argument an hour ago and she was having some time out but then when I went to get her she had disappeared. One of the doormen said she told him that she was going to see a friend so Morrie and I assumed that she must have run away to see you. Lucinda doesn't know her way around the city very well at all, but her father said that she would find her way to Highton's.' Gerda looked at Alice-Miranda expectantly.

'Mrs Finkelstein, I can assure you that I haven't seen Lucinda. She's not here,' Alice-Miranda replied, wondering where on earth she might have gone.

Gerda inhaled sharply. 'But it's almost dark out.'

'Yes, and that's why we'd better find her quick

smart. Wait here,' she instructed. The tiny child fled inside the store searching for Quincy and Ava. She found them together trying on lip gloss.

'Hey, Alice-Miranda, what do you think about this colour on me?' Ava's lips were cherry red.

'You look ridiculous.' Quincy snatched a tissue from the box on the counter and handed it to her friend.

'We've got to go,' Alice-Miranda urged. 'Hurry up.'

'Where?' Quincy asked as Alice-Miranda pulled her towards the front door. 'I hope there are some more of those delicious prawn fritters out here.'

Mrs Finkelstein had disappeared.

'Lucinda's run away,' Alice-Miranda blurted.

'Run away? Lucinda? But she has no idea how to find her way around!' Quincy frowned.

'That's just the point. Her parents think that she came here but she didn't. So she's out there somewhere.'

'In New York, at night-time and on her own.' Ava bit her lip. 'I know she wanted some adventures but that's a little too adventurous even for me.'

'I have an idea where she might be, but we need to go now. It might already be closed.'

'Shouldn't we tell someone?' Ava asked.

'What about your mother?' said Alice-Miranda.

'She just got a call-out about ten minutes ago. She's gone downtown. She said that she'd be back as soon as she could.'

'We really should tell someone,' Quincy advised. 'I don't want to end up on *America's Most Wanted*.'

'I don't know what you're planning but we're not committing any crimes, are we?' Ava glared.

'Not as the criminal.' Quincy rolled her eyes. 'As the dead body.'

Ava gulped.

Alice-Miranda looked around. Most of the guests had already made their way to the upper levels of the store. She approached a rotund security man on the front door, who couldn't stop smiling.

'Hello, my name is Alice-Miranda Highton-Smith-Kennington-Jones, and these are my friends Quincy and Ava, and if anyone's looking for us, we've just gone to the park. We'll be back soon.' Alice-Miranda grabbed her friends and they raced towards the traffic lights.

The man shook his head and grinned. 'Man, kids these days sure are independent,' he said to himself.

'Where do you think she's gone?' Quincy shouted above the honking of horns.

'Come on, you'll see.'

The girls raced through the gates into Central Park.

In the half-light the park was like another world altogether. There were shadows and branches like ghosts hovering overhead.

'Stop,' Quincy puffed. 'Where are we going?'

'Don't you remember that Lucinda said she had never been to the zoo before? Maybe she's gone there.'

'But it's after closing time,' Ava said.

'And the park's huge. She could be anywhere,' Quincy gulped.

'I'm scared, Alice-Miranda. Let's go back.' Ava's voice wavered.

'We have to find her.' Alice-Miranda was more determined than ever.

The girls made their way to the entrance of the zoo, but it was locked up tight. Low growls emanated from inside the walls.

'Lucinda! Are you in there?' Alice-Miranda called. 'Come on, we'll go around the outside,' Alice-Miranda urged. 'Maybe she'll hear us.'

'Tell me exactly why you think she's in the zoo?' Ava asked.

'Just a feeling,' Alice-Miranda replied.

'That's it? Like I said before, sometimes I just don't understand you foreign people.' Ava shook her head.

Alice-Miranda ran off down the path, under the stone archway and straight into Mr Gambino pushing his hot dog cart.

'Where are you off to in such a hurry, young lady?' Lou Gambino asked. 'Hey Harry, it's Miss Alice-Miranda,' he called to his friend who was lagging behind.

'Oh Mr Gambino, Mr Geronimo, we're looking for our friend Lucinda. She's run away and we think she might have come to the park,' Alice-Miranda blurted.

'Well honey, we need to call the police. This park is no place for a young girl after dark,' Lou replied.

'What are you talking about? It's no place for an old man after dark,' Harry Geronimo wheezed as he caught up to his friend.

'But we think she might have gone to the zoo. And now it's closed.' Even Alice-Miranda looked a little worried now.

Quincy told everyone to shush. 'Did you hear something?'

'It's just squirrels,' Ava replied.

'There it goes again,' Quincy said.

In the distance a soft voice called. 'Alice-Miranda, HELP!' echoed through the trees.

'It's her!' Quincy grabbed Alice-Miranda's hand and shot off in the direction of the sound.

'We're coming Lucinda,' Alice-Miranda called.

The three girls raced towards the other side of the zoo, with Mr Gambino and Mr Geronimo limping after them as fast as they could.

'Lucinda, where are you?' Alice-Miranda called again.

'Alice-Miranda, I'm stuck,' Lucinda cried out. 'I'm stuck in the zoo.'

The children raced over to a section of metal fence where they could see Lucinda standing in the middle of the path. Her face was the colour of her dress.

'What *are* you doing, Finkelstein?' Quincy shook her head.

'I was on my way to see Alice-Miranda and I thought I'd take a detour through the park and then I ended up in the zoo by accident and then when I tried to get out it was locked and everyone had gone. And now I'm stuck on the wrong side of the fence,' Lucinda wailed.

'Stop blubbing. We'll call someone,' Ava grinned, then started to laugh outright.

'It's not funny,' Lucinda yelled. 'I think my father is up to something really bad. We've got to get to Highton's.' There was a rustling sound in the bushes beside them.

'Hey, who's there?' Lou Gambino demanded.

A figure emerged. It was a man wearing a pork-pie hat.

'Is that . . .' Alice-Miranda squinted into the darkness. 'Is that you, Mr Preston?'

'Yeah, it's me, who's that?' he asked.

'Alice-Miranda. I saw you at the Met, with Mr Clifton,' she reminded him.

'Oh sure, what are you doing here? It's a bit late to be out in the park.'

'Our friend Lucinda is locked in the zoo,' Alice-Miranda explained. 'But what are you doing here? I thought you were staying in Mr Clifton's studio.'

'I am, but I just came to collect the last of my things. I almost forgot I'd left a bag of clothes hidden down here. She's in the zoo, you say?'

'Yes – you can see her if you come down here,' Alice-Miranda said.

'No, it's okay. Wait right there. I'll be back in a minute.'

Callum Preston disappeared back into the bushes, emerging a few minutes later with Lucinda in tow.

'Lucinda!' Alice-Miranda ran to hug her friend. 'Thank you, Mr Preston.'

'I don't know what he's up to but I heard my father talking to someone on the phone,' Lucinda sniffed. 'He said something about a bomb.'

'A bomb?' Quincy's eyes widened.

'I have proof that my father has been the one causing lots of trouble for your parents at the store, Alice-Miranda. He's been paying people at City Hall and I think one of the contractors has been in on it too. I saw the name "George" and the word "foreman" and then a really big amount of money.'

'But why do you think there's a bomb?' Alice-Miranda asked.

'Well, it would certainly ruin the opening, wouldn't it?' Tears spilled onto Lucinda's cheeks. 'I knew Papa was difficult but I didn't think he was a madman.'

Alice-Miranda thought back to her conversation with George earlier in the day. 'Oh my goodness,' she gasped. 'George told me this morning that the party was going to *go off*. Come on, we've got to get back and warn everyone,' Alice-Miranda turned to her friends.

'Does anyone have a phone?' Callum Preston asked.

The group all shook their heads.

'That way.' Lou Gambino pointed. 'Me and Harry will be right behind you.'

'Hey, young man,' said Harry, looking at Callum. 'Will you give us a hand here?'

Chapter 39

The girls arrived back at the store just in time to hear the last minute of the official speeches.

'So, did you have fun in the park?' the dim-witted guard on the door asked.

Alice-Miranda shook her head, and then raced inside through the perfume and make-up counters and towards the grand central staircase with Lucinda, Ava and Quincy in tow.

Callum Preston was helping Mr Gambino and Mr Geronimo with their carts, which they parked outside the store.

'I'm sorry folks, I can't let you in.' The security guard blocked the entrance.

'Listen here, fella, this is life and death,' Lou Gambino wheezed.

'Hey, how about a pretzel,' Harry Geronimo offered. He dug around in his cart and held one aloft.

'Man, you know, I am hungry.' The guard deserted his post long enough for Lou and Callum to duck inside the store.

Cecelia had just stepped away from the podium to rapturous applause.

'Mummy,' Alice-Miranda called out. 'We need to talk to you. It's urgent.'

'Whatever's the matter, darling?' Cecelia asked.

'Lucinda heard her father talking to someone on the telephone about a bomb, and she thinks it has something to do with the store,' Alice-Miranda blurted.

'Did you say a bomb?' Hugh Kennington-Jones strode over to the group.

'Yes, Daddy. Lucinda's found proof that her father has been making all that trouble for Mummy and now we think there could be a bomb in the store.'

Hugh scoffed. 'I knew your father was competitive, Lucinda, but a bomb? That would make him a monster. Where's Morrie? Didn't I see him arrive earlier?'

The group turned and looked down from the gallery where they could see the whole of the ground floor. Among the throng of beautifully dressed men and women sipping on their champagne and munching canapés, one stood out.

'There's my mother.' Lucinda pointed at Gerda Finkelstein, who was pacing the floor between the perfume counters and chewing on her thumbnail.

'And there's your father over there.' Ava pointed at Morrie, who was looking intently at the fittings on one of the counters.

'I can't imagine that your father would be here if there was a bomb in the store and he knew about it,' Cecelia Highton-Smith said with a smile at Lucinda. 'Surely he wouldn't put his life or your mother's in danger.'

'I think we should go and find out what this is all about.' Hugh led the girls and Cee as they headed back down the grand staircase and into the crowd.

'Lucinda!' Gerda Finkelstein cried out when she saw her daughter. 'Oh my darling.' She ran towards Lucinda and hugged her tightly.

Morrie Finkelstein caught sight of his wife and child and hastened over to them. 'Lucinda.' He arched an eyebrow, and then turned his attention to Alice-Miranda. 'So where have you been hiding her? Upstairs? In the apartment? Among the children's clothes?'

'Mr Finkelstein, Lucinda was never here. I told you that before,' Alice-Miranda explained. 'She was in the park.'

'In the park!' Morrie's mouth gaped open. 'How dare you take her to the park?'

On hearing the commotion, a small group of onlookers began to gather around.

'I didn't take her to the park. Lucinda was on her way over here to tell Mummy about all the things you've been up to and to warn her about the bomb,' Alice-Miranda said stoutly and stared up at Morrie.

The man's mouth dropped open like a fish's and his wiry hair stood on end. 'What bomb? And I can assure you that I haven't been up to anything. How ridiculous. As if I'd be here if I thought there was a bomb in the store.'

'But Papa,' Lucinda began. 'I heard you before on the telephone.'

Ava's mother, Detective Dee Dee Lee, marched towards the group with two uniformed police officers close behind her.

'Mom, I'm so glad you're back!' Ava said. 'Lucinda says there could be a bomb in the store.'

'I think I can explain,' said Dee Dee, looking from Cecelia to Morrie. 'Mr Finkelstein was indeed on the telephone earlier this evening to George, your foreman.'

'What are you talking about, Mom?' Ava asked.

'That call-out, downtown; we just arrested George.' She stared at Morrie. 'And be assured, Mr Finkelstein, he was on his way here to the store with enough plastic explosives in the trunk of his car to make a serious mess.'

'So he really meant it when he said that things would *go off*.' Alice-Miranda's eye were as round as saucers.

Morrie Finkelstein's face turned the colour of toothpaste.

Cecelia was puzzled. 'George? He's Tony's right-hand man and he always seemed so friendly and helpful. And why were *you* talking to him, Morrie?'

Morrie gulped. 'I thought he might come and do some work for me. Your store *does* look beautiful.'

Dee Dee Lee shook her head. 'Mr Finkelstein, that's a lie and you know it.' She turned to Cecelia and Hugh. 'Mr Finkelstein has been causing you considerable trouble, especially at City Hall and with your foreman. All those missing deliveries, things going astray, parades clashing with cranes – well it seems George wasn't only on your payroll, he was on Finkelstein's as well, along with several people down at City Hall.'

Morrie flatly denied the accusation. 'I have no idea what you're talking about.'

'Papa, I saw your notebook,' Lucinda said. 'It had lots of amounts of money written down and George's name was there too.'

'But a bomb?' Cecelia gripped her hands together tightly.

'That was George's idea. He just got greedy. Mr Finkelstein might be a lot of things – vain, selfish, stupid . . .' Dee Dee turned to him. 'Would you like me to go on?'

Morrie shook his head.

'But, thankfully he's not a monster,' Dee Dee continued. 'I'm sorry, Cecelia, Hugh. We couldn't risk ruining the investigation by bringing you in too early. But it's just as well we've been monitoring Mr Finkelstein's calls, or there would have been a lot more ruined tonight than just this party.'

'Papa, how could you?' Lucinda's face was crimson.

Morrie Finkelstein's lip began to quiver. 'I told George, no bomb. I had no idea he would go through with it. I thought he was just trying to get more money out of me. Do you think I'd be here with your mother if I knew?' he blurted.

The group looked at each other, shocked at these revelations.

'Is Papa going to prison?' Lucinda asked. She bit back the tears that were prickling her eyes.

'I don't think it will go that far,' Dee Dee replied, placing her arm gently around Lucinda's shoulder. 'But I imagine there will be some hefty fines and none of this will do much for your father's reputation.'

Morrie Finkelstein slumped, defeated.

Gerda faced her husband. 'I don't understand, Morrie. Why did you do it?'

'I, I don't know,' he mumbled. 'I just wanted Finkelstein's to be number one, just once.'

Gerda drew in a deep breath and shouted like a woman possessed. 'And you would risk our daughter's safety for the sake of making money. Who are you?' She waggled her finger under his nose and shook her head.

'It's her fault – that child!' Morrie pointed at Alice-Miranda. 'She's a bad influence on Lucinda. Our daughter has never behaved like this until she met her.'

'Alice-Miranda has nothing to do with you wanting Finkelstein's to be number one,' Gerda retorted. 'That's a pathetic excuse if ever I heard one.'

'Alice-Miranda is *not* a bad influence, Papa. She's a wonderful friend and for your information she just saved me from a night in the zoo,' Lucinda explained.

'The zoo? What were you doing in the zoo, Lucinda, in the dark with all those wild animals – and all that fur.' Morrie scratched his forehead and a bumpy crimson rash began to creep up his neck. 'I don't understand. She made you go there, didn't she? There's no need to protect her. She's a Highton.'

'And what's that supposed to mean?' Cecelia glared at Morrie.

'No Papa, of course it wasn't planned. Alice-Miranda found me,' Lucinda retorted. 'If it wasn't for her coming to look for me, I might have spent the whole night there. I didn't see *you* out searching. You won't let me out of the house and then when I do run away you can't even be bothered to look for me!'

'Oh my goodness, Lucinda, I didn't think you'd run away. I thought you were here. It's true, then, you really were locked in the zoo!' Morrie gasped. 'There are bears in there.'

'How did you get Lucinda out?' Hugh Kennington-Jones asked.

'A friend helped us, Daddy,' piped up Alice-Miranda. 'Do you remember I told you about Mr Preston, the artist? Well, he was getting some of his things and luckily he knows a way into and out of the zoo,' Alice-Miranda smiled. 'That's him over there next to Mr Gambino.' Alice-Miranda pointed at the two men who were peering through the crowd towards them.

'So you really *do* care about my daughter?' Morrie Finkelstein cocked his head and stared at Alice-Miranda as if he had just discovered a whole new species.

'Of course I do. She's my friend,' Alice-Miranda replied. 'My very good friend.'

'But how can that be? You're a Highton and Hightons hate Finkelsteins. They just pretend to be nice. Like your mother. She's always so kind and welcoming and she writes lovely thank-you letters and always congratulates me when things go well, but . . .' Morrie trailed off.

'But what, Morrie Finkelstein?' Gerda demanded.

'Well . . .' Morrie gulped.

'Well, *what*?' Gerda snapped. Her husband looked down at his shoes and was suddenly silent.

'Mr Finkelstein, I think there's something you should know about that silly old feud between Great-Great-Grandpa Horace and Abe Finkelstein,' Alice-Miranda began.

Morrie's eyes flicked upwards.

'Did you know that your great-grandfather was engaged to a very beautiful woman called Ruby Winters?'

Morrie slowly shook his head.

'Well, on the day that the two men were set to become partners in a store, a terrible tragedy happened. You see, Ruby worked for Great-Great-Grandpa Horace and she went with him down to Wall Street to the bank. Horace was meeting Abe so that they could sign the documents. That day, a wagon laden with explosives went off and Ruby was one of thirty-eight people who tragically lost their lives. Abe was so racked with grief that he didn't want to go through with the deal. Grandpa Horace had no choice but to go it alone. He'd already signed the papers.'

'Is this true?' Morrie asked, looking around at the gathered crowd.

'Yes, Mr Finkelstein. It was all over the newspapers in September of 1920. Quincy's Granma Clarrie, she told us about Ruby Winters and Abe, and then Mrs Oliver and I went to the library and it's all there.'

'She's telling the truth,' Dolly Oliver chimed in.

'Oh.' Morrie was thinking about that scrap of paper locked in his desk drawer. It never had made much sense. He gulped and lowered his head. No longer the image of a rich and powerful business-man, he more closely resembled a very naughty little boy.

'Is this true, Morrie?' A tiny woman clutching a walking stick joined the group.

'Oh no, not you, Aunt Heloise.' Morrie flinched and stared at his shoes.

'Morrie Finkelstein, I think you have some serious apologising to do,' declared Gerda, her cheeks aflame. 'And I suggest you start with your own daughter, then Cecelia and Alice-Miranda and Mr Gruber and everyone else in this family you've ever maligned. What's more, you will make amends for all of the terrible lies you've told about the Hightons and I suggest you spend some time at that library yourself. You will allow Lucinda to go back to school on Monday and choose her own friends, just as the boys have always done. And for the record, I'll choose my friends too from now on, and I can tell you, Rita Schwarzkopf won't be darkening the door of that salon ever again.' Gerda was wound up like a spring. 'And another thing, we are not going on holidays to Southampton this year. You will take me and the children to Paris so we can see the Palace of Versailles for ourselves whether you like flying or not. That's if you're not in prison!' Twenty years of frustration spewed from Gerda's lips. The group of guests who had been watching the exchange began to retreat.

'And you can take your mother and me to lunch every Wednesday from now on,' Heloise added.

Dee Dee Lee stepped forward. 'Mr Finkelstein,

I'll need you to come downtown with these gentlemen to answer some questions.' The two uniformed officers stood either side of Morrie.

'Don't expect me to hold your hand, Morrie Finkelstein. You got yourself into this mess and you can get yourself out. I'm going to have a glass of champagne and have a proper look at this beautiful store. Cecelia, would you like to show me around?' Gerda smiled at her host.

'Of course.' Cecelia looped her arm into Gerda's and the two women headed off towards the handbags.

'Well, I think I should go and see how everyone else is getting on,' said Hugh before also making a retreat.

Alice-Miranda put an arm around Lucinda's shoulder. 'Are you all right?'

Lucinda nodded.

'Let's go upstairs,' the tiny child directed. 'You simply have to see the toy emporium. It's amazing. There's a full-size tree house and fairies that fly too. And there's a pirate ship. You can go aboard and there are dress-up clothes and a huge box of treasures.'

'Slow down, Alice-Miranda. I want to see the whole store. Remember, I've never been here before.' Lucinda smiled and squeezed her friend's hand.

The four girls were about to head for the elevator when Quincy's palm hit her forehead. 'Oh no!' she exclaimed.

'What's wrong?' the trio asked.

'Look up there.' Quincy pointed to the mezzanine level where Granma Clarrie and Mrs Oliver had discovered the Arabian themed party in the ladies' shoe department. Finger cymbals chimed and the strains of a *zummara* led a harem of dancers, resplendent in their rainbow of costumes, prancing across the floor.

'Tell me it isn't true,' Quincy groaned.

The girls giggled as they watched Granma Clarrie and Mrs Oliver making some rather audacious attempts at belly dancing.

'Granma!' Quincy wailed. 'Stop!'

'No,' Alice-Miranda smiled. 'Let them go. I think Granma Clarrie's amazing. I hope I'm still belly dancing at ninety-seven too.'

Chapter 40

'Last night was amazing wasn't it?' Alice-Miranda slipped her hand into her father's as the family walked along Fifth Avenue towards the Met.

'Wonderful, darling,' her mother replied. 'Granma Clarrie's certainly energetic. That dance-off with Dolly was something to behold.'

'And surely there had to be a certain amount of satisfaction in seeing your old enemy get his come-uppance, Cee?' Hugh grinned at his wife.

'I thought I must be going mad with all the

things that were happening at the store. I'm just glad that Morrie's been brought to his senses. But I wish you'd have told me about Ruby Winters last week when you found out, Alice-Miranda,' Cecelia finished, looking at her daughter.

'I tried to, Mummy, but you were so busy. I didn't want to worry you with anything else,' Alice-Miranda replied.

'Speaking of busy, your mother and I promise, Alice-Miranda, no more running off to meetings and other things – we're going to make the most of our last week together,' Hugh grinned.

'And no more secrets?' Cecelia glanced at her husband.

'I promise, darling, no more,' Hugh replied.

'Is it really true, Daddy, that Uncle Xavier didn't die all those years ago?' Alice-Miranda asked.

'Yes, sweetheart, the evidence seems to suggest so,' her father replied.

The happy trio reached their destination.

'You know, the man I met when I was drawing the Degas – the one who was admiring that picture from Pelham Park,' Alice-Miranda explained, 'he lectured our class last week.'

'Was he any good?' her father asked.

'Yes, he's wonderful. He has some paintings here in the gallery. I think you might be very interested once you see them.'

The family reached the top of the steps and headed into the cavernous foyer.

'Wait here a moment,' the tiny child instructed. 'I just need to do something.' Alice-Miranda rushed over to the information booth.

After a short exchange the young woman at the booth picked up the telephone. 'He'll be here soon, miss,' she said after she finished the call. 'He'll meet you in the gallery.'

Alice-Miranda skipped back to her parents.

'Well, why don't you show Mummy and me this mysterious painting from home?' Hugh asked.

'I will, but there's something else I want you to see on the way.' Alice-Miranda led her parents through the Grecian antiquities and the Indigenous exhibits upstairs to the west galleries.

'It's in here,' Alice-Miranda explained. 'Over there.'

'Oh my goodness.' Hugh frowned and rubbed his temples. He stared at the intricate painting in front of him.

Alice-Miranda looked at the citation and

read aloud. '*Dragons and Knights* by Edward Clifton.'

Alice-Miranda looked up at her father, wide-eyed. He was mesmerised.

'That picture. And the name. That's my mother's maiden name,' Hugh whispered. 'Is it possible?'

'Daddy, I think there's someone you should meet.' Alice-Miranda stared at the tall man with the thick shock of salt-and-pepper hair who had slipped silently into the gallery.

Hugh looked at his daughter and then to his wife. Alice-Miranda pointed behind him.

Hugh spun around and Ed Clifton stepped forward and offered his hand.

'Hello little brother.'

✴

On that sparkling Sunday afternoon in Central Park, two men who had been lost to one another as boys began to get to know each other properly for the very first time.

'Mummy, come and look at this,' Alice-Miranda called to Cecelia, who was lying on the grass reading a magazine.

Cecelia stood up and went to see what her daughter was looking at.

'We're gonna miss that kid, Harry,' said Lou Gambino, as he watched the family from behind his hot dog cart. He smiled at Alice-Miranda, who was darting in and out of the trees chasing the squirrels. 'But you know, I have a feeling she'll be back.'

Harry Geronimo pulled the chess board from the small cupboard on the side of his cart. 'I think you might be right. You know, Lou, this is a good life, a very good life indeed.'

And just in case you're wondering . . .

Lucinda returned to school on Monday. She and Alice-Miranda finished their Science project in time for the fair and came in a credible second place behind Alethea and Gretchen, who had produced an outstanding experiment on how to identify counterfeit bank notes. Gretchen convinced Alethea to leave Alice-Miranda alone, on the threat that she would unfriend her immediately if she didn't. Alice-Miranda hadn't given up altogether on her and Alethea being friends one day – but she was smart enough to know that it might take a little while longer to get there.

Lucinda's mother invited Ava, Quincy and Alice-Miranda to the salon on Saturday afternoon, but Lucinda suggested they go for frozen hot chocolate instead. Out on bail, Morrie agreed and accompanied the girls himself. Mrs Oliver insisted that she go along to make sure that he behaved himself. Morrie couldn't remember having so much fun in ages.

Gerda Finkelstein told her husband about her visit to Louisa. He suggested she go as often as she wanted. Gerda said she wasn't asking his permission.

Morrie Finkelstein turned over a new leaf. In fact, he raked a whole lot of leaves when he nominated park duty for his community service. A judge sentenced him to one thousand hours which, strangely, he found quite enjoyable. Morrie wrote a formal apology to Cecelia and offered to terminate the contracts with the suppliers he'd stolen from her. Cecelia said the suppliers could make up their own minds about that. After all, there was more than enough room in New York City for both of them.

Callum Preston adored his job as Ed Clifton's assistant. In his spare time he painted and drew as much as he could. Gilbert Gruber saw the picture of Alice-Miranda and the tamandua and invited the young man to hold his first exhibition, *Zoo Creatures*, at Highton's on Fifth. It was a sell-out.

When Alice-Miranda had seen the little book with the drawings in her father's study alongside those mysterious notes, she'd written to Mr Clifton via the Met and suggested that he might like to meet her family. She didn't know for sure if he'd come but she'd had to take the chance.

The man now known as Edward Clifton spent several days with his younger brother, filling in the gaps for forty lost years. Ed explained how he had fought bitterly with their father when he told him he wanted to study art. Henry Kennington-Jones said that if he walked that path he would walk it alone. On a wet winter's night Henry banished his son from their home. But his mother Arabella couldn't bear to see her beloved boy disowned. She took a painting from the wall in one of the guest bedrooms, one she especially loved. It was a mother and her son by Renoir. She told him to sell it and use the money to take care of himself. But just the next night, there was the terrible car accident. Edward couldn't bear to part with the only thing that linked him to his mother. He worked three jobs to put himself through art school and gave the painting anonymously to the Metropolitan Museum of Art so he could look at it whenever he wanted to. And everyone else could too. His father hated art, so Edward wasn't concerned that he would ever find out where the painting was. Xavier used his middle name, Edward, with his mother's maiden name and over the years made a life for himself in New York, too angry to look back. His mother had always said 'no regrets' but Edward wasn't so sure about that. He had no idea that his father had told everyone he'd died alongside his mother. As far as he was concerned, he thought his younger brother mustn't have wanted anything to do with him.

Then when he met Alice-Miranda he knew it was fate. And if his own brother was anything like this tiny child, with the cascading chocolate curls and brown eyes as big as saucers, he knew he had nothing to lose, just a family to gain.

Cast of characters

The Highton-Smith-Kennington-Jones Household

Alice-Miranda Highton-Smith-Kennington-Jones	Only child – seven and three-quarter years of age
Cecelia Highton-Smith	Alice-Miranda's doting mother
Hugh Kennington-Jones	Alice-Miranda's doting father
Dolly Oliver	Family cook, part-time food technology scientist
Cyril	Pilot
Gilbert Gruber	General Manager of Highton's on Fifth Avenue
Seamus O'Leary	Chauffeur

Students and Staff at Mrs Kimmel's School for Girls

Miss Jilly Hobbs	Headmistress
Mr Felix Underwood	Fifth grade teacher
Miss Andie Patrick	Sixth grade teacher
Miss Cynthia Cleary	Receptionist
Mr Whip Staples	Doorman and handyman
Lucinda Finkelstein	Fifth grade student
Quincy Armstrong	Fifth grade student
Ava Lee	Fifth grade student
Gretchen	Sixth grade student
Thea Mackenzie	Sixth grade student

Others

Morrie Finkelstein	Lucinda's ambitious father
Gerda Finkelstein	Lucinda's mother
Ezekiel and Tobias Finkelstein	Lucinda's elder brothers
Aunt Heloise	Lucinda's great-aunt
Granma Clarrie	Quincy's great-grandmother
Eldred Armstrong	Quincy's father and a famous musician
Maryanne Armstrong	Quincy's mother
Isaac Armstrong	Quincy's elder brother
Dee Dee Lee	Ava's mother and a NYC detective
Lou Gambino	Hot dog vendor
Harry Geronimo	Pretzel vendor
Callum Preston	Young artist
Ed Clifton	Artist
Hector	Private investigator

About the author

Jacqueline Harvey has spent her working life teaching in girls' boarding schools. She's never had an art lesson at the Met but she has come across quite a few girls who remind her a little of Alice-Miranda.

Jacqueline has published eight novels for young readers. Her first picture book, *The Sound of the Sea*, was awarded Honour Book in the 2006 CBC Awards. She is currently working on Alice-Miranda's next adventure.

For more about Jacqueline and Alice-Miranda, go to:

www.alice-miranda.com

and

www.jacquelineharvey.com.au

Have you read the first four Alice-Miranda adventures?

Book 1
*Alice-Miranda
at School*

Book 2
*Alice-Miranda
on Holiday*

Book 3
*Alice-Miranda
Takes the Lead*

Book 4
*Alice-Miranda
at Sea*